sidelined

the contract

Bianca Williams

Bianca Williams Books

Bianca Williams Books, LLC.

Print ISBN: 978-0-9985146-4-2
eBook ISBN: 978-0-9985146-5-9

~-~-~-~-~-~-~-~-~-~-~-~-~-~-~-~-~

SIDELINED is a work of fiction inspired by true events. Certain characters names, businesses, incidents, locations, and events have been fictionalized for dramatic purposes.

ABOUT THE AUTHOR

Bianca Williams is the award-winning author of the sports romance series Sidelined. Book One, "The Draft", was released in 2017 and won the USA Best Book Award and was a finalist in the National Indie Excellence Awards. To the delight of readers everywhere, Book Two, "The Penalty", was released in 2018. Sidelined is the story of  event planner Bryn Charles and her unexpected romance with her client NFL superstar Shane Smith. The contemporary novels are inspired by Williams' dating adventures in her hometown of Baltimore County, MD.

She discovered her love for creative writing while pursuing a double major in Finance & Management at Chestnut Hill College in Philadelphia. After graduating at the top of her class, achieving a successful career in finance, and co-founding an event planning company, Bianca began penning her debut novel. When she isn't writing, Bianca uses her platform to empower young women in personal development, business, and relationships.

Her signature slogan — know the plays, or get sidelined — reminds her to have a strategy for success in everything that she pursues.

Praise for Bianca Williams' novel, Sidelined The Draft

"No time is wasted in Williams's fun, fast-paced page-turner. The love interest is introduced on the first page, and things only get hotter from there until the thoroughly satisfying conclusion."
-The Book Life Prize

"Going down easy like scrambled eggs, pancakes, syrup, bacon and orange juice on a Sunday morning, William's literary flow is effortless, like a real pro. For all readers who love a great, old-fashioned girl meets boy story, *Sidelined* is your perfect match."
— Omar Tyree, *New York Times* bestseller author

"Sidelined: The Draft by Bianca Williams is a page-turning, stress-filled romance, with tries, fouls, and of course goals, or in this case, perhaps agendas would be more to the point. Written in the present tense, it follows Bryn and her surprising infatuation with NFL superstar Shane Smith, a spoilt man-child. The story is heavily character driven and easy to follow, whether you're a fan of sports or not. The characters are developed, and I often found myself getting frustrated at some of their actions. Ms. Williams shows poise and talent for creating atmosphere throughout her plot. This is the first book in the series and, given the ending, it's easy to understand why." - Reviewed By K.J. Simmill for Readers' Favorite

For the untouchable and for those who have been sidelined

ACKNOWLEDGEMENTS

I started this labor of love in 2013 and in 2020 it has come to its end. It was bittersweet saying goodbye to my beloved characters, Bryn, Bailey, Jen, Mandy, Terry, and last but not least, Shane. I hope you loved them as much as I did. I will forever be grateful for this story and the individuals who inspired it. The journey of writing this series, although tough at times, helped me to realize a dream. I'm officially a writer, y'all!

Honor to GOD for being my foundation. He gave me the vision and through this undertaking, brought healing. I'd like to thank my support system for this project. Jasmine, for your perseverance in reading every chapter as it's written, as well as, the final draft at least a hundred times. Malica, for your continued support and always finding typos before we go to print. Briana, for your maturity and understanding as a daughter and allowing me to finish this project without the fear of being judged. Gail, for being the best editor a new author could find. I hope we have more projects in our future.

To my readers, thank you for taking a chance on SIDELINED and allowing me to take up space in your life. "Are you not entertained? (In my Russell Crowe voice.) ☺

To love, peace, and happiness. I will conclude this salutation with one of my favorite quotes.

"It's the possibility of having a dream come true that makes life interesting." – The Alchemist

CONTENTS

sidelined

the contract

1

<u>THE PERFECT GIRL –</u>
<u>ACCORDING TO SHANE</u>

Ask Carice why I'm in jail right now and she'll tell you it's Bryn's fault. Ask her what happened to us and she'll tell you it was because of Bryn. According to her, anything bad that happens is caused by Bryn.

For real, it's all bullshit. I'm here because *she* put me here. And now the Nighthawks are involved, which means she done fucked up. What's worse is that she don't get it. She thinks she just did some extra wild shit to get my attention. Nah, this time, her crazy ass can actually ruin me.

I was crazy once, but I've changed. Carice? She's still doing the same dumb shit from before. She lazy as fuck. She don't cook, she don't clean, and she don't do the laundry. I be having to call my auntie to come and clean the house. Shit's crazy. She don't even watch the kids. They asses go to daycare all day. When I come by to see them, she in her room wearing the same clothes from the day before. Shopping is a thing of the past and she barely gets her hair done. I'm tired of seeing that dry-ass ponytail. That's why everybody keep asking me why I got her, of all people, pregnant.

When I first saw Carice, she reminded me of the cop from CSI, Vanessa Ferlito. I think that's why my cousin Qmar chose her for me. He knew what I liked. Anyway, I was the man of the hour, so she came straight over and started dancing on me. Her hair was long, black, and shiny. She had a thin waist, a plump ass, and legs for miles. That was her winning quality. I love 'em tall. We were eye to eye with her in them clear heels. I felt it in my soul; I wanted her to have my kids. My kids gotta be tall, I thought. She was freaking on me, nasty as shit, just the way I liked it.

My fiancée at the time had given me a pass for my last night as a single man and I was free to do what I wanted. It wouldn't have mattered anyway. Carice was on it and she wasn't backing down. She had confidence, swag, and focus. She knew what she wanted and went for it. She had me hooked.

I called it quits *that* morning with my fiancée, cut her a fat-ass check and let it play out the way she wanted, letting people think she left me at the altar so she could save face. I ain't give a fuck. I knew deep down inside that I couldn't marry her. She was beautiful. The most beautiful girl I'd ever seen. . . but she was ugly on the inside. I'd ignored it for long enough. Meeting Carice was perfect timing.

We got along good. We was on some crazy Bonnie and Clyde type shit. She ain't care what I did as long as I came home to her. She was loyal. I had all kinds of bitches. She even let me bring a few home. Sometimes she'd watch. Sometimes I'd watch. But most times she'd join in. Those were the good ol' days. It was cool like that. She was cool like that. Ain't give me no mouth. We had an understanding, an arrangement, which kept us both happy.

Things started to change when she got pregnant. She got in her feelings and started wanting me home. Shit, I was a twenty-two-year-old millionaire and she wanted me home. That shit caused chaos. I rebelled and turned to music. She turned to her best friend. The more popular I became, the more women threw themselves at me. I swear, I was with a different one every night of the week. The only time I saw Carice was on my day off. Even then, I was with someone else that very night.

Then Riley was born. My angel. I wanted to be home. Except Carice started having some postpartum and wanted to argue all the damn time. While Riley was pulling me back in, Carice was pushing me away. I didn't even want to touch her, not like that anyway. That's when she started verbally attacking me every chance she got. She was insecure and always accusing me of fucking somebody. Well I had to, because we wasn't.

Then I decided I had to get another spot. Being away a couple of days a week helped. We started talking again. She calmed down a bit. She started coming to my games again and during off-season she was helping Qmar with forming my R&B group, TGS. We became one big-ass happy family. That's how I got her ass pregnant, *again*. It was cool for a minute. Then, I don't know what happened.

Bryn.

Man, I knew the perfect girl existed, I just didn't know she was going to walk into my life. I remember the day we met like it was yesterday. It was at this Italian spot in Little Italy, Tony's. She was with her business partner, Jen. She was dressed in a business suit. Her jacket had a deep V-neck. My dick gets hard just thinking about her breasts. Real set of Ds. Beautiful. They was popping that day. I'll never forget that cleavage. She was short, really short, with these big brown eyes. And when she smiled, I felt like I was home.

For the first time in my life I felt unsure about everything. I noticed I was underdressed, like I needed to sit up straight and speak proper English. I popped some Tic Tacs to make sure the breath was minty fresh. I don't know. It was something about her that made me want to be better. It was instant. I liked her. Like I *really* liked her. I knew right then, I had to make her mine.

She was quiet, unlike Jen. Man, Jen ran her mouth non-stop about the event she wanted to plan to launch my music group. I tried to sit still as long as possible, but all I did was sneak a few peeks over at Bryn, who just smiled, batted her long lashes, and took notes. I wanted to cover my face. She had me blushing and shit. I ain't know dark skin could turn red. I never felt what I was feeling before. She had me all bubbly and responding to questions all goofy. I was sweating, stuttering, and fumbling trying to pass her the salt. I wanted to run out and come back in to start over, but instead I calmed myself down and started following her lead on everything, hoping I wouldn't fuck up and ruin the chance to ever see her again.

When the meeting was finally over, I walked them out. We said our goodbyes. I wanted to kiss her hand and shoot my shot, but I punked out. I just blurted out, 'I'mma go wit' y'all.' They knew what I meant. I had to see her again. I needed another chance.

After I signed the contract, I wanted to spend time with her almost every day. I felt this crazy energy when I was around her and I always wondered if she felt it too. Every chance I could, I requested an in-person meeting, invited them everywhere: dinner, basketball games, nightclubs, football games, you name it. And each time trying to flex my muscles and show her I was the man. But she was unimpressed. I'd try all kinds of things to get her to see me, the real me. Or maybe the new me. I would bring her flowers. I ain't ever buy a woman flowers before her, not even my momma. She would smile, thank me, and that's it. I was definitely looking for more, but I knew I wanted to get to know her on a deeper level. But every time I wanted to try, I was scared she was going to turn me down.

First, I thought she was seeing somebody but when I found out she was single and it was just her and her daughter, it was game-fucking-on. I turned up the charm and my pursuit was on a thousand. I was about to be man *and* stepdad of the year. But even when I stepped up, she didn't give me a break and still was so damn independent. Sometimes too independent. She wouldn't let me do shit. I had to be like, 'let me be a man'.

With Carice, I was the man. I was responsible for everything. Everything, to the point I started to resent it. Then I started to resent her. She could see it. Shit, she felt it. I was changing, each and every time I stopped by, I felt like I was becoming a different man. Eventually, the more I saw Bryn, the less time I'd want to see Carice. I'd only come by to see Riley and once she was asleep, I was out, ignoring the fact that Carice's stomach was getting bigger. It was a dick move, but I felt dead around her. And it wasn't because she was pregnant and we wasn't fucking. I wanted more. I needed more.

Bryn made me feel alive. She was the reason I wanted to be a better man. I don't know exactly when it happened. I could say it was at first sight because not only was Bryn a knockout, she was smart, kind, and had the biggest heart. The fact that it was taking forever to win her over only made me want her even more. Finally, I relaxed and took my time. I started paying attention because I wanted everything to be special. And each time I chilled with her I felt at peace. I could totally relax and quiet my mind. I wanted every moment with her to last forever.

Then, she finally agreed to date me. I became Prince-Fucking-Charming and relished every minute of it. I was patient, caring, and most of all, strategic. And when she finally invited me into her personal space, I knew I was in. She couldn't resist.

The sex. Man, the sex was on-point. Like a drug, it pulled me back every time. I don't think I've ever felt that before. Everything with Bryn was new. She was so trusting, unlike any of the many, many women I'd been with in the past. Everything with her was special. I started to fall in love with her and I damn sure knew that she was in love with me.

I knew it because she studied me. She knew my likes, my dislikes. She knew what I would say before I said it. She knew what I would do before I did it. Sometimes, I felt she knew me better than I knew myself. She just got me. We shared the same likes. We both loved Disney movies. She'd flip back and forth whenever I'd talk about kids. We both knew we wanted six. She introduced me to travel. I even started reading again.

There isn't anything she wouldn't do for me. And I know there isn't anything I wouldn't do for her. She's my something special. I don't even know what that means. I just know I don't have the words to describe what we've got. Some shit I made up that's just for us 'cause I never knew it was possible. That's why I made her a promise, always.

And now. . .

I don't know how the fuck I am going to keep it.

2

SOUL MATES

The room pulsates as Jen and I watch the breaking news footage, of my man, in handcuffs and being led into the police station. *NFL Linebacker Shane Smith arrested for alleged kidnapping* flashes in bold red and white text at the bottom of the screen. *I knew it,* I think, as I inhale deeply to try and calm my breathing. As insane as it seems, I could have predicted this. I know who and I know why. Shane's ex, Carice Charles. She's been threatening him with the police for the last two years, except this time, she actually followed through. But if she thinks an arrest is going to tear us apart, she's got another think coming.

"Carice?" asks Jen, breaking our silence.

It's times like this when I most appreciate having my best

friend right next door. She has a cabinet full of liquor that she doesn't drink. I notice I'm clenching my jaw, and release it as I grab a shot glass from her collection. "She finally did it." My voice is sarcastically kind. Closing my eyes, I shake my shoulders and flail my arms to release the tension. "I've got so much crazy energy coursing through my body right now I could run a marathon in record time." I peek at Jen through my good eye, the one that isn't twitching. "This is exactly what she wanted."

"She must have found out. . . about the. . ." she points at my finger, "you know. . ."

I rub my face and gently massage the pressure in my temples. "We are about to do *this*. . . AGAIN!" I take the shot of vodka. It burns going down, causing me to choke. "I can't let her win."

It was only a month ago that I had an ah-ha moment and promised myself I would end this game with Shane. With all the back and forth, he'd lost my trust and I finally called it quits. The only reason I agreed to take him back was because he said he wanted the same thing I wanted, a commitment. But if this is what our future is going to look like, I'm not having it. You know what? I can't let my mind go there at this moment. I need to talk about something else.

"Whatever. I'm hungry."

"Wow, your reaction. That's different." Jen shrugs her shoulders. "I just expected you to be flipping out."

"If I flip all the way out, she wins. Not today. I'm not stroking out over this bullshit. We all know Shane didn't kidnap his kids. That accusation is ridiculous enough. You and I both know there's nothing in this world he loves more than his kids. Not even me. He wouldn't do ANYTHING to jeopardize losing them."

"But he did." She flips her left hand like Beyoncé's single ladies.

"This doesn't count. It's not fair."

"She's playing for keeps."

"Well, if she thinks publicly humiliating him by telling the world that he fucking stole his kids will have him running back to her with open arms, she's wrong. She threatened him with this last time, remember? The publicity stunt from Hawaii?" I refill my glass.

"You're right!"

"She's recycling threats. She just happened to execute this time." I grab the remote to turn the television off. Just in time, my impressionable little girl is rushing down the stairs with Jen's younger sister, Taylor. "Anyway," I widen my eyes and perk up, letting Jen know that I'm changing the subject. "Bailey babes, I feel like cooking!"

"But Mommmmm! But we just got dressed to go out to brunch!" She stands with her hands on her hips.

"Great, you look chic. So that means you can go inside the grocery store and do my shopping for me. I'll add French toast to my list just for you." I pinch her cheeks.

"Works for me," says Taylor. "I like your French toast."

We leave the house and Jen turns to me. "I'll drive."

Taylor pouts, "No, I want to ride in Bryn's car." She likes to ride in it whenever she visits. When she tries to get in the front, Jen delivers a look of death and she proceeds to the back seat.

"Don't even try it," says Jen through her teeth.

Taylor rolls her eyes at Jen and sulks. "You get to ride in her new car all the time."

Jen whips around in her seat. "Get over yourself. You're not nine years old like Bailey!"

"Shane bought you this car for your birthday, right?"

"He did," I nod, backing out of the driveway.

"That ring too?" asks Taylor.

Jen turns and faces the back seat. "DJ Bailey, you're in charge of the music."

I thought she was going to fuss out Taylor.

"I got you." Bailey takes out her iPod and *Freeze* by T-Pain and Chris Brown starts to play. She starts dancing in her seat. "I got this one from Shane."

Shane, Shane, Shane. There's no escaping him. Our lives have been so intertwined, it's hard not to think about him even when we try. I put my car in sports mode and speed to the store. When we arrive, I give the girls door-to-door service. As soon as Bailey and Taylor jump out, Jen immediately picks up the conversation where we left off.

"You don't have to put up a strong front for me. I think you should call someone. I mean. . . he *is* practically your new fiancé." Somehow, I sense Jen is being slightly sarcastic so I ignore her. "What about Terry? I'm sure his bestie assistant or whatever he is these days can at least tell you if he's okay."

"He's fine. But I'll call Terry to ease your worries." Even though Terry is the last person I want to speak with right now, I put my pride aside and dial his number. As I figured, he doesn't answer. He could be busy, but deep down inside I have a feeling he's ignoring my call. He's probably looking down at the phone from filing his nails and mouthing, 'I told you so.' He tried to 'warn' me about Shane from the beginning, but I didn't listen to him or anyone else for that matter. Not even myself.

When he picked Shane up from my house this morning, it was the first time he'd officially seen Shane and me together as a couple. Terry had been professing his love for me for over a year. It's not his fault. I didn't have the heart to tell him, he *never* had a chance. It was always Shane. From the first time we met.

I can always tell when the big dick walks into the room. He has a certain edge about him. So, I can admit, I was checking for Shane that first moment he sat across the table from me. I kept it cool. But it was hard because he flexed his beautiful muscles every chance he got. I would just laugh. The last thing I wanted was to entertain an athlete, especially one I was working for. So, I turned down his countless advances and kept it strictly business. The only problem was even after the event he kept coming around, and the cold shoulder I gave him eventually started to warm.

When I noticed the dynamics of our relationship starting to change, I wondered if I could take a man like him seriously. First of all, he was too unpredictable, a bit of a wild card. That trait drew me to him, but it also pushed me away. He had a sweet sensitive side, but then more times than not, the crazy eventually came out. After working with him, I noticed that he could go from hot to cold in seconds. Jen said he was bipolar.

I think it was the freedom in him that made him so unpredictably likeable. He was daring and he took chances, something that I've always been averse to (being a single mom at twenty tends to make you live a risk-free life). But under his uncertain tough-guy exterior, he also had a gentle spirit. When he wasn't taking quarterbacks out on the field, he was running around being a big kid at heart.

I developed a trust with him. I believed him when he said if I gave him a real chance, he'd never hurt me. Then I started believing in us. And when he put on a full court press, I barely had any strength to resist. I finally felt safe. I took a chance on him regardless of his circumstances. I didn't question the details of his situation, because he assured me that it was over. Carice was a thing of the past and as for me, I was his future.

I'd like to believe it's still the case.

I rub my ring and as much as I want to believe, my heart betrays me and starts to fill with doubt. Carice manages to outmaneuver him every time. Unfortunately for him she has the advantage, his kids. And now that he's been arrested, I'm sure this only helps her case. I don't want Shane to choose between his kids or me, because I know it's a losing battle.

"Umm, earth to Bryn."

Snapping out of a daze, I put my phone in the side of my car door. "No answer. I'll wait for Shane to call." I exhale loudly.

"If you marry him, you think you can deal with this level of drama? She's going to be around at least for the next sixteen years. It's only going to get worse. In fact, if she does know about the two of y'all, I have a feeling she's going to make it a lot harder for him to move forward with his plans."

I let my mind wander and picture Carice running into our wedding ceremony and causing a scene. My anxiety starts to grow.

"Umm, hello, am I talking to myself?"

"I just have to wait to hear from him. No use in speculating and raising my blood pressure, again. I feel like it just went down." I crack my window to let some cool air in.

"The reality is, she's got a hold on him with those kids. If you move forward, you are stuck with them, all of them, including her."

She's right. I cringe at the thought.

"And then you would be exposing Bailey to that foolishness and—"

"Don't make me hand him this ring back." I cut her off.

Jen raises a brow. "I'm just saying to look at the shit-uation without your love goggles on."

"I've come too far to go back now. I just need to speak with him. I have doubts, but I want to hear all the facts no matter how ugly. Saying 'she's crazy' isn't good enough. And maybe, if this is going to continue, I'll change my mind and he can have his ring back. I can go my way and he can go his."

"Umm." She purses her lips. "It sounds good." Jen takes another dig.

"Jen, let's not and say we did. Save the tough-love speech."

The thing I admire most about Jen is her ability to keep it real, but I don't want to hear it right now.

"Whatever you do, stay strong. I know when you love a man, when you really love a man, you will sacrifice."

"Yeah, and with Shane, I'd rather have many sleepless nights next to him than not have him at all."

"I know you do, and it pains me. Loving him has always been a slippery slope. I just don't want to see you crying this whole year like last. I'm only saying this because I care. I truly do."

"And I appreciate it. And I appreciate you for always telling me the ugly truth." I pause. "I take that back. I'm still pissed about that ugglass dress you had me wear to his first event. Things were much simpler then." I smile.

"It's been two years. You act like it's been a lifetime."

"Every day with Shane feels like a lifetime," I swoon.

"Jesus, please make it stop." Jen raises her hands in prayer.

I hold my hand out and watch the flawless diamond catch the light. "She *is* pretty."

"Wow, you couldn't have paid me to believe that this could happen. I mean, I meet him based on a referral. Two crazy-ass years and two events later, y'all are 'engaged', promised or whatever, and we're about to plan a third event. Well, maybe. Depending on how this entire thing plays out."

"Crazy, right? The part that's the funniest is that he got on my last damn nerves."

"You never did tell me when things between you two changed from professional to personal."

"And I never will." I grin.

"Y'all had me fooled. Disrespected Platinum Events. I swear."

"We fell in love." I sway in my seat to *Un-thinkable (I'm Ready)* playing in my head.

"Yuck." Jen sticks her finger down her throat.

"I would tell you about the amazing sex we had this morning in my closet. . ."

"Another time," says Jen, cutting me off and holding her stomach as if she's in pain.

"We're soul mates."

"You really believe that?"

"I do actually."

Jen holds her head. "God help us."

3

<u>ALWAYS</u>

The day passes slower than I can bear. I find myself waiting by the phone, checking and rechecking it to make sure the ringer is on so I haven't missed his call. This is one hell of a way to bring in the New Year. After checking my phone for the hundredth time, I realize stores will be closing soon and being hungry and alone is a recipe for disaster. So, I toss on some sweats and even though it's cold out, slip on my flip-flops. My purse is by the door, so I grab my keys and rush out.

One thing I'm thankful for is that I don't have the baby daddy drama. Never did. Bailey's father and I never needed to establish custody. We always had an understanding and respected each other and our positions. In fact, she's with him now. This is the first New Year's Eve we've spent apart. I've heard that bringing in the New Year with someone is the sign of good things to come for that year, so I like to bring each year in with her. But this year, I decided to share the love with her dad.

At the supermarket for the second time today, just my luck, they are locking their doors. *Great.* The Wendy's drive-through is still open. Ugh. My stomach hurts just thinking about it, but beggars can't be choosers. As I make my way over, I see a couple leaving a small Italian restaurant. Instantly relieved, I park and run inside to place a to-go order for myself and Shane, just in case he's released tonight.

Only my excitement doesn't last long. At the bar while I'm waiting to place an order, the news coverage of Shane being arrested is on repeat. The embarrassment makes my stomach ache all over again. People sitting at the bar start to point and loudly share their opinions. "He cheated!" screams some random woman. "Lying, cheating, S.O.B."

Tell them how you really feel, why don't you? Shame. I shrug my shoulders and look down at my phone. It's flat out humiliating. For him and for me.

As soon as the bartender comes over to take my order, my phone rings. I signal that I need a few minutes.

"Hey," Shane's voice is low and slightly muffled.

"How are you?" I feel my heart beating in my chest.

"I'm alright. Just got to deal with this bullshit."

Asking him directly 'what happened' might be off-putting at this time so I decide to wait. "Is there anything I can do? Do you want me to bring you something to eat? I'm out grabbing something now."

"Sure, but I need a minute 'cause I'm about to get on a call with my lawyers. I just wanted to let you know not to worry. I'm sure you saw the news."

Not wanting to make matters worse, I omit sharing that I'm watching it now. . . on repeat. "I'll order your favorite. I'll text you when it's done. I love you."

"I know babe. Thank you. Love you too."

To my surprise, people are still talking about Shane's situation when our order is ready. Then it hits me, and I get butterflies. After all this time, I can't believe I'm feeling anxious when it's time to see him. I need another drink and I don't have any wine at home. I hope the liquor store next door is still open.

The inside looks empty but the lights are still on, so I'm relieved when I try the door and it opens. I head straight to the back to the chilled white wines to find Shane's favorite, a Chateau Ste. Michelle Riesling. No luck, so I search the shelf and find a warm bottle out of my reach. I jump, step on the bottom shelf, and try to use another bottle to scoot it forward.

"Allow me," says a familiar voice, causing me to flinch. Nick's long arm reaches over my head to assist.

"Oh wow! How are you?" I smile and give him the tightest hug.

He smiles sweetly, just as he did when I saw him last, which feels like yesterday. "I'm doing well. How about you?" He steps back and gives me a once-over. "Wow, you look great."

I blush. Bumming it never felt so good. Besides, he's never looked better. His beard is low and a bit scruffy. I can barely contain my excitement. "What are you doing out here? Don't tell me you own this liquor store too," I joke, remembering the last time I saw him. I was at his bar when I got totally wasted, fell on the floor, and banged my head on someone's knees when trying to stand. I hope he doesn't remember. I continue smiling through the embarrassing memory.

"I'm celebrating at my dad's. He lives in Greenspring and this was the only liquor store still open." He looks around, rakes his hand through his dirty-blond curls. I notice his finger is still ringless. "How's Jen?" He hands me the bottle of wine he retrieved from the shelf.

"Thank you. Jen's good." I nod. "Jen is Jen. Always wheeling and dealing."

"Your little princess?"

"She's well. She's with family tonight."

"How about the big guy? I see he's got some drama right now. You talk to him?"

"He'll be fine." I wave it off. "I'm sure of it."

"Awesome. What are you getting into tonight? Got any plans?"

"I think so." I look up, letting my eyes wander the store.

"You think so?"

"Yeah." I sway back and forth, not offering more details and avoiding all eye contact.

"Well, I won't hold you up any longer from your unsure plans." He smiles again and reaches in for another hug. "You still have my number, right?"

"I do. It's always good seeing you, Nick." I wave and leave him in the wine aisle and head towards the register. *Wow, he looks great.* I don't know if he knows that I used to have a huge crush on him. Oh well, it doesn't matter anymore. I stare down at the wine bottle. *I'm taken*. Ha, ha. Even I can't think it without laughing. For some reason, it's starting to feel like a cruel joke.

My cell rings.

It's Shane. "Hey babe. You coming?"

"Yes, I'm picking up your favorite bottle of wine. I'm waiting to check out." I lower my voice to a whisper. "It's taking a while because the lady in front of me is buying $60 worth of pick 3s and she's ordering them one by one."

"Wow."

"I know, right?" I laugh. "And there's no shame." I'm momentarily distracted when Nick gives me a final wave as he walks out.

"Do me a favor though."

"Yes?" I come back to reality. "What do you need?"

"I'm at my other house. My kids' house. I'll send you the address."

"Oh." I get choked up. "Sure, send it. I'll put it in the GPS." My butterflies leave and awkwardness settles in with 'my kids' house' on repeat in my head.

Still, I make a quick detour home to freshen up and dress comfy but cute. I leave my hair down, add a touch of gloss, and finally slip on my new accessory. "I'm taken," I say, staring into the foggy mirror. My distorted reflection doesn't even take me seriously. It's because she knows my deepest secrets and all of the craziness I've been through with Shane. *Is it still even possible for us?* I think. I'm thankful that I don't have a clear view of her face when she responds, *Am I hopeful or absolutely crazy?* Whatever it is, I lift my chin, square my shoulders, and exhale. It's now or never. I'm not going down without one last fight. It's me against his vengeful ex. I can do this. We're going to make it. I'm *almost* sure of it.

The GPS takes me to a palatial house hidden in the hills of Greenspring Valley. At the end of the winding driveway, I park between Shane's Black Range and his Blue Hummer. It's the one she drives. I remember, because I'll never forget the day she showed up at my job in it. *That shit show.* I feel a twinge of anger, but still I get out and walk down the blue-lit walkway carrying my sweetheart's food. When he opens the door, I smile the biggest smile. Just seeing him standing at his six foot five, leaner at two hundred and fifty pounds, I start to feel secure and believe anything is possible. "Hey," I say, giving him a kiss. "I come bearing gifts."

He flashes me a slight grin, kisses my forehead, and takes the bags from my hands. I follow him past a massive spiral staircase and into the kitchen, which is right off of an attached great family room.

"It's beautiful in here," I say, looking around and chuckling when I notice his house is painted the same color as mine.

"Thanks. This is the one I gave up."

The colors make sense now.

Shane unwraps the food and sets out our plates. "You can sit down, you know."

He must have noticed me standing as still as a statue. It feels weird being in here. I grab a bar stool and sit with my hands folded in my lap.

"Get comfortable. Well, actually can you get the wineglasses? They're back there." He points to the cabinets behind him.

"Sure." I get up and cross the kitchen to the glasses even

though I don't want to touch anything. A note on the counter for Carice confirms my hesitation, and I can't hold back from zooming in and reading, *Carice, carpet cleaners are scheduled for Wednesday – Darshell.* It's a note from his aunt. I act like I don't see it and continue over to him with the glasses. He stays quiet as he pours a red. Afterwards, he grabs the food and wine, and invites me over to the big comfy sofa in front of the TV.

Shane kicks up his feet. "Have you ever seen *Weeds?*"

"No, never heard of it."

"It's really good."

"Let's do it." I force a smile.

Shane starts the television series and we eat in silence, except for when Shane bursts into laughter every now and again. I'm thankful for that, considering what he's been through today. When we're done eating, he clears the plates, turns on the fireplace, and pulls me onto him to cuddle.

I know I doze off a few times because when I hear him laugh, I wake up. I'm beginning to wonder why he hasn't said anything yet.

"You want a blanket?" Shane asks, starting the next episode.

"Sure." I watch him as he walks away and goes upstairs. This is so weird. Besides that note, there isn't any sign of Carice or his children, but I still feel like an outsider. It's like I shouldn't be here. I put on a fake smile when Shane returns with the blanket and the bottle of wine.

"You going to try and stay up until midnight?"

"I'll try." I laugh.

Shane fills our glasses, pulls me close. "Where's my girl?"

"Bailey? She's with her dad." After hearing myself say it, I immediately regret it.

He goes silent and stares into the flames. "They're gone."

Afraid to say the wrong thing, I simply wait for him to say more.

"I don't even know where they at. I can't call the police on her 'cause she got temporary full custody." His eyes begin to glisten.

"I'm sorry." I rub his arm.

"Shit's crazy, right? She knows I went to your work party." Shane nods and takes a gulp of wine. "It was my weekend with the kids, but Qmar was watching them. I stayed by you. She was blowing my phone up leaving messages that she was coming to get the kids. I text her back like, hell, no you ain't. I was with you, so I didn't get them home in time. She was at my house when I got home. We got to arguing. Riley was crying. Qmar is my security now and left a gun on the kitchen counter. It had a safety on it. Don't matter. She told the cops saying I was trying to hold the kids hostage. Now I'm a kidnapper. Now, she fucking with my paper. Fucking up my paper fucks up hers. She don't think. She reckless. The Nighthawks are involved now. They want me to put this shit to bed."

My thoughts exactly.

Shane turns the channel to *Ryan Seacrest NYE*. He goes silent again.

When the countdown begins, he refreshes our glasses.

". . . five. . . four. . . three," Shane looks down at me, ". . . one. . . Happy New Year, babe!" He plants a big wet kiss on my lips. I cuddle in close to him and close my eyes.

"Babe." His voice startles me. "Go get in the bed." He looks down at me, stroking my head.

"What time is it?"

"It's 3 am."

"You've been awake all this time?"

"I can't sleep. Go upstairs and get in the bed."

"I don't want to leave you." I cuddle in close to him.

"I'll be up. Change. There are t-shirts in my closet. Go stretch out."

Maybe he wants to be alone, so I don't put up a fight. I give him a kiss goodnight and leave him and the blanket on the sofa and walk up the massive staircase. On the top floor I pass his daughter's room. It's decorated in a princess theme. Across the hall is his son's room furnished with racecars. I continue down the long hallway and open the double doors to his master suite. Since I have to use the bathroom, I look around there too. It's completely empty with the exception of toilet paper, soap, and a roll of paper towels. After I wash my hands, I take a peek in the medicine cabinet. That's empty too. On my way back into the room I enter the walk-in closet to find a t-shirt. It's been cleaned out. Only a Nordstrom bag sits on the floor filled with white t-shirts. *This feels soooooo wrong.* This was their home. I change and fold my clothes and place them on an empty shelf. A million thoughts flood my mind and not one of them is positive.

Staring at the bed, I don't even want to get into it. I know it was hers, even theirs at one point. I sit at the foot of the bed and can't bring myself to getting comfortable. Instead, I walk back downstairs to find Shane sound asleep on the sofa. I won't wake him, so I cuddle next to him. My presence wakes him anyway.

"What are you doing?" He rubs his sleepy face.

"I came back to get you." I reach for him.

"I can't sleep up there. I miss my kids too much." Shane looks up at me like a sick puppy. "I've got to get my kids back. Carice text me. She and the kids are in New Jersey at her cousin's house. If I agree to her arrangement, she'll bring them back and drop the charges. If I don't listen, she'll ruin me. I'm nothing without my kids and I ain't shit without football."

My heart sinks and as the room falls silent, I stare at Shane feeling completely deflated. And for a moment I sense that somehow this is my fault and I want to disappear. I sit next to him and force a smile. Then he leans closer and I console him until he finally falls asleep. As for me, I lay my head on his chest. I want to cry for him. I can feel his pain. His joy has been taken away. I stare at the flames for what feels like hours experiencing a plethora of emotions and agonizing over my next move.

An arrangement? I'm all too familiar with Carice's definition of an arrangement. Whether he wants to admit it or not, we both know this 'arrangement' includes Shane with an end game of forcing us apart. She can't be trusted. She would do anything in her power to come between us, including using his kids.

I close my eyes. I love Shane. I love him in all his madness. But now I feel robbed. At my company holiday party, I got the chance to see a glimpse of the old Shane that I've been dreaming to get back. And I know, as I sit here cuddled in his arms, that we are right back where we started and we can't move forward like this.

I slide from under his arm without waking him and kiss him tenderly on the forehead. As I walk towards the kitchen knowing it's the end of a beautiful relationship, I wipe tears away before flipping over the note left for Carice.

My hand shakes as I write, *Always.*

Placing my ring on top of the note, I glance back over to Shane before gathering my belongings and skulking out the door.

4

<u>NEW YEAR NEW ME</u>

It's officially morning and I wake up feeling like shit. That's why if I had it my way, I'd roll over, cuddle under the covers, and lie around all day doing absolutely nothing. But I can't. Today is Jen's inaugural New Year's vision board brunch and if I don't make an appearance, I can forget any and all babysitting favors for the rest of the year. So, despite my wish, I untangle myself from the covers, sludge out of the bed, and start to put myself together.

As I soak in a hot bath filled with lavender-scented Epsom salts, I feel my stress levels reduce a few notches almost immediately. But I'd be lying if I said everything is okay. I'm hurting. More than Shane will ever know. And I have to hide it, at least for today. Turning Jen's shindig into my pity party is the last thing I want to do.

Jen's door is unlocked when I arrive, so I let myself in. The aroma of buttery biscuits greets me. "Happy New Year!" I force a smile. "I see you've gone all out." There's an arrangement of red roses and white hydrangeas down the center of her dining room table. "Your display is lovely."

"And I decided to cook. I was talking to my Aunt Jackie this morning and she was telling me all about her breakfast spread." Jen cooking is a rare event. "Fried potatoes with onions and red peppers." She points with her spatula. "Bacon, sausage, scrapple, eggs, pancakes, waffles, baked cinnamon apples, and honey butter biscuits."

"I'm glad you're inspired. I assumed you were getting it catered. Let me try one of those biscuits." I smile and grab a warm one off the baking sheet.

"Those are made from scratch." Jen looks up. "My God, you look dreadful. Shall I ask why?"

Did I not do a good job with packing on the concealer to cover the dark circles around my eyes? Acting like I don't know what she's referring to, I add more butter to this delicious biscuit. "Really?" I ask between chews.

"You can try that fake stuff with someone else. Remember, I know you. Your eyes are the windows to your soul. Right now, they are screaming disappointment."

"There's nothing to discuss." I flash her a close-lipped smile and drizzle honey on my final bite.

"If it's the usual. . ." Jen takes off her mittens and checks her phone. "Be quick about it. Bae and Sasha are five minutes away."

"Are you sure?"

"Bryn, I know you and I know Shane. Start talking."

"Shane managed to outdo himself this time. For starters, when I finally talked to him, he had me meet him at his old house. The one he said he 'had' to give to Carice last year."

Jen frowns. "What was he thinking? What was that like?"

"Eerie. I was not comfortable at all. I'm guessing we were there because he wanted to feel close to his kids."

"Did he say that?"

I shrug and help myself to some orange juice. "He didn't have to. He's trying to be transparent, I guess. Either way, we both had a hard time sleeping. For different reasons, I'm sure."

"What was his reason?"

"Long story short, as it turns out Carice wants another arrangement, and he's going to agree to one."

"Bryn. . . oh my dear Bryn." Jen shakes her head, removes her apron, folds and places it in her kitchen drawer.

"It's bad, I know. But I'm not taking this lying down." I flash my ringless hand. "I left it."

Jen's eyes light up. Her look of disappointment is now a cross between shock and horror. "You didn't?" She runs over to hug me. "I don't know if I'm sad or proud, but you definitely need a hug. My God! How did he react?"

"I don't know. . . yet."

"Can you be more specific?"

"I left a note and placed the ring on top of it."

"Oh my. You literally kicked him while he was down? I assumed you guys would have talked about this."

"It's for the best. I'm confident that I will be fine. . . in the end. I deserve to be happy, and all I keep feeling is pain. I've lived just fine without him in my life before." I try and convince both of us.

"Umm, hmmm."

"A few weeks ago, I came back from Trinidad refreshed and focused on moving on. And then you and Bailey fall for his okie doke and decide to help him get me back. I fall for it and end up with a 'promise'. Carice loses her shit and now we're here. I mean, who am I kidding to think this was really going to end in happily ever after." I pause. "Enough is enough."

Jen bites her lips and spares me the 'I told you so' stare-down. "Would you like to hear my honest opinion?"

"Just spit it out."

"You are in denial. This right here. . . is only temporary. He's going to come after you as soon as he wakes up." The doorbell rings. "Chew on that for a bit." Jen leaves me to answer the door.

She's right. This isn't any different from the last time and I need to be ready for when he shows up. My phone chirps, alerting me to a new voicemail. My stomach churns when I hear his voice.

"Not you too. Call me."

My heart melts. I drudge up the strength to press delete, put a smile on my face, and turn to receive Jen's guests.

"Hey lovely." Bae gives me a kiss on each cheek. "You look nice. . ." He sounds unsure but I'll thank him anyway.

"Why thank you, darling." I bat my eyelashes. "New Year, new me."

"I like that! I'm going to use that this year. It's the start of a new decade. Why not?" He cases the food display. "This looks delightful."

It's time to be seated and Jen takes her place at the head of the table. "Before we dig in—"

My phone rings loudly, interrupting Jen. "Sorry." I cringe and turn my phone on silent.

"I just want to say thank you for coming and being a part of my life. I appreciate each and every one of you. I decided to prepare a special meal curated by my beloved Aunt Jackie, so I hope you brought your appetites." Jen bows her head, blesses the food, and tells us to keep the compliments to the chef coming.

Even though I just lost my appetite, I make a plate with a little bit of everything while my cell vibrates non-stop on the table.

"You need to get that?" asks Bae.

"It can wait." I wave dismissively. "It's nothing."

Jen raises a brow. "I wouldn't say it's nothing but you might want to take care of it before—"

"I got it. I'll take care of it." After I make my plate, I look at my phone notifications. I have ten text messages, two Twitter mentions, and three Facebook posts. All from Shane. I unlock my phone and respond to his last text.

I'm not at home so please don't come.

Where you at?

I'm busy. Can't talk right now.

Who you wit?

I'm with friends. Then I've got to get Bailey. Promise I'll call you later.

I'll be waiting at your house.

I tuck my phone away.

"We good?" Jen's eyes widen.

"Let's just say, you were right." I try to keep a smile from creeping across my face.

"Umm, hmm." Jen rolls her eyes. "Oh, and one more thing. I read an article recently that said some people discuss blessings they received in the prior year so they start the New Year in a state of gratitude."

"I'll start." Sasha raises her hand. "I'm thankful you made that call and I was available. Being a part of the Platinum Events team has truly been a blessing. I'm able to express myself creatively while also having fun. What more could an artist ask for? Thank you, Jen and Bryn."

"You're welcome, Sasha. Thank you for your kind words and honestly, we couldn't have done it without you." Jen looks over at me to go next.

"Where do I start? I guess I'm thankful for realizing that the definition of insanity is doing the same thing over and over and expecting a different result." I raise my glass. "To finding our voices, enforcing change, and staying off the sidelines!" I lower my glass. "That's all I've got."

"Ooookaaayyy!" Jen turns to Bae. "Bae, how about you?"

"I'm blessed. And this year I was able to be a blessing to my family. Not just financially, but emotionally. We experienced a lot of loss this year and because I was in a good head space, I had the ability to be there for others."

"To higher heights. That's what I want to be. A blessing to others. Service is so important. Speaking of which, I want to plan an event for a day of service this year." Jen takes a few bites.

"Now just wait a minute, Jen. What about you? What are you

thankful for?" Bae asks.

"I'd have to say my biggest blessing is the fact that I lost my job and started a business I've been able to maintain off of word of mouth. People love our work. Our clients love us, and I don't want to return to Corporate America. So let's keep up the good work! I'm thankful for another year of good health. Not just for me, but for my friends and loved ones. May the blessings of God continue to rain down on us. Now let's eat before the food gets cold."

Thirty minutes and a full stomach later, I stare at a blank canvas, which will soon be my 2010 vision board. I'm not going to lie. I'm distracted and everyone can tell, so I do my best to refocus. I excuse myself and return home to grab my board from last year to help get me started. It's covered in cutouts of a bunch of my favorite designer items from Chanel, Dior, and Burberry. Lots of fur coats in various lengths and colors. At the very top, a photo of me and Dwayne 'The Rock' Johnson's head cutouts pasted over a couple getting married on the beach. Needless to say, since taking Shane back, the Rock's face has been covered with a small photo of Shane.

When I return, Jen is sharing the story of when we first started vision boards a few years ago. It was her idea from the beginning. At first, I thought it was going to be some illuminati type of ritual, until she showed me a book titled *The Secret* by Rhonda Byrne. She told me that she watched a video about the law of attraction and visualization, which is the concept behind the board. If you can visualize something, you have the power to will the universe to manifest it in real life. So, we tried it and since we've witnessed the results, we've been doing them ever since.

This year, I think I'll take a different approach. Right now, I'm over the material stuff. It doesn't bring the happiness the marketing ads promise. Now don't get me wrong, I love luxury items. I love products that are made well and stand the test of time. But they have their place. It's not a replacement for love and happiness. In the moment, gifts feel great and I feel even better when I wear them. But if I'm not wearing them for the one I love, they become just things or a nice to have. In fact, it's been so long since I've carried my Chanel purse, I completely forgot that I even owned one. Also, those things that I've accumulated from my vision board over the last two years don't keep me warm at night. This morning was the perfect example. When I returned to an empty house, not one of those handbags mattered. Not one designer shoe showed up for me when I needed it the most. With that said, my 2010 vision board theme is the reinvention of happiness.

I flip through some magazines with that thought in mind and come across a few words, statements, and blurbs that speak to my soul. *Face anything. Stronger than ever. No drama. Know your worth. Plan of action.* I like them. They make me feel good. Positive energy flows through me when I say them aloud. Then I find a few fitness photos. Last night when Shane and I were watching *Weeds,* this perfectly toned woman was changing her clothes and Shane was practically drooling on himself. He was like, *Damn! You can tell she works out.* But I wouldn't be doing it for Shane. It's going to be for me. Part of my new self-care plan. I want to be both mentally and physically fit. And since I'm a hopeless romantic, I leave a place for love and repurpose the cutout of Dwayne and I at our beach wedding. Last time I checked he was single. There's hope still. As for Shane, I'll listen to what he has to say but until then, I attach his face on the sideline.

I deserve love.

Healthy love.

And while mouthing my 2010 mantra, *New Year, New Me,* I add the finishing touches to my board.

5

THE CONTRACT

As expected, there's a knock at my door. I open it, and Shane's down on one knee covered in snow flurries. "Is this what you want?"

I pause and think. "Actually. . . yes! It's exactly what I want."

He looks up with puppy-dog eyes. "Can we talk?"

Waving him in, I leave the door open and walk into the living room. Bailey must have heard his voice because she's trampling down the stairs to get to him.

"Hey you!" Shane high-fives Bailey. "Happy New Year."

"Happy New Year to you!"

"How have you been? Your mom told me you've been having dance practice a lot."

"Yup. We're rehearsing for our spring show." She does a halfhearted pirouette.

"When is it?

"It's in April!"

"Cool. I'mma holla at your mom for a bit and then I gotta fly out. But I'll check my schedule to see if I can make it back for the big show. Give me a hug."

"Have a safe flight."

"Thank you, Bailey baby."

Bailey runs over to give me a hug and kiss goodnight before she heads back upstairs.

Shane walks over and sits next to me on the sofa. After leaving Jen's, I had no idea when he'd pop up, so I made sure I looked my best. My hair looks effortlessly sexy even though I just spent hours in the mirror.

He takes my hand and puts the ring back on my finger. "Don't take this off again. I made a promise."

"Umm. . . when were. . ."

"Let me finish. You know how much you love Bailey. You know how much I love her. Just imagine if her dad had complete control over her and you couldn't see her. It would suck, right? You can't understand what I'm going through. I'm not a part-time dad. I ain't sign up for that. I need to see my kids every day. This situation is killin' me. It's like a part of me is missin'. I don't want to lose you as well."

"Even I can see that Carice is using your kids to manipulate you and she isn't going to stop until she gets what she wants, and that's you. You're juggling. You're like a double agent. A bad one, I might add." I pause. "So I assume you agreed to her terms."

Shane opens his mouth to speak.

"You know what? You took too long to respond. I'm not doing this." *Go Bryn.*

"So you just gonna let her win?"

"Do I really have a choice?"

Shane jumps up and starts pacing. "For real—"

"I'm not going backwards. I'll be thirty this year. *Thirty*! I'm not getting any younger. I want a family. Damn, I *may* want another kid. We're so far away from a happily ever after, it doesn't seem like it's even a possibility. The best thing I can do for me is to be honest with you and speak my truth."

"What do you want from me? My hands are tied."

"Seriously?" I lean back on the couch, close my eyes, and take a deep breath. "Maybe I should take a page out of Carice's book. It seems to work for her."

"What you mean?"

I stand up, making direct eye contact. "Hell, I want an arrangement! That's what'll get me to stay."

"Done."

Oh shit! It worked. "Better yet," I fold my arms across my chest, "I want it in writing."

"You for real?"

Hold your ground, Bryn. You're doing great. "I am," I say matter-of-factly.

"Let's do it!" Shane claps his hands loudly before extending his arm to give me a fist bump.

"I'll draw up a contract."

"Have it to me in the morning. Preferably before I fly out."

"It's going to be official. If you break it, Carice won't be the only one taking you to court." It's hard for me to keep a straight face. This is all too ridiculous.

"I gotta go to court wit' you too?" Shane makes his way to the front door.

"Are you saying you are going to break it already?"

"I ain't say that."

"Umm, hmm." I squint my eyes before continuing. "It's going to be airtight. Now *I* can always release you. But *you*, you can't quit."

Shane shakes his head, laughing. "You trying to make it like my NFL contract? Then I can't wait to start negotiations." He grins and flashes a wink.

"Did you negotiate with Carice?"

His smile disappears. "Not *dem* types of negotiations."

"Well, I can tell you one thing." I twirl around in front of him, making sure he gets a three-sixty-degree look at me. "You're not getting this until we have a signed contract on file."

Shane tries to smack my ass but misses. "Have your people call my people and let's make a deal." He grabs my arm and pulls me in close.

I push him away. "No touching."

"I should warn you. I'm an expert at negotiating." He laughs, grabbing his dick as he walks towards the door.

"Just for that display of cockiness, I'm adding guarantees! Laugh at that."

"Bye Uncle Shane!" Bailey yells from upstairs.

Shane flinches. "Was she listening to us?" His eyes widen.

I shrug my shoulders. "I hope not." I walk behind him, nudging him out.

"Bye, Bailey baby!" he shouts. Then he turns to face me. "Can I get a hug goodbye? Like a real one?"

"Sure, because it's going to be the last one you get for a while." I stand on my tippy-toes and wrap my arms around his strong neck. He leans in and kisses my lips ever so softly. And just like that, my panties are wet. I pull him in closer and our small peck turns into a long passionate kiss. He backs me into the house and up against the wall.

"You know I always get my way, right?" Shane whispers. Picking me up, he pins me against the wall. He's quick with his hands. "She wet, just like I thought. You can't resist the Hulk."

"You better put me down before Bailey catches you."

Shane instantly drops me. "Can I come sneak over tonight? Like old times?" he grins. "Leave the door unlocked and I'll sneak into your room after Bailey's asleep. We can have silent sex again." He smiles at the thought.

Don't get weak. Stay strong. "Not without a signed contract," I remind him.

Shane takes out his phone. "Negotiations begin in twenty-four hours. I'll delay my flight."

"Don't worry, Mr. Smith. You'll have your contract." I pat him on the ass as he leaves.

Carice gets an arrangement, and so do I. Even if I don't sleep, I don't care, I'm writing this contract tonight. I lock the door and peek out the window, watching him jump into his Range.

"Whelp, I guess we're giving this another shot. Third time's a charm." I set the alarm and turn the lights out. When I get upstairs, Bailey is on her laptop. "Lights out, munchkin." She puts her laptop away and I go into my room and pull mine out. "Let's make this happen."

I still have a blank page an hour later, so I call Jen for help. When I tell her what I'm putting in place, she's ecstatic. "And he's going to sign it?" she asks.

"Yes, he's going to sign it. I think he trusts and knows that I have his best interests at heart, and I would never do anything to deliberately hurt him. I know he knows that."

"You sound like you've got your head on straight, but I'll believe it when I see a signed copy. Do you know what you want?"

"I think so."

"Because if you don't know, you need to figure it out. Otherwise, you'll forever be doubting and constantly looking over your shoulder."

"Well, that's kind of the point, isn't it?"

"I mean, just like a ring don't keep a man faithful, neither will a signed copy of a piece of paper."

"What if I put in a clause for marriage?"

"I'd say you were on the right track, but is that what you really want? Are you ready to be a wife? Or are you just saying that because you want to lock him down and you probably only have a handful of years left before you become a high-risk pregnancy? Would you really want to have his kid and be tied to him for the next eighteen years? Ugh. The thought. I need some Pepto."

"Here we go. I'm doing this because clearly, Carice plays this game better than me. So now, I've got to one-up her with one of her own tricks. If this arrangement means being tied to him forever, then so be it. I don't want to waste any more time with him. Either we're headed someplace serious, or he can go play games with someone else."

"I hear you. I'm still trying to figure out when y'all got on good terms again."

"Don't hate. He showed up like you said he would."

"I'm not hating. My concern is always what's best for you and Bailey. If marrying Shane is the end game and that is what's going to make your life complete, so be it. But if not, you need to be honest with yourself first. I don't know if I can see it."

"Maybe it's not for you to see." I roll my eyes at the phone.

Jen goes silent and I hear her clear her throat. "Listen, as long as you see it. I don't have to wake up next to crazy every day. You do."

"He makes me happy."

"He also makes you sad. I've been the one nursing your tears."

"I'm happiest when I'm around him."

"If you're only happy when you're around him, you need to find a hobby or do some additional self-work. He should only be enhancing your internal joy."

"I like who I am around him."

"And who is that?"

"Okay Jen. You've made your point."

"You're the one who just called me and mentioned marriage. That is not a game. It's not something you jump in and out of. And the last thing you want to do is to be tied to a fool. I'm just keeping it real. As real as possible without getting you all upset. I just want you to think before you mention marriage in the contract."

"You're ruining this for me. It's supposed to be fun."

"Then make it fun."

"You don't think marriage is fun?"

"I swear y'all have had an equal amount of drama since y'all started seeing each other. I swear it's been half great and half insane. I think it's premature to start talking forever."

"But when you know, you just know."

"Does he know?"

"I think he does. We've got something special."

"I swear if I hear you say that one more time. . ."

"But we do. It's like Bobby and Whitney. They were crazy as a bag of cats. But they loved each other."

"It takes more than love to make a marriage work."

"Okay, since when have you gotten so well versed in marriage?"

"First of all, I'm educated. I read. And secondly, Aasim is married. And the latest, if I haven't shared because we've been so consumed with talking about Shane, is that he's living with his ex-wife. Crazy, I know. It doesn't change the fact that he's infatuated with me. Now, the only reason why nothing has happened between us is because of me. I refuse to sleep with a married man. It's against my moral code."

"I thought you said morals were taking up a lot of space in your bed at night."

"They are. If I could just push them off, I'd have room for more dick. But as it stands today, I won't do it. I believe in karma. I would never want something like that to come back to me. But back to you. I don't want to rain on your parade. Do what you need to do. I'll be here for you either way. Let me know if you want me to look it over when you're done."

"Of course. I wouldn't have it any other way."

6

ROSES ARE RED

It's the first day back at the office for the New Year and as soon as I park my car, I receive a text from Mandy announcing that she wants to quit. Followed by another saying she's only mentioned it to me. Since I care, I'm now responsible for talking her off the ledge. It's another reminder that this year is getting off to a rough start.

I walk into a dark office. "Good morning. Happy New Year!" I sing, trying to bring levity.

Mandy swings around. "Harry sold the company!"

"What?" I click the light. "How do you know? Did I really just ask you? What I meant to ask was did he tell you that?" I think for a second. "Never mind." I hang my coat and place my purse on the center table. "Let me guess. You used your special skills."

"You got that right." She claps her hands and leaps from her chair.

I want to put my lunch in the fridge but I know she's not going to let me get away, so I let her continue while I stand in the center of the office holding my bag.

"I saw a wire confirmation for $10,000,000 on the fax yesterday referencing a Major Taylor." Her eyes widen as she walks towards me. "It's a code name," she whispers.

I would not have figured that out, but okay. "Before I even get into everything else. . . you were here yesterday, why?"

She walks back to her desk. "After the party, Harry was a little drunk and started talking about how next year we'll have the chance to buy stock options. So I came to the office yesterday and checked his files." She whips out a thick stack of papers. "The official records, bank covenants and all. And he lied." She points. "We can't buy stock. It's above our pay grade."

"Why am I not surprised by *anything* you've just shared?"

"Are you going to stay?"

"Let's not make any rash decisions. I'm willing to wait and see what happens."

"I'm thinking about doing my own thing." She tosses the papers onto the center table.

"You should look into that for sure, but not right now. We're technically in a recession." I use the break in convo to put my food away. When I return, she starts thumbing through the document.

"The equity firm Harry partnered with is bringing in a CFO. His name is Leroy Kelley. I've got his employment agreement right here. I've already done my initial screening and background check."

"Mandy. Your stalking is at a whole other level. Seriously." I chuckle. "I don't know. I may need your services soon."

"Girllll! I heard about Shane! Carice dropped the charges, according to the morning news."

"They act like they have nothing else to report on."

"That's good news, right? Y'all looked mighty cozy on that dance floor at the holiday party."

"Mandy. . . there's a lot that I need to catch you up on. Much has transpired between Shane and me since that party." I try to keep from smiling. "And it involved a diamond."

"Holy shit, Bryn! Why didn't you call me?" Mandy leaps up from her chair and hops onto my desk. "That's probably why he got locked up! Where's the ring? I wanna see. I wanna see."

"It's at home. I'm not ready."

"Girl, you crazy!"

I shrug.

"It's expensive, I'm sure!" Mandy's blue eyes twinkle.

"Let's just say, he got that part right."

"Why can't he get it *all* right?"

"Mark my words! He's about to, or else. For real this time. In fact, I'm literally making him sign a contract to ensure he does."

"What?" Mandy stares at me blankly.

I shrug my shoulders. "Yes, I'm putting my terms in writing to essentially stay in his life while he sorts out this mess. He's going to agree to it and I think it's going to work. Negotiations begin tonight." I grin.

"I don't know. . . it sounds like you've finally cracked, but I think I like it," she squeals. "If you need any ideas, and I've got plenty, I'm right there." She points to her desk.

"Appreciate it. I think I've got this one." I smile at Mandy and then turn away to reclaim the start to my day. I need to concentrate because I've got a contract to write.

We're about halfway through our quiet workday when we get a visitor at our office. A tall lean suit with designer stubble leans on our doorframe with an iPad and today's paper tucked under one arm and introduces himself as our new boss, Leroy. "I insist you call me Lee," he says with a slight southern drawl. I catch Mandy assessing him as he continues. He enjoys his morning coffee at Starbucks, long business lunches, and his days off to spend at his beach house. He also slips in that he'll be working remotely from there a few days during the week, especially in the summer months. "I've got young ones at home." He finishes his intro by sharing that he's a huge Cowboys fan. "And you?" he points to Mandy.

With an unimpressed gaze, she crosses her arms and responds sharply, "I'm Mandy and I prefer to be addressed as Mandy."

Unlike Mandy, I stand to shake his hand. "Hi Lee, I'm Bryn. I look forward to working with you." I shoot Mandy a play nice look. She completely ignores me and remains silent.

"Mandy, want to come with me? I've got big plans for your new department." Lee turns and springs away.

"Already making changes, huh?" Mandy huffs under her breath.

I really hope he didn't hear her. I shake my head and continue with my work.

I'm in the zone when Mandy marches back into our office and slaps her notebook down. "It's either him or me. So I need to find some dirt on him."

"He doesn't seem that bad."

"How can you take him seriously? When I look at him all I see is Rob Lowe. You can't trust anyone that has a permanent smirk and spends that much time styling his hair."

I Google Rob Lowe and shake my head at the similarities. "This is funny. They do look alike."

"I was going to tell him he needed to button his shirt, this isn't a movie set."

"Oh, Mandy."

"He's splitting us up! Whoop de!" Mandy plops down in her chair and pouts.

"Now I have to act like you didn't just come in here and tell me."

"I don't care if he knows. You're up next. He's waiting in his 'new corner office' for you. I can't believe Harry gave him that office."

When I approach Lee's office, he's inspecting his teeth, so I pause at the door.

"Come on in." He stands and pats his hair in the mirror. "I've heard nothing but great things about you and Mandy. But as with all mergers, there is organizational change. I've had some time to evaluate the various back offices and I've decided that I'm removing Mandy from finance completely. She'll be our senior accounts officer and as for you, Ms. Charles, you're my new controller."

"Really?"

"Yes. And we'll be pulling support staff from the other entities so you can both lead your new departments."

Looks like my vision board is in full effect. Things are turning around. "This is great news! Thank you."

"Don't thank me, I'm just the messenger. Harry insisted. I usually come into companies and fire the existing team and build one of my own, but the two of you were identified as key. He mentioned that you both take good care of him."

"Harry said that?" *Seems so unlike him.*

Lee laughs at my reaction. "Please, go through these resumes and you and Mandy take your pick."

I leave his office with a new pep in my step. Controller. It's so unexpected. I return to my office and toss the resumes on our center table and take my seat. Mandy still has her arms folded across her chest, as they were when I left.

"First day and he's already changing things. He didn't even consult with us." Mandy grabs a few of the resumes. "What if I don't want to leave finance?"

"Honestly, all things considered, it could have been a lot worse."

"I've been with Harry for a long time. I just don't know if I want to be working for Lee. In fact, I'm calling him Leroy. I'm not letting him take over my job."

"But he's not. He's going to be focused on his own work, I'm sure."

"I don't like it. He's pulling me out!" Mandy pouts and paces the office. "Looks like I'm going to have to turn up the heat now that I've found his social."

"Mandy. You want to do some investigating? Forget about Lee. I've got something that's actually worth your while."

"Please hire me. Covering the Shane drama would be perfect.

Did you tell Leroy that you're dating Shane?"

"Absolutely not. It's none of his business. Besides, there's nothing to discuss."

"Well then, I should tell you it accidentally slipped out when he bragged about his Nighthawk season tickets."

"Was he really bragging? Because he doesn't seem like the type."

"I don't like his hair!" Mandy blurts, making me laugh.

"I can't with you today."

"I just have a bad feeling about him," Mandy pleads.

"Give him a chance. Time will tell. Just like everything else in life."

Leroy stops by, poking his head into our office. "I'm off to a meeting." He speed-walks out the back door.

Mandy wrinkles her nose. "I smell something fishy."

"I think it's your filet-o-fish, from lunch," I say, pointing at her trash. "Make sure that goes out tonight."

The end of the workday nears and I want to be prepared for Lee's return, so I put aside drafting the contract to finish reviewing the resumes. Half are good and the rest, mediocre. Any resume that exceeds two pages goes straight into the trashcan. Anyone with that much experience isn't suitable. I only need an entry-level accountant and I think I found the perfect one, Lisette, a University of Maryland graduate with two years of accounting experience. She seems perfect. I can teach her the ropes.

When I check on Mandy, instead of going through resumes, she's reading through Lee's profile on MD Case Search, on both screens. She has no shame. I leave to get water and when I return, I warn her that I can see her screen. "I could have been Lee."

"No, I just saw him about five minutes ago pulling into the parking lot in his convertible Porsche. What a showoff. Doesn't he know that today is calling for snow?"

"Mandy, Mandy, Mandy." She's headed off the cliff. "I see you aren't going to give him a break. At least try and play nice. Because I know—"

We're interrupted by the dragging of a box as tall as Lee. "Special delivery!"

Mandy quickly minimizes her screen and runs over.

Lee throws his hand up, practically mushing her in the face. "Bless your tiny little heart. It's for Bryn. . ."

I glance at the box excitedly. Meanwhile, my mind is screeching, *What on earth?*

Lee lays it flat and grunts, holding his back on the way up. "Feels like there's a small child in there."

I walk around the box a few times with my mouth wide open. *What is Shane up to?*

"Well, don't just stare at it! Open it! I'll wait. I want to see what's inside!"

When I turn to get a pair of scissors, Mandy is ready and waiting, placing them in my hand like a surgical assistant. "Thanks." My heart pounds and I cut the tape along the edges of the box. Mandy has her phone out filming my every move. "Here goes nothing!" I say, lifting the lid.

"Oh my stars! Are those real?" cries Lee.

Lying in the box are a dozen six-foot long-stemmed roses along with a four-foot glass vase.

"They are beautiful." My hands tremble as I arrange them in the vase. I walk around them a few times admiring their height and find a small cream envelope. *Negotiations start tonight. Love. S*

"Girl. . . good luck with those negotiations!" cries Mandy.

Oh, he's not playing. Let me get back to drafting this contract.

1

THE NEGOTIATION

Shane shows up exactly twenty-four hours later. When I open my front door, he's dressed in a cream sweater, which looks flawless on his muscular chest, and a pair of European-cut pants. He's holding a dozen red roses. "Hello, beautiful." Handing me the roses, he leans in and kisses me on the cheek.

"Hello, handsome. More roses?" I smile. *And he smells delicious. I see he's on a mission.* Now, I slightly regret not having shaved my legs.

"I know you're the kind of woman that appreciates them."

"You're right about that. Let me put them in water before we leave."

He follows me to the kitchen. "Well, we could just stay here, and I can handle all negotiations." His hand trails down my back. "Have we ever fucked in your kitchen?"

I shrug his hand away. "I would appreciate if you would take this seriously."

"Look at me, I am." He licks his lips. "You look sexy."

"We can't solve all of our problems with sex."

"Is that what you think we do?" He hugs me from behind as I fill the vase with water. I feel his hard dick pressing against me.

My eyes water a bit. I know I'm sensitive right now. I'm definitely PMS'ing. I bite my lip to keep it from quivering. "I think. . . In the past. . ."

"Babe. . ." He can tell I'm getting emotional and so he hugs me. "My bad. I ain't mean to upset you. I was just trying to have fun. Remember, it's good that my dick gets hard when I see you. If it didn't, we'd have problems."

"I know. But I don't want that to be the only thing that holds us together. I'm not trying to discount it either. I mean chemistry is necessary, but what happens after that?"

"You gonna start holding out on me?"

"I didn't say that. But—"

"But. . . what?"

"I'm just saying. . ." I look back at him. "Sex—"

"Is a non-negotiable. No deal." Shane reaches over my head, snatches the flowers out of the vase, and runs for the door.

"Shane! Cut it out."

"Ouch!" Shane comes back and drops the roses in the vase. "Fucking thorns." He sucks his finger. "Babe, I'm just keeping it light. I'm fittin' to go so I can lay out our terms."

"Our terms? I'm calling the plays!"

"Wrong."

"Excuse me." I immediately get an attitude.

"I'm fittin' to make this fun." Shane does the two-step, humming the hook to *Forever* by Drake, as he leads me out the door. It begins playing when he starts his truck. When it's over, he flips to a new playlist as we drive downtown. I thought he'd take us to our regular spot, Ruth's Chris, but it seems as though he's got another place in mind. "So how was your day?" he asks me.

I fold my hands primly atop the envelope that contains the infamous first draft of our contract. "Eventful. A lot of change is happening. Good things. But change all the same."

"I had a fantastic day." Shane nods his head to the beat.

"Fantastic? Do tell!" I shift in my seat to face him.

"I talked with my babies."

"Sweet! How are they?"

"Missin' their daddy." He starts thumbing the steering wheel. "Just missin' their daddy," he repeats. He looks like he wants to cry.

"Well, I'm sure they were happy to speak to you." I rub his shoulder. "It's going to be okay."

"I just wish she ain't have the power to keep takin' them like this."

"I can't imagine what it's like."

"It's hell. Pure hell."

We ride the rest of the way in silence, listening to his latest playlist. When he pulls up in front of Oceanaire, the restaurant we visited on our first date, my mouth drops. He hates seafood. "Shane, you didn't have to."

"I'm fittin' to soften you up." Shane gives me a wink and

jumps out. The valet opens my door and helps me out. Shane slips him a hundred and offers me his arm. I'm grinning ear to ear as we approach, and turn to warm butter when we're seated at the same table.

"Did you arrange this?" I look up at him, smirking.

Shane scoots into the booth and makes himself comfortable. "This is where we started." I slide in close to him. He strokes my hair. "It was just you and me. None of this crazy shit we got going on now." He smiles. "I was so scared you wasn't gonna give me a chance."

"Were you really? I thought you noticed I was checking you out from across the table."

"I mean kinda. I do have that natural effect on women." He laughs. "But for real, I couldn't read you. Not really. Not around that time."

"So, you can read me now?"

"Fa sho!"

"Wow, we've come so far. I remember you wore your hat everywhere we went. Oh, and the gold chains."

"Ha, ha." Shane reminisces. "You right. I've grown up a bit. I guess you gonna take credit for that?"

"Of course."

"You changed too. You was all scared to date me. You hit me wit' that ol' dating an athlete bullshit. Now, you love me. You can't get enough of me. You ain't neva gonna leave me and that's why you keep giving me more chances."

"Really, what else do you know?"

"I gotta stop playing games. Time's up."

"So, you're admitting to playing games?"

"Stop, you fucking up the moment."

I raise both brows.

"That ain't come out right. I'm trying to be serious and you joking."

So sensitive. I look him in the eyes and blink for him to continue.

"I admit I've made mistakes. I ain't neva said I was perfect. And for the record, neither are you."

I open my mouth wide to speak but then clamp it shut, give him a tight grin, and allow him to continue.

"Neither one of us is perfect. You stopped trusting me and rightfully so. I feel like I've earned back your trust. Well, I'm earning back your trust."

I nod in agreement.

"Last time we was here, I asked you about your dreams. You said you just wanted to be happy. And this is me puttin' it all out in the open. I want to get this right just as much as you do. I don't even know what I'm about to agree to, but I know if it means keeping you in my life, I'm wit' it."

Our waitress arrives at just the right time to take our orders. When she walks away, Shane holds out his hand.

"Now let me see this contract."

"I need you to brace yourself. You do realize this isn't an ordinary contract?" I hand it to him slowly.

He reaches in the manila envelope and pulls out the two-page typed contract. He rubs his eyes and shakes his head, then begins to read. "Wow! You know I read slow?"

I fold my hands tight, place them in my lap, and wait for him to finish.

Our food arrives by the time he finishes. He loudly exhales and slides the contract back inside the envelope.

I stare at him, searching for a reaction, a response, something.

He places his napkin on his lap and slices into his sizzling hot steak. After taking a huge chunk in his mouth and starting to chew, he chuckles. "Teabagging, huh?" He continues to chew.

"That's all you remember, teabagging?"

His mind always goes there.

"I'm saying it caught my eye." He snickers.

"Nothing else caught your eye?"

"One of your guarantees did."

I bet I know which one and grin, showing all my teeth. "Right here, you sat right where you are now, and you asked me what my dreams were. I didn't have an immediate answer. But now I do. I've even got it all drawn out for you."

"I don't know if I'm ready for marriage." Shane sets down his knife and fork.

"Well, that's where this needs to lead. I can't keep playing the game of Carice and her 'arrangements'. I need to know that you're serious and we're not just wasting time. I need to know for sure that at said time, we will be together, in marriage. If not, then we can part ways now."

Shane narrows his eyes. "I need time to think. I gotta read this again, digest it."

Doubt fills my mind and my eyes get watery. He notices and reaches across to rub my leg under the table. "Why are you 'bout to cry? Please don't. I feel like it's my fault."

"You don't love me enough to marry me?" *I really need to bleed.*

"Bryn, of course I love you. I just don't know if I'm ready."

I attempt to blink my eyes dry and then avoid all eye contact with him. "I didn't say we had to get married tomorrow. I'm saying that if we're committed to each other and we're happy together and it works, then the contract should end in marriage. If it doesn't work, you're free to walk away."

Shane scratches his head. "We can't spend every holiday together. I got kids. And. . . and. . . no social media. It causes too much drama. I can't have you and Carice fighting." He thinks for a moment. "And no cruises. I seen *Titanic* too many times."

"How about a trip to Disney?"

"Yeah, yeah, that'll work. Oh, and add a threesome."

"Excuse me?"

"Ha, ha. I'm kidding. No, not really." He hands me the envelope. "Go ahead and make those changes and come over tomorrow night and I'll sign it."

"You really want me to add that?"

"I mean, is it a deal breaker?"

"Really?" I narrow my eyes.

"Yeah, really. Is it?"

"Nope," I lie, crossing my fingers as if it really works.

"Give it here. I'll mark it up and sign it right now." He snatches the envelope from me.

"As long as we're married first."

Shane's excitement vanishes. "You just took the fun out of it." He hands it back. "Never mind."

Whew! "You don't like that word, do you?"

"Marriage? I mean. I tried it once, it ain't work out. We ain't even make it to the altar for real."

"I'm not her."

"Well, ain't we lucky."

"You're getting distracted. Let's start from the top."

"One. We don't go more than two weeks without seeing each other. Done. My schedule is gonna be ridiculous but we'll work it out."

I smile.

"Two. You wanna meet my family." He gives me a dumbfounded look. "You already been around my family. What are you talking about?"

"Romello. Qmar. Fake cousin Will? Are they your only family members?"

Shane rolls his eyes. "Bet. Three. You want to go to every game? I already said you ain't going to Shitsburg. It's too dangerous. Scratch those two."

"Fine, no Steelers games."

"Four. We get a place together." Shane strokes his chin. "Like, I want that but that's kinda difficult considering I'm trying to figure this thing out with my kids. I mean. . . we haven't even told Bailey!"

"Don't try to use Bailey to get out of this one."

"Let's exchange keys until the timing is better. Will that work?"

"I guess I could make an exception."

"I mean, just still let me know when you coming. Qmar be having bitches over sometimes and I'd hate for you to walk into the house and they fucking."

"Five! Thanks. I didn't need that visual."

"You're welcome," he giggles. "Five. The trip. We covered that. Six. Holidays. We covered that. Seven. Man, you typed it in all caps. NO MORE LIES. We've been through too much for that. I promise that I won't lie to you anymore."

"About anything."

"Nothing, I promise."

"Last but not least—" Shane's eyes widen.

I interrupt, "And you do all of these things, and you will be the recipient of all the things listed below."

Shane's eyes glisten and his smile widens.

"Yes. In the end, I want this to be official." I point to the ring. "I want to be married."

"I gotta sign this?" Shane bites his lip. "What about we do Oprah and Steadman. Life partners."

My smile disappears. "No."

"I'll think about it."

"You've got twenty-four hours. This offer is only good until then."

"And what's up with these guarantees? I'm for real not going to get any cookies until I start checking stuff off this list?"

"Correct." I take the paper from him. "I'll make the corrections and bring it to you for a final signature."

"You didn't like your roses? Didn't it make all the ladies at work jealous?"

I blink. "Uh-uh, you're not getting out of this."

"Let's do it. Whatever it takes."

8

THE FINAL DRAFT

It takes me all day to put the finishing touches to our contract. Between Mandy acting up, and starting to pack up my files at the office, I barely have time to finish it. Since I don't have a printer in my office, I save it on my flash drive and take it by Jen's for her to review the final version.

She takes her time reading through it, and if looks could talk, she'd be screaming. She nods in silence and refers to her phone every now and again before finally speaking. "Are you just doing this out of formality to say you gave it one last chance?"

"We talked. He's aware that it is now or never."

"Understood. Do you seriously think this contract is going to turn him into the man you want him to be?"

"It doesn't matter because he's already the man that I want."

"Really? Interesting." Jen taps her foot.

"Let me clarify. I just want him to address his unresolved issues. And meeting the terms of this contract is the only way I'll stick around while he cleans his mess up. If all goes well, I'll get what I want in the end."

"But do you believe it will work?" Jen sucks her teeth.

"I wouldn't be going through the motions if I didn't."

"Have they worked in the past, these arrangements?"

"So many questions!"

"Look, you asked for my help."

"Seriously? Obviously, this is my first one."

"I mean, the ones he's had with Carice?"

"I don't fucking know. How would I know that?" Now she's pissed me off.

"Relax. I'm just checking to see if there's been a pattern to these arrangements of his. Are you prepared to move on, for real, if he doesn't do these things?"

"Yes!"

"I hope so, for your sake." Jen hands me the final version of the contract. "The saga continues." She has a fake smile on her face. "I'm done with my edits. I added a few extra guarantees. You can thank me later." She's kind enough to print a copy for me since my printer is on the brinks. She thinks it's a sign. "Are you otherwise prepared?"

"I think so."

"Well, nothing beats another failure but a try. I mean, if he fucks this up, I think you can walk away saying that you've tried everything, and you've given him every opportunity to make things work. And for goodness sake you have it in writing to prove it. And you can finally, finally, be free! Hallelujah!"

"Is there something you want to tell me?"

"Oh, nothing. Go forth and prosper." She shoos me away. "Be sure to text me and tell me how it goes."

"I will. What are you about to do?" I stand and collect my things.

"I'm going into meditation and prayer."

"Okay. Have fun. Here goes nothing." I text Shane that I'm on my way, call Bailey downstairs, and we jump into my car to drive over to his house. I know Jen was being a smart ass tonight and that's why I didn't buy into it. She's probably PMS'ing as well. I've got too many other things to worry about, and her opinion of Shane and me isn't one of them. The reality is that I'm in this relationship and she isn't.

"I don't think I've been to his house before," says Bailey.

"Really?" I think for a few moments. "I guess not."

"Are his kids here?"

"I don't think so. I think he'll be leaving soon to go and see them. They've been out of town lately."

Bailey gazes out of the window. She also feels sad when he leaves town.

I turn on music as a distraction. Adele's *Don't You Remember* is playing and I quickly change the station. The last thing I need is her crying as well. I turn to 92Q. It's guaranteed to be playing some rap music. "Don't be sad. I know it hurts, but the time passes quickly. He hasn't left yet so you technically still have time to smile." I stroke her hair. "Look at me."

Bailey wipes a tear away. It breaks my heart to see her like this.

That's when I think about his kids and what they must go through whenever he leaves. It sucks. Life isn't ever fair. Someone is always making a sacrifice to make someone else happy. That's when it starts to sink in. I'm feeling like the bad guy. In my happy little world, Shane is with me and Bailey. In order for that to happen, his kids lose a full-time dad. That's the reality. *Yikes!* I don't want to think about it. Not tonight. Not right before I get this contract signed. I force a smile on my face and pull into Shane's driveway.

Bailey grabs the envelope, unaware of its contents, and walks at my side through the garage to the interior door. I peek in first; the lights are low and romantic music is playing throughout the house.

"Wait here," I say to Bailey. The last thing she needs to see is a naked Shane strolling around the corner. I take my phone out and text him.

Bailey is with me so get DRESSED!

Within seconds, we see bright kitchen lights turn on. I take it as my cue that it's safe to come in and continue into the house.

"Bailey baby!" A disheveled but fully dressed Shane is there to greet us.

She leaps into his arms. He's giving me all kinds of looks and mouthing me off over her shoulder. "I didn't know you were coming. I would have stocked up on some of your favorites. Actually, I may have some golden stuffed Oreos. With some Fanta orange soda?"

Bailey nods yes.

Shane looks at me and wipes his forehead. I know he's thinking that it was a close call. I probably should have told him she was coming with me, but I wanted to surprise him. Instead, it looks like we were the ones about to get a *huge* surprise.

I shake my head and laugh as I leave them in the kitchen and take a seat in the living room in front of the fireplace. He's got it lit, with a bottle of wine and two glasses on the coffee table, and *Aladdin* on the TV on pause. I should have suspected he'd try to seduce me with *Aladdin*. I take the remote and press play.

Shane comes in with a tray of Oreo cookies, Fanta, and popcorn with syrup drizzled over it. They join me on the couch. "Movie night!" shouts Shane. "I see you brought a reinforcement," he whispers. "I guess you got scared." He chuckles to himself.

"Ain't nobody afraid of you. We were just bringing your contract and then we were going to leave."

"I'll sign it after the movie." Shane rolls his eyes at me. "Right, Bailey?"

I can't help but laugh at his sulking. "I meant what I said."

Shane turns up the volume as the *Arabian Nights* song starts to play and he turns the lights low. I know it won't be long before we're all asleep.

Bailey is the first to go out. She's stretched out on the sofa and snoring as Aladdin is about to take the magic carpet ride with Jasmine. I tap Shane on the shoulder. "You want to carry her to the car for me?" Bailey weighs three times as much when she's asleep.

"Seriously? This is my favorite part!"

"Sorry, I figured you could press pause." It's not like he hasn't seen this movie a thousand and one times.

"Be patient. Where are you rushing to?"

"I have to work in the morning and she actually has school."

"And? I have a flight." Shane hushes me and holds up his finger. When *A Whole New World* finishes, he turns to me. "What were you saying?"

"Bailey is upset you're leaving."

"You aren't?" Shane creeps over and tries to kiss me.

"What did I say?" I point to the contract. "Guarantees first."

"You are really taking this contract thing too far." Shane stands and walks into the kitchen. He digs through a drawer, holds a pen up, and then drops it on the kitchen counter. He returns, sits back down and turns up the volume. "There's your pen in the kitchen."

I take the contract into the kitchen and wait for him, sitting in a chair and looking around, daydreaming about what a life living together would be like. His kitchen is at least three times bigger than mine. Lord knows I'd have to take cooking classes. I still cringe thinking about the first time I made dinner for him at game night. I fried boneless, skinless, chicken breast. He hated it. I laugh at the memory.

"What's so funny?" Shane catches me in a trance.

"Laughing at the first time I cooked for you. You made fun of my chicken."

"Yeah, it was pretty bad." He retrieves a glass from the cabinet and fills it with ice. "Who fries chicken with no skin?"

"Apparently I do. And remember those dry-ass red velvet cupcakes I baked that time?"

"Now *they* were awful."

"You ate one."

"I know. They were dry as hell. I ain't wanna hurt your

feelings."

"You do love me, don't you? You eat my terrible cooking." I laugh. "I can't wait to cook for you full time."

"You would want to do that?"

"Why not?"

Shane's eyes shift. "I mean. . ."

"I'll take cooking classes."

Shane exhales. "Thank God. That will work."

I throw the pen at him. "What are you trying to say?"

"I ain't 'trying' to say nothin'."

"You make me sick."

"You are mistaking me with your cooking."

My mouth drops open. "That's mean."

Shane lets out a boisterous laugh. He even wakes Bailey. "I'm fucking wit' you. Come on, where's the contract? Is it ready for my signature?" he asks, using a proper British accent. He has to brace himself against the counter he's laughing so hard.

I slap the contract on the counter, pick up the pen, and hold it in his face. He's barely able to contain himself long enough to sign. "Do you need a copy?" I ask.

"Yeah, there's a copier in my office. I'mma send it to my lawyer to see if I can get out of it." He continues to laugh as I walk away towards his office.

"You're not funny," I say, but chuckle. I hear Bailey ask him what's so funny. He only laughs harder.

In Shane's office, I walk around his solid redwood desk and reach for his desk lamp sitting next to his massive Apple screen, the size of a television. I had no idea they made them this big. *What on earth is he using this for?* When I hit the light, it illuminates a picture in a frame of him and his kids. The three of them are all smiles. Lying in front of the photo is an envelope addressed to Carice Charles from the District Court of Maryland. I can see that it's opened at the top. My heart starts racing. I want to look inside. I look towards the door. Technically, I have time. But when I reach for it, I instantly feel like the bad guy again. *Do what you came here to do*, I tell myself.

I take my copy, place his on his desk, and turn the light out.

When I return to the kitchen, Bailey is cheering. She runs up to me and hugs me. "Shane is coming to my show."

"He is?" I look at him. "That's awesome!" I mouth 'thank you'.

He places his hands over his heart. 'Anytime,' he mouths back. There's a softness about him I haven't seen in a very long time. Maybe he really is fighting like he says he is.

"Well ladies, I know y'all got busy days tomorrow. I will see you both very, very soon." Shane walks us to the car. He opens Bailey's door first and then comes to open mine. Leaning on the door, he stares down at me and I up at him. He steals a kiss, reaches into his pocket, and places a key into my hand. "Cross that off your list. Mi casa, su casa."

I smile. *This motherfucker just gave me a key to his place.* On the inside, I'm screaming and running in circles. On the outside, I remain as cool as ever. "How do I know that it works?"

"Why don't you sneak over tonight and find out?"

9

HOLDING A GUN

Taking Shane up on his offer, I convince Bailey to stay by Jen's with Taylor and return home to freshen up and change from loungewear to leather in minutes. When I return, I park in the driveway and walk around to the front door to use my key. The alarm chimes an alert and luckily for me it's disarmed. One small detail he forgot to share. The house is dark, so I head straight upstairs. Shane lies naked, his flat sheet barely covering him.

"My, my. What if I hadn't come back?" I set my cellphone and keys on the dresser.

"I knew you would," he says, pulling the sheet completely back before standing up. He's already ready. He gets closer and tugs at the strap of my trench.

"Ummm. I just came to cuddle." I swat his hand away.

"Not dressed like that. Love the boots, by the way. Who bought you those? They look expensive." He grabs the back of my neck and kisses me.

"My man, remember?"

"Oh yeah." He walks me backwards through his master bathroom into his closet. Turns me around then hits the light switch. Half of his closet is empty. One pair of shoes sits on the shelf, a pair of cobalt blue Swarovski FiFi Strass.

"You found them!" I scream at the top of my lungs.

"The last pair in your size. What, he only make one size per pair of shoes?"

I pick up the coveted shoes and admire them. I'm so happy I want to cry. They are absolutely beautiful. *My something blue!* I think. "I love them." I smile and literally jump for joy.

"So, I know you said you wanted to go on a shopping spree."

I did? My eyes shift. *Oh shit, Jen's edits.*

"Well, I hate the malls. Too many damn people—"

"I love them!" I give him a hug. Then I set them down and bend over to take off my boots to try on the shoes.

"Wait, what are you doing?"

"Trying on my shoes."

"Oh, hell naw!" He grabs me and swoops me up over his shoulder, carrying me to the bed, ass out, like a rag doll. "You keeping dem on." He bites my upper thigh.

"Ahh!" Naturally, I kick.

Shane shouts back. "That was a close one!" He lies me down and kisses me on the lips. "You almost hit the golden jewels." He kneels over me and undresses me with his eyes.

That's when I decide to put my foot on his chest and reach for his dick. "Fuck me like it's the last time you'll ever touch me."

Shane's eyes get big and he gives me a sexy grin. "I want to hear you scream my name."

"Fuck me, pool boy."

"Pool boy?" Shane's facial expression deflates.

"I don't know. I couldn't think of anything else." I laugh.

Shane sits back and furrows his brows. "Gladiator, warrior, titan!"

"Ooh, water boy!" I laugh.

"Keep it up, it's going to go soft."

I place my hand on Shane's face. "Fuck me now, gladiator." I burst into laughter.

"Watch what you ask for, Princess Padme. You should be afraid. Very afraid." Shane leans in and bites my shoulder.

"Whoa, now." I gasp for air. "Don't go there. That shit hurts."

"Issa good kind of hurt." Shane grins.

"How would you know? I've never bitten you."

"You want to?"

"No, actually. I'd rather slap you."

Shane sits back. "Seriously?"

I can see him thinking.

"In my face?" he continues.

"Yup." I nod.

"Hard?"

Squinting my eyes, I do like he does and respond with a question. "Do you bite me softly?"

"Sometimes. But why you wanna slap me in my face? I mean you can slap my chest. Like this." Shane lightly smacks his bare chest. "Love taps."

"I can't with you."

"I can't believe you want to smack me across my face."

"You asked." I laugh to lighten his mood.

Shane eyes me. "I ain't realize you was violent. I gotta watch you."

"You should, because if you cross me. . ." I laugh. "Just kidding."

"I believe you."

"You should." I smile.

"Whatever. You ain't never going to leave me." Shane takes one of my legs and places it on his shoulders. 'cause nobody lays pipe like me."

Damn. He's right. My body is tingling all over and I don't even bother to respond. I simply lay back and let the pipelaying commence because I know that his stroke is breathtaking.

Afterwards, my head on his chest and my body cradled in his big strong arms, our breathing is in sync. I notice, as I listen to the beat of his heart, he's sound asleep. As for me, I'm a little restless. It's because I'm hot. His body radiates heat. I try to get comfortable but I simply can't. It doesn't help that my mind is racing. I can't stop thinking about all kinds of random things. My anxiety is kicking into overdrive. It tends to do that when I'm feeling that things are too good to be true. It's like I find things to start worrying about. Meanwhile, he's completely at peace.

I can't help but worry about us. Part of me wants to believe that this contract, our arrangement, is going to hold us together while he fights for his kids. But deep down inside I feel like my worst nightmare is waiting around the corner.

I quit staring at the ceiling and roll over, turning my back to him. He readjusts as well. Now facing the television, I watch the beginning of a Disney movie, close my eyes, and wish upon a star for our happy ending.

I'm standing in a courtyard with an ornate stone fountain. I admire it and the surrounding foliage. I walk around taking photos. I'm alone. I know this because there's no one to take a photo of me. Yet, I continue around the fountain taking photos and plan to return for a photo shoot.

When I reach a busy highway, I stop taking photos when a tarantula, a really fucking big black tarantula, attaches itself to my back. I struggle to get it off but it's not budging. There's a shopping center just a few feet ahead.

"Excuse me!" I call out to a group of teenagers. "Can you help me get this off my back?"

"Go into Taco Bell, they should be able to help!"

I yank the door open.

I suddenly awaken. *What the hell?* I roll over to get comfortable again. I do not want to dream about spiders, so I try to think about anything else. *Baseball, flowers, candy. Anything but spiders.* I think, and close my eyes.

It's hot standing in front of this oven wearing only an apron and a pair of heels. Shane returns home from work wearing a suit and tie and carrying a brown briefcase. There's a lavish spread of hotdogs, sausage, and freshly popped popcorn on the dinner table.

He kisses me on my forehead and smacks my ass. "What are you making?"

"Funnel cake. You hungry?"

"I'd rather have you."

"But I have a tarantula on my back." I show Shane my back.

"I think it's from the neighbors. We've been having a tarantula problem

around here."

I snap out of my sleep. Again? What is the deal? I look over at Shane who's knocked out, and reach for my phone. I pull up the internet and Google 'dreaming of tarantulas'. My search reveals many results. I tried to go to the most reputable looking site. Dreams About Tarantulas – Interpretation and Meaning. It reads that I should be careful. There's a person who will betray me when I least expect it. I continue to scroll through my phone to find more information.

Shane and I are lying in bed. Lights from the TV flicker in the room. I roll on my side and the bedroom door flies open.

Carice charges through the door with a tarantula perched on her shoulder, screaming nonsensical words at the top of her lungs.

I stare at her, still distracted by the enormous black tarantula on my back.

Shane jumps up!

She pulls out a gun.

Points it at me. Then at him. Then at me again.

Shane pulls me behind him.

Bang. Bang. Bang.

I'm shaken. Opening my eyes, I see the battle of Sparta is playing out on television. I can't possibly go back to sleep. I roll over and take the remote from Shane's sleeping hand. He must have woken up in the middle of the night and turned on *300*. I turn back to the Disney Channel and try not to fall asleep again.

In the morning at breakfast I can't stop thinking about my dreams. I mean. . . they were rather haunting. I want to share them but he's skipping around the kitchen and I'd hate to ruin his mood. So I let him enjoy the moment. I sit on a barstool at the kitchen counter and watch him make us breakfast. A bowl of Frosted Flakes with a glass of orange juice. It's endearing.

In between sips of my juice, I sit and stare at him while he eats. I've never felt more in love. Waking up next to him could never get old.

"What you thinking about?"

"Us."

"You thinking 'bout last night." He nods, taking a spoonful. "I put it on you." He rubs his abs then flexes his biceps.

"You take a lot of pride in your sex game, don't you?"

"Nobody lays pipe like me." He starts flexing like it's his turn during a body building competition.

"Here we go again." I drop my head. "I hope you realize I don't love you just for sex. I love you the person. And I hope you feel that way too."

"No doubt." Shane stands and kisses me on the forehead. "Whatever you need to tell yourself. "So, what are you doing today?"

"Work."

"Stay here," he says. "We can make love all day." Shane gives me a playful wink.

I reminisce over last night, him hovering over me from behind and repeatedly whispering my name in my ear and saying he couldn't get enough. "Yeah?" I smile devilishly.

"Yeah, and then you can drop me at the airport."

"What time is your flight?"

"Three."

"I'll have to get Bailey's dad to pick her up from school because Jen has an appointment."

"Have y'all always gotten along?"

"Her dad and I? I'd say for the most part. I've never experienced what you're going through. I mean, the first five years weren't easy. We had our share of disagreements, but I don't ever remember not letting him see his child. In fact, it was the complete opposite. I was like, you need to spend more time with your daughter."

"Did he?"

"He was trying to figure his life out. Now that he's married and settled, it's easier."

"I need to see my babies every day. This is killing me."

"When will you be able to see them again?"

"I don't know. She said she may bring them to Indiana."

"Right. . ." I keep my extra commentary to myself and continue eating my cereal.

"What was that about?"

"I don't trust her."

"Well, I don't blame you. She hates you. Right before I was handcuffed, she – and I quote – said she's not losing her family to 'that bitch'."

"So it is because of me?"

"Everything is your fault."

Now my dream is starting to make sense. *She hates me.* "Has she ever been here at this house? Like lived here? Stayed here?"

"Nope. Only been in the driveway to drop my kids off. Why?"

"I just want to make sure that I'm not occupying a space that was once hers."

"Nah, never that. But I want you to know we gotta court date coming up. Things might get a little crazy. Just chill."

"I thought y'all are talking arrangement and trying to settle out of court."

"I'm fittin' to get my kids. That crazy chick got me arrested."

"Speaking of crazy. . . I had the craziest dream last night."

"What about?" Shane collects our empty bowls and places them in the sink.

"Carice. She tried to shoot us. Or maybe just me."

"What did you eat before coming over?"

"I think it was your fault."

"My fault?"

"You turned on *300* and it was loud as fuck and when I woke up they were killing each other."

"She ain't THAT crazy!"

"You sure about that? Considering what you're currently going through."

"I may have to rethink that. But I'm good. I hired the best lawyers. I've gotta team of them working my case. I'm gonna win and get my babies back." He rubs my shoulders to assure me.

Taking Shane's large hands, I wrap them around my waist. "I honestly don't want you to leave."

"Come with me." He kisses my neck.

"You know I can't." I lay my head on his chest. "I actually have a career. I can't just pick up and go like you. But I'll see you in two weeks," I snicker.

Shane steps back and lifts my chin. "Do you trust me?"

And just like Lena Headey told Gerald Butler in *300*, I tell him, "Spartan. Come back with your shield, or on it."

Shane's eyes smile and he replies, "Yes, my lady." He kisses me. "No retreat. No surrender."

10

OPPORTUNITY KNOCKS

While Shane's in Indiana fighting his battle, I'm fighting one of my own. It's week eight of the battle of the back office and today, Mandy is in full Dwight mode. I think it's the beginning of her ending here at Pearsons, formally known as The Lawson Company. I can't imagine her being here any longer. She's absolutely miserable. I just hope she holds it together long enough not to scare off the new hires. They will be here in a few hours and I still have to relocate to my new office.

"I think he has a drinking problem." Mandy states today's accusation matter-of-factly.

Here she goes again poking the bear. She's on a mission to try to find something, anything, to get Harry to get rid of Lee. She's preparing for an out-of-office lunch meeting with Harry next week and she wants me to go. I conveniently make myself unavailable but support her by entertaining her accusation.

"When you say drinking problem. . ."

"I'm saying that he's a drunk. AA kind of drunk. He keeps Listerine in his desk drawer. And I also found a rotten banana in there. He's disgusting. I'm documenting everything." Mandy huffs and continues to type.

"That is some combination." I laugh. "Listen, let's not focus on Lee today. Just think. Today is our last morning of being office mates. Let's crank up the music and celebrate while I pack. Come on, Mandy, do the honky-tonk one last time. Just think, now you'll have to walk down the hall to visit me."

"I don't know why he doesn't just leave you here and give the new girls an office to share."

"Mandy," I scold.

"I know. I'm going to miss you, that's all."

"I will still come visit, but only on R&B days."

"Oh snap!" Mandy jumps up and turns on the radio. "You're right. It's country day!" Carrie Underwood blares through the speakers. And when *Cowboy Casanova* ends, she proceeds to ask me for a Shane update.

"He's consistent. What more can I ask for." I flash a cheesy grin.

"That's why you've been smiling so much lately."

I nod. "Could be. He Skypes me every night just to say goodnight." I swoon.

"Girl. . . I guess that contract worked!"

"The contract, the vision board, I don't know, but this year is off to a great start."

"I so hate that you're leaving," Mandy pouts. "Are you going to tell the new girl about Shane?"

"Lisette. I don't know." I already know that once she starts, I've got to shield her from Mandy's craziness as much as possible. Mandy's new hire, Reba, is starting today as well. I remember her saying she shared a name with her favorite artist, Reba Macintyre, so she was perfect for the job. "Can you please not to tell Reba?"

"Sure, no problemo."

I really hope she can keep a lid on it. It's bad enough she mentioned it to Lee. You never know why Mandy does the things she does.

Mandy and I dance to country music as I pack up my belongings and take them down the hall to my new office. It's smaller than the office we share but it's got a huge window with a lush courtyard view, unlike the parking lot view I'm leaving behind. Mandy, though, likes that view. She can keep tabs on who's coming and going. When we had to decide who would move to a different office, it was a no-brainer. She wasn't going anywhere.

"Where is what's-her-name going to sit?" Mandy follows me down to my new office with a box of binders.

"Lisette," I remind her, "at that desk." I point to the desk opposite mine.

"Man, y'all can't fit a table in here."

"It's tight, but we'll manage."

Mandy shrugs her shoulders. "You should make Lee knock down that wall and let you sit in the office next door."

"It's fine. We'll manage just fine."

"He makes me sick. I think he's separating us on purpose."

"How does he benefit from doing that? This is beneficial for all of us. Both of us are advancing our careers. That wouldn't be happening if we'd stayed where we were. Also, let me remind you that he intended getting rid of both of us."

"Not before I get rid of him." Mandy storms out and sprints down the hall. For her sake, I hope she finds another job because if not, I fear it won't be long before she's gone.

I make my last trip down the hall for the rest of my things, pile my personal belongings in the chair, give Mandy a hug, and roll back to my new space. It's small and a bit cozy but more importantly it's mine.

Around lunchtime, Lisette arrives at my office and I take her around to meet everyone. When we get to Mandy, she's wild-eyed and sweaty. "Look at this." She reaches into her satchel and whips out the folded packaging of what looks to be foreign beer. "It's a twenty-four pack. I caught him sneaking it into the dumpster out back."

"Excuse me?" I blink. "Where did you find that?" She would pick today of all days to go dumpster diving.

Mandy places her hands on her hips. "I got it immediately after he threw it there. I wasn't in there long."

"Eww, Mandy." She has stooped to an all-time low.

"I'm telling you. He's got a drinking problem and I'm taking it to Harry."

"What if he had a party this weekend and he was just cleaning out the car?"

"This!" She holds up the box. "It was concealed in a brown paper bag. I'm telling you; I know the signs. It's gut instinct and

I'm trained for this."

We're still in her office when the HR lady brings Reba in. We all exchange greetings and almost immediately, Mandy starts grilling Lisette. "How old are you? Do you have a boyfriend? What school did you graduate from? Where are your parents from? You have a tan and I know you're not mixed."

Lisette turns red in the face. "I'm sorry?"

"Please ignore her," I say.

Meanwhile, Reba is snapping gum and nodding along with Mandy. She answers Mandy's questions for herself.

"Well, *I'm* twenty-seven, I have a boy toy. I graduated from Loyola and my mother is Italian and my dad is Latina. And yes, my hair is naturally red."

"I'm one fourth Puerto Rican!" Mandy shouts.

I can tell they are going to get along just fine. "Well ladies, it was nice chatting. I've got a million things to show Lisette. Perhaps a late lunch? Or not."

"Alright, come back and visit." Mandy waves us goodbye.

"I'm sorry," I apologize to Lisette when we're out of earshot. "That's Mandy. Long story."

"Don't worry," she waves casually. "I have a crazy aunt."

"She can be a lot to take, but she's really sweet. Right now, she's got it in for Lee and I'm trying to squash it, so wish me luck." Speaking of Lee, I've got a one on one with him in fifteen minutes. Before I rush to my meeting, I show Lisette our new space and around the office. She's at the coffee machine when I leave her.

Lee is scrolling through his iPad when I arrive at his door. He glances up and invites me in. I take a seat and look around his office. He doesn't have anything personal set out. Thanks to Mandy, I keep thinking about the rotten banana and breath freshener.

"Bryn, how do you like your new office?"

"It's nice."

"How's getting away from Mandy?" He raises his hand. "You don't have to answer. I know it's refreshing."

Yikes. I guess their feelings towards each other are mutual.

"She can be *a lot*. But she's got a huge heart."

Lee puts his hands behind his head and leans back in his chair. "How was your weekend?"

"Great!" I'm not sure where this is going. "Yours?"

"Exhilarating. I went to Virginia with some college friends and we rode the fastest rollercoaster in the United States. I blacked out like three out of the five times I rode it."

"That sounds concerning. You kept getting back on it after blacking out?"

"Well, I kept missing it, so I got back on it until I got to enjoy the entire ride. But the Mrs. asked the same thing when I told her. She stayed at home with the kids and she had schoolwork to finish up. By the way, do you have your MBA?"

"I don't." I hope that's not a bad thing.

"Why not? What's stopping you? The company will pay for it."

"I thought about it. . . I said I'd do it when my daughter got to high school. I'm a single mother so I don't want to take away any more time from spending with her."

"I had my first set of kids young, so I understand. My wife said the same thing. She's doing hers online. The University of

Maryland has a great online program. You should consider it."

"I'll give it some thought. Thanks for the advice."

"I see huge potential in you. You'll achieve important things in your career. You just need to surround yourself with the right people. Lisette was a thoughtful choice. I expect great things from your department."

"And great things you shall receive."

"Good. That's all. I need to run and get a drink, espresso of course, before meeting with Mandy." He jumps up. "Ladies first."

Grabbing my notepad, I leave and head to Mandy's office while Lee goes for his coffee. *Those two.* I'll tell her that I was right. He was partying with friends this weekend.

"Mandy," I tap her on the shoulder before leaning down to whisper in her ear. "He was partying with old college buddies this weekend."

"I want to know," Reba interrupts. "It's not polite to whisper. If it's about Leroy, Mandy already told me about her recent dumpster-diving excursion. I personally think she's right. He seems a bit sketchy."

"I'm out of it. Do what you need to do. I've got work to do." I wave goodbye and leave them to their plan. As for the rest of the day, I plan to finish unpacking, train Lisette, and look into an MBA program. Ignoring Lee's advice would be a bad idea.

When Bailey was just two years old, the deacon at the church randomly approached me and asked if I'd been to college. At the time, I had not. I'd landed a full-time job that paid enough for me to get by. It was just a job, not necessarily a career. I responded that I didn't need to go to college because I was going to marry a rich man and become a housewife. He literally laughed in my face.

Once he got himself together, he gave me a very stern look and said that I needed to secure a stable future for both Bailey and me. Until today, it was the best advice I'd ever received.

When an opportunity comes knocking, it's best to open the door. That's why while Mandy is playing detective, I'll be advancing my career.

11

UNCONDITIONAL LOVE

Leroy looks frustrated when he arrives at the door of our office. "Headed to my 2 o'clock with Harry. You ladies need anything?"

Lisette hands him a stack of checks to sign.

"Bryn, have you been added as a signer on the bank account?"

"Not yet."

"That's changing today." He huffs, takes them, and speed-walks down the hall back to his office. He returns moments later, tosses the folder of checks on the corner of Lisette's desk, and says before he walks away, "Look out for an email from the bank."

Lisette smiles and says to me, "You better not tell Mandy."

"She shouldn't care."

"I've only known Mandy for a few hours and even I know she's going to take it personally. While you were meeting with him, she stopped by and kept saying that Harry should have promoted her instead of hiring Lee. So, with Lee empowering you—"

"Don't worry, he's empowering her as well. She's just resisting it. The reality is, it's a good thing and she should be happy."

"Don't say I didn't warn you." Lisette's a sweet kind soul. She's already looking out for a sista. I haven't told her about Shane, even though I'm sure she must have seen the framed photo of me, Shane, and Harry hanging in Harry's office. Harry wants me to get Shane to autograph it for him. I told him not to hold his breath. Shane's weird about signing stuff if it's not for a kid. But seriously, who on earth besides Harry would want or pay for a signed photo of the three of us? Nobody in their right mind.

Shortly after Lee leaves the office, I hear the pitter-patter of Mandy's shoes making their way down the hall. "Lee made you a signer on the bank account?"

Lisette turns around in her chair and looks over at me and then back at Mandy.

"I think so. Lisette gave him a stack of checks because he was running out and appeared not to have time to sign them." My eyes shift. "Why?"

"I got an email about it."

I turn to check my computer and see that they cc'd the finance alias on their email. "Yup, this is the email." I turn back towards her.

"This just isn't fair." She turns red in the face and starts balling her little fists.

"Mandy!" I shout. "You've got to let it go."

She flips her hair back, taking a deep breath. "That's the final straw. I'm leaving this bitch." She storms off down the hall.

I look at Lisette, who turns back to her desk. I get up and rush after her. "Mandy!"

Reba, sitting at my recently vacated desk, looks up while thumbing through a contract binder and starts grazing on a handful of mixed nuts. "Yeah, she's pissed." She points at Mandy, who's sitting at her desk with her eyes shut tight.

"No Bryn, I'm quitting. I deserve better." Mandy's eyes are wet.

"Don't leave. We need you."

"It's either me—" she hits her chest, "— or him." She points in the direction of his office.

I rub my face, forgetting that I have on a full face of make-up. "Hand me a tissue, please."

"You know he drinks." She tosses me the box.

I stare blankly at her then turn around when I hear someone walk in. "Oh, it's you." Lisette walks over to Reba.

"Ladies, help me talk some sense into Mandy," I say. "We don't want her making rash moves."

"He's a drunk! And I'm not working for someone like that."

"Really? That's some accusation."

"He's always running out of here and he's always using mouthwash. What kind of man keeps constantly rinsing with Listerine?" rants Mandy.

"A metrosexual. I know. I used to date one," snaps Reba.

"See. He's probably just extra clean," I plead.

"It's not. . . I just need to go do my own thing. I'm tired of this anyway." Mandy shuts down her computer.

"We finally have the help we need and you're ready to leave." I'm getting really frustrated with her now.

"We can run it without him. Right?" Mandy's looking for back-up.

"We can do a lot of things, it doesn't mean we should," chimes in Lisette. She's so smart. I knew I made a great hire. We think alike.

"I'm going tell Harry I need to meet with him, today." Mandy grabs her phone. "I'm calling him now."

"He's with Lee. Leave it alone. The last thing you want is for this thing to backfire."

"I've got nothing to lose."

"Okay." I shrug my shoulders and turn to leave.

"So, Bryn, when do we get to see that ring?" Reba smiles.

Tilting my head, I look at Mandy.

"Not me this time."

"No, not Mandy. I want to date an athlete just to see what it's like. Like my last boyfriend lifted weights. He was like a fake body builder. But I hear it's not the same." She winks and smiles. "So, I stalk this NFL girlfriend website and I just happen to see a thread on Shane Smith. It's like really long. It mentioned a ring. I figured it was you since you're seeing him. I saw the pic in Harry's office."

"Wow! That was totally unexpected."

"I mean, why beat around the bush? You're dating a millionaire and like, I want to see the ring and I like hearing about it. I'm obsessed with all of the housewives shows. Have you ever heard of WAGS? I have aspirations to be on one of those reality shows but until then, I want to live vicariously through you. Please?"

"I really don't like to discuss Shane in the office."

"Yeah, I hear you, but can you make an exception? I mean, there's nothing to be embarrassed about. I won't judge." She shrugs her shoulders and rolls her eyes back. "All men cheat."

I'm sure I have shock written all over my face. Reba has no problem with speaking her mind. "There are other women for sure. I don't know if they ALL cheat, but. . . let's just say there are lots of women and they don't ask, don't care, if the guy says he has a girlfriend, fiancée, or wife," I answer matter-of-factly.

"I feel like we need to have this conversation over drinks. Let's do dinner tonight. I mean technically, we didn't have our new-hire lunch. That's what HR said, so I say let's make it a new-hire dinner. Besides, Mandy needs a drink. Just look at her."

We all stare at her and she looks as if she just got released from a mental facility.

"I do." Mandy nods helplessly.

"Fine, I guess." I shake my head and text Jen, asking her to get Bailey and that I have a work function.

After work we meet at On the Boarder, located near our office, because Reba is convinced they have the best margaritas and guacamole in town. I'm not going to lie, from the lack of upkeep in their ladies' room, I'm slightly afraid to eat anything from here.

Back at the table, our drinks arrive and our spritely waiter comes to our table carrying a bunch of supplies.

"Oh, he's going to make it in front of us." I survey his display.

"Yes." Reba shimmies in her seat.

"I never had guacamole," says Mandy. "You like it because you're half Mexican, right?" she asks Reba.

"Ummm, I'm Latina." Reba makes a face. "There's a difference."

"I've never seen a red-headed Latina." Mandy, obviously tipsy, finishes her first margarita.

"Mandy, you need to get out more. I mean, you can be any ethnicity and have red hair. It's from a mutated gene. Anyways. . ." she flicks her hair, "I love being a ginger. I frequently get mistaken for Cintia Dicker."

"Dicker?" Mandy starts laughing.

Our waiter fights to keep a straight face but he can't keep from turning red.

Mandy's laugh grows louder. "Dicker!" She slaps her knee.

"I guess that's all you've been thinking about since your husband got deployed," Reba snaps.

"Jimmy? Nah, I keep a pink 'dicker' in my nightstand," Mandy tries to whisper. "It's nine inches too."

Our waiter hurriedly places our chips and guacamole on the table and turns away.

"Mandy, you are embarrassing. We can't take you anywhere." Reba calls back our waiter. "Can you refresh her drink please?"

"I think we need to cut her off." I reach in for a chip and take a scoop of the famous guacamole.

"Well, speaking of dick, how big is Shane?" Reba asks outright.

I hold my hand out to stop her.

"No, like seriously," she insists. "I heard that, you know, black guys have larger dicks."

"I can't provide any insight. I've only dated black men. Mandy is better equipped for this topic."

Mandy's already nodding and smiling but when she opens her mouth to speak, Reba talks over her. "No, don't say anything. Our waiter is on his way over here. You don't know what to say out your mouth around company."

"Mother, may I?" Mandy pleads.

"Ugh. No one will ever call me mom. I'm never having kids." Reba smooths her shirt, highlighting her flat stomach. "I have a six-pack to maintain."

"Is that the only reason? You can always lose the weight," Lisette chimes in.

"I just don't want them. I'm wayyyyy too selfish. I enjoy my freedom too much. My mom says there's no use in me getting married if I don't want kids so, you know?" She reaches for the salt. "I'll be forever single. Besides, I'm too irresponsible. Just last weekend I accidentally locked my niece in the basement."

"You what?" Lisette looks appalled. I think we all do.

"I know. I know." Reba rolls her eyes. "I swear I thought my sister had put her down for a nap. So, when I heard her screaming and calling for her daddy, I just assumed she didn't want to sleep. You know, I was just going to let her cry it out. Well, it wasn't until my mom came in the house and was looking for her, she realized that she was locked in the basement. This is why I can't be trusted with children."

"Why didn't you check on her to be sure?" asks Mandy. "That's what I would have done."

"I don't know. I just don't have that motherly instinct, I guess. My sister was pissed."

"I'd be pissed as well. I'm assuming she's okay."

"I mean she was red from crying her eyes out but she's alive."

I shake my head. "That's the thing. When you have kids you constantly worry about them. For the longest, I never wanted to send Bailey to daycare. As a working single mom, you really don't have that many choices. Then, you're so exposed. You become so vulnerable. I'll tell you that. There's nothing you love more than your kids. You would literally give your life for them. No doubt. I would run into a burning building if she were in it to try and save her." I grab another chip. "Okay Reba, the guacamole is awesome. Let's change the subject. I'm getting all emotional just thinking about it."

"I want another before it's too late," Mandy chimes in.

"Ummm, didn't you tell me that your husband jumped off the sixtieth-floor balcony to get away from your current kid?" Reba asks Mandy.

"What?" shouts Lisette.

Mandy turns red in the face and tries to contain her laughter so she doesn't choke on her drink. When she finally swallows, she lets out a crazed laugh.

"Yeah, he like jumped out of the building to get away from a kid," Reba continues. "That's why I know I can't deal." She flicks her hair back.

"It wasn't to get away from the kid. He planned on jumping that night and the kid was crying, so he was just joking," Mandy says.

"Excuse me? What do you mean he planned to jump?" I raise one eyebrow, concerned.

"I didn't tell you that Jimmy is a BASE jumper?"

"No, you failed to share. I knew about the military but not that he jumps for fun."

"Well, to be considered a base jumper you have to jump from a building, antenna, span, and earth. Like a cliff, ya know. Well, he hasn't done any buildings in a while and certainly can't jump off a building during the day, so he usually does it at night. Well, he did."

"That is the craziest thing I've heard. I would freak out if I was on the balcony and saw a man falling from above."

"I'm with Jimmy. I'd jump to get away from a crying kid." Reba eyes the dessert menu.

"Josh and I just had our first anniversary and I can't fathom loving anyone more than him," says Lisette. "We want kids, but we're going to wait until he's finished up with grad school before we start trying."

"That's sweet. I didn't marry Bailey's father, but a love between a parent and a child is completely different. I can't even think of a word to describe it. I guess it's like how God loves us. Or maybe we can't even fathom that kind of love. Like, it's not even possible to understand since it's a divine love. I'm not saying you can't love a spouse as much. I'm just trying to say that it's different. And, I wouldn't trade my life for no man. I don't care how big his dick is," I joke, hoping to lighten and change the conversation.

"Funny you say that. Josh and I were talking, and I presented him with a scenario where I had complications during childbirth. I asked him if he had to choose between me or the child, who would he choose? He said the child! I threw a pillow and yelled at him. He said he wouldn't kill his child. But I was upset because I'm like we can always have another child. Men are weird. I would choose him."

"You think you would. Give it time." I smile. "We can have this conversation again after you spit one out."

Our waiter returns with a round of waters and takes our dinner orders.

"Well, I've got both." Mandy collects the menus and hands them over. "Bryn is right. It's different. I love the kid more. I mean, what wouldn't you do for your kid?"

"I'd do anything." Just thinking about it brings tears to my eyes. "It's an unconditional love."

"My point proven. That's why I'm not having kids." Reba turns to the waiter. "I'll have a hot fudge sundae with sprinkles." Then she turns back to us. "I love myself too much."

12

<u>WINNER TAKES ALL</u>

Jen's door is open when I arrive home, and I know it's not because she's looking out for me. She knew that I'd be arriving late. I grab the bags of groceries I picked up on the way and go inside. She's in her living room dancing and what she calls singing. "It's my house. . ." Her high-pitched squeals kill my ears, so I make an abrupt entrance hoping to cut her off. She only gets louder.

"Excited, much?" I yell over the noise.

"Platinum Events just landed our next big client. Can you say 'bar mitzvah'?" she asks, snapping and shimmying her shoulders. Then she starts dancing like she's a part of TGS. "I haven't had a client this big since Shane. I was almost wondering if it was still possible. I mean, I stay up at night worrying that I was a one-hit

wonder. But now, I know for sure that my talents are limitless."
Jen continues to dance to the music playing in her heart.

I shake my head and laugh. "Congratulations, Jen. You deserve it." I give her a hug.

"What? You've quit Platinum Events again? This is our win! I got the business, I still need you to make it happen."

"Of course I'm in! How? When? Fill me in on the details."

"I have Aasim to thank. It's one of his colleague's kids. They live right up the street in Pikesville. I met with the wife today. She has a rock the size of a walnut sitting on her finger. It was insane. I kept staring at it."

"When is it?"

"In the fall."

"Oh, good. Because. . ." I smile. "I have great news to share as well."

"Do tell!"

"Lee, my new boss, encouraged me to enroll in a grad program. My job is going to pay for it!"

"That's fantastic!" Jen gives me a high-five. "Man, Bryn, if you do that, you will certifiably be *that* bitch. You will be so accomplished in your own right." Jen gives two air snaps. *"Girl!"* she screeches and dances in place.

"I know, right?" but I start stressing at the thought of doing it and Jen notices.

"Stop finding reasons to stress. You're always waiting for the shoe to drop. Celebrate your accomplishments."

"I know, I know. Where's Bailey?"

"She's downstairs practicing for the spring concert. She says she has to practice extra hard since it's four weeks away and Uncle

Shane is coming. And by the way, when do you plan on breaking the news to her? She's going to be really confused having to switch from calling him Uncle Shane to Paw Paw Shane, or whatever y'all are going to have her call him. I know you ain't crazy enough to have her call him Dad. You-know-who would have your head on a platter."

"First of all, he's married now so he shouldn't care. I'll tell her when Shane and I are married. I'm not wearing my ring at the moment, so we'll address it when the time is right. I've got enough to worry about."

"You're right about that. I'm going to call Sasha and have her set up a series of meetings starting this weekend, so I need you to start thinking about themes."

"I thought that was your job? I'm just execution." I smile and call for Bailey. "I'm just kidding."

"Coming!" Bailey yells back.

"Anyway, how was your work function?"

"Interesting. It was a happy hour. This new team is going to be something. Mandy wasn't holding anything back."

"That's it?" Jen asks, throwing up her hands.

Because I know she's looking for more of a response, I start telling her, "Reba, the new girl, asked if black guys have bigger—" I stop when I hear Bailey coming up the stairs.

"No, she didn't!" Jen bursts into laughter. "I'm just going to assume Reba is a white girl."

"Actually, she's Latina."

"Oh my! Did you tell her?"

"No, I don't think I answered. I didn't have any experience to compare it with. Apparently, Mandy does."

"Mandy! How is she?"

"Off the chain as usual." I clasp my head.

Bailey hands me her book bag to carry. "You ready?"

"Yup."

"Here, you carry the grocery bags. Your breakfast for tomorrow is in there."

She takes them from my hand and walks out the door. I wave Jen goodnight.

Settled at home in my bed, I light incense and lay awake listing to some British neo-soul soundtrack on Pandora. It's a real chill vibe. I'm trying my best to keep the stress levels low. It's been a while since I had a panic attack and I want to keep it that way. Sometimes when too much change happens all at once, it brings it on.

While I'm laying here thinking about all of these great things happening to me, I can't wait to tell Shane. Lifting my bed sheets, I search for my phone to call him. He answers on the first ring.

"What's up?"

"Just lying here thinking of you."

"Really? This late? What are you thinking about?" he asks. I can hear the sly note in his voice.

"How much I love you." I giggle.

"Blah, that's boring. I thought you was gonna tell me you were thinking 'bout baby maker."

"That too."

"Good. So, you not stepping out on me while I'm out of town."

"Have I ever given you a reason to be concerned?"

"No, but I just had to put it out there. I'll be there in two weeks to lay it on you."

"Gee. Thanks. How are you these days?"

"Yeah, about that. . ."

His tone feeds my anxiety and my heart starts racing. "Should I even ask?"

"Well. . . I gotta get surgery. My injury from last year didn't heal properly. It's going to be outpatient. I gotta go to a special doctor in North Carolina."

"I'm sorry to hear. When?"

"Right after Bailey's show. They wanted to do it now, but I already told her I was coming back."

"She'll understand."

"Nah. It's all good."

"Well, maybe I can take some time off and go with you. I have a nurse costume from Halloween I can wear. I'll take care of you. Wait on you hand and foot." I giggle.

"About that. I would love you to come and take care of me. But Carice is bringing my kids, and. . ."

"Say no more." That name. It literally gives me chills when I hear it fall from his lips.

"I didn't want to tell you over the phone, but—"

"Umm, hmm. So you want to break the first rule already?" My vibe is instantly ruined.

"Bryn—"

"Oh, you're not asking for my permission. This deal is done. I see."

"I know you're not intimidated by her?"

"You're joking, right?"

"Honestly, I don't *want* to do it. I ain't breaking anything. I'm just pushing it out a bit. I think my surgery can be an exception."

"I'll come to you and stay at a hotel."

"Bryn, I know what I'm telling you ain't right to you in a million different ways so I'm gonna try and use the time wit' them to my advantage. I don't want to argue with you."

"Carice's doing what she does best and turning up the heat. Carice seems to always have the upper hand. You do realize this isn't a win-win type of situation? Someone is going to lose. And if your little plan doesn't work, it could ruin *us*."

"Man, this shit is crazy. I feel like I can't catch a break."

"It shouldn't be this hard."

"Don't sound like that."

"Honestly, I had a good day and I wanted to share all of the good news with you, but now I'm feeling discouraged. I feel like everything else in my life is great except this one thing. It's like a thorn in my side. She is a thorn in our sides. What she does to you, it indirectly impacts me as well. Bailey too. I mean, when is this going to end?"

"This is it. Stick with me, Bryn. I'm in it to win it, and this time, it's winner takes all."

"I hope, for your sake, you're right."

13

NEVER SAY NEVER

This week is unusually calm. Mandy is quiet. She's focusing on training Reba. Skypes with Shane are consistent but since telling me the news about his surgery, they seem to have shortened. I can't lie. I'm still a little pissed about it. I've got to find a way to take some time off to be with him. But instead of worrying myself with this so far in advance, I fill my morning with the business of getting Bailey out the house and off to school. Besides, I don't want to walk around angry. This morning, I'm enjoying a cup of hot tea and meditating on my vision board and debating if I should move Shane's face. By the time my drink is finished, I decide the answer is yes. I fish through the kitchen drawer for some clear tape and place him back in his rightful place, next to me dressed in all white.

As for the rest of the day, Jen and I are scheduled to spend the day together doing one of the things we love the most. Shopping! Event shopping. The bar mitzvah money came in fast in one lump sum, so we're off to one of our exclusive shops to design florals, and pick out furniture, linens, vases, and lots more.

When Jen arrives, she's wearing a little black dress showing her thighs.

"Well excuse me, sexyatta. Where do you think you're going? You have a hot date at noon?"

Taylor pushes past her and heads downstairs to my basement where Bailey is playing on her Wii.

"I just might." Jen walks past me carrying two pairs of shoes. "Open toe, or closed?" She puts one on each foot.

"Hmm. Turn to the side? I like the open toe, but it's forty degrees outside, so I'd say wear the closed.

"I want to wear what looks best. There's nothing practical about being sexy."

"Listen. I know. There's been many a day."

"Great. Are you ready?"

"Don't you think we're going to look odd walking around together? You're in a little black dress and I'm in jeans, a shirt, and Uggs?"

"You have a man. I don't. And I'm trying to land one before it's too late. But where's your ring? And at least put on a pair of heels."

"Seriously? We're running around today."

"Less competition the better." Jen throws her hands on her hips. "Besides, you don't wear it to work, so the best time to wear it is on the weekends."

"Fine." I run upstairs, take my ring out of its case, and place it on my finger. I take one more glance in the mirror and decide not to change my jeans. I'm comfortable. But I change my top and slip on a pair of black pumps. I return, and Jen gives me her nod of approval.

"Now let's go and do tell about your mysterious new beau," I say.

Jen giggles on the way over to my passenger door. That's the cue that I'm her driver for the day.

"Ya know, you can still drive," I say.

"When I get a brand-new BMW, I'll drive. My back hurts and I need the heated seats and the hip rotator."

"Or we could just do a spa day and go shopping tomorrow."

"No, there are like a thousand bar mitzvahs going on and they all have crazy money and at the moment, they're all using the same vendor. We've got to lock everything down early before it's gone. I had dinner with the owner last night and he suggested that we come today."

"We're going shopping. It makes more sense to drive your truck."

Jen tosses me the keys. She's acting all weird and giggly, so I know there's something she's not telling me. "So. . . this owner. Is he your new guy?" I guess.

"He wants to be, but no, never."

"Never say never. I'm just saying."

Jen laughs. "Don't judge me."

"Exactly!"

"No, seriously. Listen. I'm about to tell you. Okay?"

I nod.

"Last night, well, late last night, I got a call from an unrecognizable number. At first, I wasn't going to answer, but something told me to, and I did. I picked up and said hello."

I can tell I'm about to get the blow-by-blow version of this story, so I turn the music down.

"And then, he sent pictures."

"Wait, back up. I missed something."

"That's because you aren't listening and you're messing around with my radio."

"I'm all ears. I just don't know how you go from hello to receiving a dick pic." I laugh.

"It wasn't a dick pic." Jen holds her phone out.

"Oh, he's cute."

"Yes, and he used to play for the Saints."

"Okay. I really need you to start over."

"You should have been listening. Long story short, we're meeting up and I can't wait to experience sex with an athlete for myself."

"Girl, we go for hours and it's still good."

"Like I said. And apparently an athlete's dick is also magical the way it's got you walking around here."

"So, you just going to fuck him to find out?"

"I'm strongly considering it." Jen lifts her nose. "You can't be the only one having all of the fun."

"Listen. I'm not one to judge."

"Well, speaking of fun. I have a surprise for you." Jen goes all giggly and I'm getting suspicious. Her eyes get shifty and I can see all of her teeth.

"What is it?" I narrow my eyes at her. "What have you done?"

"I made us an appointment." She gives a wide grin.

"What kind of appointment?" I sing.

"Well, the kind of appointment that I know you weren't ready to make on your own. But you know I'm a planner and I can't leave this to chance."

"Oh Lord. What have you done?"

"You'll see in about ten minutes." Jen laughs and then turns up the music. She's bobbing in her seat to Frank Sinatra's *Love*.

Jen's definitely in a mood. I shake my head and laugh while joining in with the lyrics. When Sinatra's *The Way you Look Tonight* ends, we're outside a bridal showroom. "This is why you had me wear my ring." I shake my head. "And heels? No, you didn't!"

"Yes, I did! Now get out and let's try on some dresses!"

"This is a bit premature."

"You won't know what you want until you try it on. Trust me. I've done this before." Jen is opening my door and ushering me out.

"Have you? With no husband on the horizon."

"I wanted to know what it was like and I've got my dress picked out. So now, all I need is a man." Jen pushes the door shut behind me. "Don't worry. It will be fun. I had a celebrity stylist pull everything. Just sit back and be a princess for a few hours."

I cover my face as she escorts me in.

The first dress I try has me looking exactly that, like a princess. "I don't care for the sweetheart neck. My boobs are popping fresh."

"You said Shane loves your boobs. This is a way to highlight them. I like the dress." Jen holds her hands to her face. "You look like Cinderella."

I spin a few times. "Umm. Okay. I'm ready for the next dress."

"Perk it up!" she shouts.

I curtsy, grab the heavy tulle skirt, and inch my way back into the dressing room. Next, my dresser places me into a long-sleeved lace number. It's form-fitting and has a long train. It feels nice but it doesn't complement my height. "I need to be at least five nine to look right in a dress like this."

"That's what heels are for. Alana, can she get a seven-and-a-half stiletto?"

I twist and turn in the mirror while waiting for my shoes. The dress is starting to grow on me. "I like the fit. . . it's a possible."

"No, I need you to be excited about this dress. Next!"

The next dress is a high low and I immediately turn it down, refusing to try it on. Alana gets an attitude and storms out. *Well, this has been an interesting turn of events.* I guess she's off to tell on me. While she's gone, I see it, *the dress*, hanging on its lonesome. When Alana returns and pulls out the next dress, long and beaded, I stop her and point to the V-neck lace and tulle dress and ask if it's been claimed. She leaves to check and returns with a big smile. *Now, let's see if this is my size.*

"It's perfect!" screams Jen at the top of her lungs when I walk out. "Say YES to that dress, girl!"

I laugh at her and just stare at myself in the mirror. It is the perfect cut for me. A few alterations and I'll be ready to walk down any aisle. I think I feel sick.

"He is going to lose his mind when he sees you."

I give Jen a look. "I feel warm. Shortness of breath. I need a Valium." I fan myself.

Jen leaps from her seat and grabs my arms. "Breathe. You are fine! Life is to be lived! Celebrate. It's okay. I know you are always worst-case scenario, but that man loves you and he signed the contract. Stop worrying so much. Touch and claim, girl. And I don't even believe in that foolishness. Touch and claim. In fact, this princess needs a tiara!"

Jen is in full bestie mode and there's no stopping her. "Please bring a bandeau tiara and two glasses of Champagne to calm her down."

I take a deep breath, exhale my worries, and clink glasses with Jen. Shane and I are at the one-yard line and we just need to score.

"Mazel tov, bitch, mazel tov!"

We're a bit tipsy leaving and since I value my life, I take the keys from Jen.

"I can drive," she slurs, wobbling in her heels.

"Get in." When I open the door, I notice a person sitting in a blue Mustang or Dodge point a camera at us. Jen sees it too because she starts yelling.

"Excuse me? Excuse me? Did you just take a photo of me?" Jen is walking towards the car. I don't like the way this feels.

"Jen," I call after her. "What are you doing?" The car backs up and speeds off.

"That person just took a picture of us!"

"I mean, you do have them thighs out today," I joke.

"It's not funny." Jen gets in the truck and rolls her eyes. "You remember what happened last time someone snapped a picture of us. We ended up on the front page of the *Baltimore Sun* and it landed me in Pete's office."

"It wasn't the photo. It was the comment. Don't worry. We'll be laughing about it when we're old and grey." I can't keep from snickering. It was taken on the hottest day downtown at the harbor in Baltimore City. We were leaving Gallery from just having lunch on a casual Friday, when someone snapped a picture of us. Turned out it was a reporter and she was interviewing people on Baltimore's hot summers and how they were coping in the workplace. At the time, Jen and I were working at a top asset management firm. Very blue suits and ties. Guys not wearing a tie were considered casual. That day, Jen was dressed inappropriately. She was wearing open-toe shoes, a sleeveless shirt, and a long skirt with a split. To top things off, she said, and I quote, 'They will just have to judge me on the quality of my work and not based on what clothes I wear.' The next morning, every accountant on our floor had a copy of the paper on their desk and Jen got a personal note with one from the CFO. It was pretty bad. She was pissed and obviously still is.

"I know exactly what it was about!" she shouts. "I was humiliated."

"So sensitive." I try to look away to keep from laughing again.

"I don't like people I don't know taking photos of me. They don't have my permission." Jen is fuming.

"Just think. You work for yourself now, so you don't have to worry about getting fired."

"If you're trying to make me feel better, you're not, so please stop trying. He's lucky I didn't pull out my machete."

"You have a machete?"

"Right here!" She pulls a twelve-inch machete from between her seat.

"Who are you? What do you have that in here for? You would

never. . ."

"Never say never!"

14

ALL IN

We all have butterflies. Bailey, who's prepping for her show, and me because I'm waiting to see my love who's back, finally! Shane texts me as soon as the lights go out in the auditorium to ask where I'm sitting. *Seriously? You're late.* I discreetly text back that I'm on the left side, about ten seats from the front.

He texts back.

Move over

I look over my shoulder to watch for him making his way down the aisle so I can grab him, but there's no sign of him. *What did he do, text me from the car?* I wouldn't be surprised if he did. Shane is the type of person who would be like 'open the door' and then show up five minutes later. Why? I could have opened it when you arrived. He doesn't like waiting. I remember he and Jen used to have it out because she was always late. She's gotten a lot better. Today, when it was time to leave the house, she was on time. She knows I don't play when it comes to Bailey's shows. She will get left behind.

About two minutes into the first performance, Shane plops down beside me out of breath.

"Did I miss her?" he whispers loudly.

Placing my finger to my lips to hush him, I shake my head no.

"Okay, good. Traffic." Shane shifts in the small seat trying to get comfortable. He finally uses the aisle to stretch out one leg. "I like this song." He pulls out his phone and gets the app to identify it. "John Mayer."

"Shhh." Before these parents start trippin'. Then again, it's Shane. They will let him get away with anything. I watch him add it to his playlist while at the same time, trying to shield the light coming from his phone. Eventually, I give up and simply look forward at the stage and act like he's not with me.

That changes of course when it's Bailey's time to hit the stage. Shane starts hooting seconds in.

"You'll distract her." I nudge him.

He huffs and finally sits still. Jen on my left thinks it's funny because she always secretly records each show on her phone, knowing good and well that she shouldn't.

"I can't take y'all anywhere," I say. "It's ballet, not a football game."

"Whatever," they say simultaneously.

I know these performances are dry, but they've gotten better over the years. The schools really need to work on getting diversity in their dance department. We'd like to leave when Bailey finishes her piece but unfortunately, we have to sit through another forty-five minutes. Shane looks like he wants to cry. "It will go by fast," I lie.

When we stand for the final ovation, Shane barks, "Thank GOD!"

"Y'all are embarrassing." I point at both of them.

"Let's get out before the house lights come on." Shane grabs my hand.

I pull him back. "We can't. We've got to wait."

"People gonna recognize me." Shane starts getting antsy.

"We'll stand guard," I say, and switch places with Shane, putting him between Jen and me. But as soon as the lights come on, a man with a long ponytail seated in front of us turns around.

"I had a feeling that was you. Ready for this season? Shouldn't you be training? I thought you weren't coming back here until July?"

"I'm here for my daughter's performance," he responds politely.

"My man. Can't wait to see you back on the field. Go Nighthawks!"

Jen and I just stand there with stupid grins on our faces. People can't help themselves, I guess. Then I see Bailey running with her bags. We're overjoyed that she came out so quickly.

"Uncle Shane!" She runs right over to him.

"What am I? Minced meat?" I hold out my arms.

"Mom!" she gives me a hug second.

"Come, come. Let's go before everyone tries to talk to you." Bailey grabs Shane's hand and starts leading him out. We surround

Shane, taking baby steps through the crowd trying to block as much as possible. It's really of no use.

"I'm so glad you made it." Bailey smiles.

"You rocked. I got flowers for you in my truck. I ain't bring them in. I was rushing."

"Thank you, thank you." Bailey skips ahead.

"Y'all had some hot music too. I added a few to my playlist."

"They let me help with the music for the contemporary pieces."

"Nice." Shane gives her a fist bump.

We finally reach Shane's truck quickly because he's parked in a handicap spot directly outside of the school doors. So trifflin'. He opens the passenger door and hands Bailey a bouquet of lavender roses. He gives her a hug and then turns to hug me. "Have any plans tonight?" he whispers.

"There he is!" screams Jen at the top of her lungs, startling all of us.

"Who?" I look around.

"Auntie!" says Bailey. "Goodness! You're loud."

Jen takes off. "The blue Dodge."

I spot the car but they clearly see her coming towards them and peel off again.

Jen jogs back, out of breath. "I knew I wasn't going crazy. Somebody is following us. You, me, I don't know."

"I have no reason for someone to follow me." I shrug. "Or do I?" I squint my eyes at Shane.

"Me either!" says Jen. "Well, not really. I don't think Aasim. I don't know. But I'm going to call him right now. What if his wife thinks we're sleeping together?"

"Jen, is there something you need to tell us?" Shane smiles and gives me a wink.

"What about the wrong number guy? Or the designer guy? Girl, you better get these men under control," I joke.

"Jen got men like that? I knew she was a ho," jokes Shane.

"I heard that." Jen lifts her fist. "Don't make me punch you and knock you out in front of these kids. Because I will," Jen threatens.

"No one is punching anyone." Bailey is protective of Shane.

"That's right. Bailey has my back." Shane looks over at me. "You got your keys, right?"

"Yeah." I retrieve them from my purse.

"Use them."

I laugh. That's code for 'come over tonight'. "We're going to Ruth's. Care to join?"

"Can't. Nighthawks got me on a strict diet. I don't want to be tempted."

"Fair enough." When I give him a hug goodbye, I whisper in his ear, "But you want dessert though." I try to look innocent.

"Yeah, bring me some of that." Shane smirks. "Goodnight Jen, goodnight Bailey. Great performance and have fun at dinner."

We have reservations so we don't have to wait. We're seated in Jen's favorite booth. Our waiter comes right over and instead of asking if we need anything, he focuses on Jen. "I recognize you from somewhere," he blurts out.

"From here?" Jen questions, since she comes here at least once a week.

"Oh, you used to work here?"

"No!" shouts Jen, her tone indignant. "I dine here," she

corrects him.

"Then not from here then," he says apologetically.

She reads his name tag. "Murphy, is that your first name?"

"No, my last name."

"Do you play football?" she continues.

"I wish. I wouldn't be working here." He laughs.

"I just asked because I work with a lot of football players."

"You be hanging out with the Nighthawks?"

Meanwhile, Bailey and I are hungry watching this hilarious exchange, trying not to interrupt, so I kick Jen under the table.

"Never mind, can we order? We'll figure it out later, I guess," she says.

"I want the usual, BBQ shrimp," says Bailey, setting down the menu.

"Stuffed chicken with sweet potato casserole." I hand him my menu.

Same here," Jen says, pointing to me.

"That was easy," says our waiter. "I'll get it right in."

I wait for him to be out of earshot. "Are you fucking kidding me? I can't believe you asked him if he played football because he was a big black dude. That was so ignorant."

"I swear I know him from somewhere."

"Match, perhaps?" I ask sarcastically.

"You might be right." Jen laughs.

"That was funny, Auntie." Even Bailey finds the exchange ridiculous.

"Anyway." Jen rolls her eyes. "How's venue searching coming along?" she asks, quickly changing the subject.

Placing my glass down, I swallow and clear my throat. She's

caught me off guard. "Me?"

"I'm not asking Bailey, she's not the VP of Platinum Events. Yes, you. It's been three weeks and you haven't presented me with any options."

"Well, I. . ."

"Duh. Duh. You haven't been looking, have you?" Jen squints at me.

"Honestly, I haven't. I know I need to." Actually, I forgot. "Did I tell you I ran into Nick on New Year's Eve?"

"No! How are you going to just slip that in? There's been a lot you haven't been telling me."

"Yeah, I did. He told me to keep in touch." I fight to keep a huge smile from creeping across my face. Just then, our warm bread arrives.

"Is Nick the guy you liked from that building?" Bailey asks. "You used to say, 'Nick is so cute. Nick is so cute'."

"He still is." I laugh.

"Ha, ha!" Jen erupts. "You should call him." She raises her brows, grinning. "See if he's got a venue we can use."

"I just might." I take a bite of bread. "Smart ass," I mutter.

Dinner continues to be full of laughs. Bailey, Jen, and I critique each performance and Bailey gives us the backstory on the entire production. When we arrive back home, Taylor shows up at Jen's unannounced. It works out perfectly because Bailey wants to stay with her, and I want to stay with Shane.

"Have fun!" I say, seeing her off to Jen's with her overnight bag. *Time to get sexy*. It's April and the forecast is calling for snow flurries, so I put on a chunky sweater with a pair of leggings and Ugg boots, but underneath, it's sultry seductress. I'm finally breaking out this black lacy playsuit I ordered online from Agent Provocateur. I pose in front of my full-length mirror to get a peek at what Shane is going to see and I guarantee he's going to love it. I fix my sweater and let my hair down and apply a red glossy lip. For dramatic effect, I apply false lashes. I want my eyes to pop!

And last but not least, I reach high into my closet and retrieve my Chanel Box. I often forget I even have this bag. Grabbing my everyday Louis Vuitton tote, I transfer all of the contents and head out the door.

Shane's house is dark when I arrive, so I use my key. "Hello?" I tap on the bedroom door and slowly walk in. "Shane, love. . . it's me." I enter and close and lock the door behind me. Setting my purse on the dresser, I search the room. "Shane?" I check the bathroom. "Where is he?" For a moment I panic, thinking about the dream I had last time I was here. I flinch at a bang on the door.

"Bryn," says a booming voice that I'm so happy to hear. "Why did you lock the door?"

I rush to open it. "Well, I expected to find you in here."

"I had to run downstairs to my basement and turn off some stuff." He reaches for an embrace. "Your heart is racing."

I laugh off the crazy thoughts.

"Relax. You good? You're safe with me."

"How was your day?" I ask, stroking his back.

"It was exceptional." He gives me a genuine smile. He feels the lace and beading under my sweater with his free hand. "What's this?" he asks, tossing away the phone and lifting the sweater over my shoulders to drop it on the floor. He tugs on the waist of my leggings and peeks inside. "You're wearing a onesie?" His smile turns devilish. "I wanna eat you." He stares at me with dreamy eyes.

"Is that all you want to do?" I ask, kicking off my Uggs, knowing full and damn well I want the same exact thing.

"Shut up and kiss me."

When he kisses me gently there's so much heat, my clothes practically melt off. Still kissing, he guides me backwards to the edge of his bed and lies me down. His gaze is intense, almost ravenous, as he separates my legs. I look up at the ceiling, feeling a tear form in my eyes from the anticipation. I hear the unsnapping of my bodysuit and feel the fullness of his tongue. My legs tremble uncontrollably.

"You like that?"

I look down at Shane who's biting his lip.

"I love it. I think I'm about to shed a tear."

"Damn, I ain't made you cry in a minute. I'mma have to step my game up." Shane kisses every inch of my body. "Dis my pussy, right?" Shane teases me, standing naked and flexing every muscle.

"Yes." I reach for his waist because I can't take it anymore. I want to feel him inside of me.

"Patience. I ain't done yet. I want to see you squirm." Shane goes back down on his knees. Propping my butt up, he goes in for round two. I barely have any strength by the time he comes up for air. "This is Shane's pussy." He flips me over and gives my ass a smack. I assume the position. My body is ready and impatiently waiting. 'cause. . ." I sink into the bed as he climbs on top of me, "nobody. . ." he spreads my knees even wider, "and I mean nobody. . ." he arches my back, "lays pipe," he rubs his hard dick against my very, very wet pussy, "like me."

After three orgasms, I'm face-planted in a pillow, practically drooling on myself. But Shane wants to cuddle. I think I need a Gatorade or something to boost my electrolytes. Wearing one of Shane's T-shirts, I cuddle in close and he wraps his big arm around me. It feels so safe. I close my eyes as Shane channel surfs for a good movie. "You know, we haven't been out to the movies in a while," I say, rubbing his chest and gently tracing his tattoos with my finger.

"I know. I'm trying to keep a low profile until this thing with Carice is resolved."

Ugh, that name. I just got dicked down. The last thing I want to talk about is Carice.

"Don't go quiet on me."

"I. . . don't know what to say." I purposely yawn and close my eyes, hoping he gets the hint.

"I was hoping for your support."

One eye snaps open. Now I'm awake. "You always have my support. Don't insult me."

"I need to know that no matter what happens, you're all in."

"Is there something you need to share with me?"

"Her and I are beefing right now and I'm about to get my surgery. I ain't going to see you for a minute so I want to make sure we good."

Sitting with my feelings, I pause before responding, "I'm all in."

"That's what I like to hear." Shane kisses me, pulling me on top of him. "Daddy is ready for some more. Dis gotta hold me over."

I'm so weak and exhausted, I start to cry.

15

FAIMLY FIRST

According to my calculations, I wasn't expecting to see Shane again until it was time to report to camp. So when I get a text that reads

        Get to the airport, your flight leaves

    for Vegas in two hours

I completely freak out.

He can't be serious. Who does this? How does he know if I have any plans this weekend? I technically have a paper to write. Then it dawns on me; I suspect he's been talking to Jen.

When I call her, she answers and says, "Yes, I'm aware. You need to get off the phone with me and pack. You can thank me later."

"Context. I need context at least." I'm breaking into a sweat running down the stairs to get my suitcase.

"Shane asked me what you wanted for your birthday this year and I told him you wanted something that money couldn't buy — him. He said he was headed to Vegas for the weekend, so you're going to meet him there."

"Clever girl," I snicker.

"I know. Anyway, go pack," she says. "I'm on a mission to schedule my own dick appointment. You aren't going to be the only one around here getting dicked down on a regular."

"Calling our waiter from Ruth's Chris?"

"Bye, Bryn." Jen hangs up on me.

I laugh. That's what she gets for being a smart ass. I wouldn't call once or twice every few months 'regular'. But since I know it will be going down, I toss the closet looking for something extra-sexy.

At the airport, to my surprise, through a sea of hundreds of people at an airport, I spot Terry, Shane's long-lost assistant. He's sitting in the Southwest Airlines waiting area fiddling with his cell. A part of me wants to turn around and hide but it's too late. It's almost like he sensed me coming. He glances up from his phone, his face lights up, and he jumps to his feet. "B!" He rushes over to me.

I give him a polite wave.

"Wow! I can't believe I ran into you! Where are you headed?" He gives me a tight hug. It's so tight, my foundation leaves a spot on his shirt. I try to wipe it off, but he doesn't care. I figure since he's still Shane's assistant, and we're flying out on the same flight for MY birthday, he knew I would be here.

"Vegas!"

"Really? That's amazing! So am I. And we're on the same flight?"

"Seems so."

I raise my brows with an awkward smile since he still hasn't made the connection.

"Yeah, I'm headed out there to meet Shane and the crew."

"Apparently I'm joining the party!"

"Cool! DeShaun is here. He's on our flight too."

"Wow. I haven't seen him in a while." I feel a hand on my shoulder followed by a kiss on the cheek. "DeShaun, DeShaun." I tap his hand. "I see you haven't changed."

"Hey babes! You traveling with us? You can sit up front with me. Terry likes to sit in the middle of the plane." DeShaun takes my carry-on bag and leads the way to the 'A' boarding line.

As soon as we're in our seats, he charms the flight attendant and sweetly asks for two vodka and cranberry cocktails.

"Such the gentleman," I joke. "I see you still have a way with the ladies."

"I never had my way with you." He fishes for his straw with his tongue. Even I know he's just trying to show off how long it is.

"Oh, DeShaun. Never." I shake my head. "Ever."

"I'd rather hear you say that while I'm staring down from on top of you."

I cover my mouth. "I just threw up."

"You phony."

"I don't think Shane would appreciate your sexual advances."

"Are you saying you would?"

I give him a side eye. "You know Shane and I are in a committed relationship."

"Man. I don't be in Shane's business like that." DeShaun exhales loudly and leans back in his seat and finishes off his drink. "You know he can't fuck right now."

"What on earth? You're keeping tabs on his dick?"

"He's got one leg."

I raise a brow. "And your point is?" I question with a smirk.

"I stand corrected." He puts his sunglasses on and lays back against the headrest. "It was worth a try. I mean, I ain't know you was coming. Shane didn't mention it."

"It's my birthday."

"Ahh. What, you going to go shopping and shit? I mean, that's what the other ones do."

His words strike a chord. "The other ones?"

"Oh, right. They was before he. . . he locked you down, right?"

I turn to him, narrowing my eyes.

"I'm fucking with you. Chill!"

I turn back and see Terry just now boarding the plane. He smiles and inches his way to the back. I'm thinking I should follow him.

"Or am I?" says DeShaun, peeking over his shades.

I'm happy that our five-hour flight feels like two. When we deplane and finally get to baggage claim, I see him. He looks even more pitiful than I had imagined. Sitting in a wheelchair, his leg in a cast elevated on a suitcase.

"Hey, babe!" I reach around and give him a kiss on the lips. "Boy, am I glad to see you."

"You look nice." He looks me up and down. "You're like

sunshine on a cloudy day."

"Awww. So sweet." I smile. "How are you feeling today?"

"Better than I look. Where's Terry?"

"He's coming. DeShaun and I sat up front."

"Fuck! He try to holla?"

"You do know your boy, right?"

"I'mma fuck him up." Shane winces and rubs his cast. "It itches."

"When do you get it off?"

"Next week. I'm about to remove this bitch myself. Once it's off, I'm going to rehab."

The thought of his surgery makes me weak in the knees.

"Okay, change the subject. How was your flight?"

"I think our plane got struck by lightning."

"What!?"

"Shit's crazy, right?"

"Nigga!" says DeShaun, cutting Shane off and grabbing the handles of his chair. "Wheels up." He pulls him back and heads towards the exit. Meanwhile, Terry is struggling with all of the bags. I offer to stay back and help.

It's a quick ride to the Aria Hotel but I swear we've traveled a couple of miles through the casino to the front desk and then to our room. So by the time we arrive at our corner king suite, I'm in need of a shower. DeShaun parks Shane in the bedroom and he hops on one leg to the bed, wincing and exhaling the entire way. DeShaun points and mouths, 'I told you so.'

"Thanks, I've got it from here." I escort him out.

"Girl, you know you want this!" he sings.

"Boy, bye!" I shut and lock the door behind him. Before I can get back to Shane, I hear another knock at the door and open it again. "Romello!" We embrace and he walks in to find Shane. The door can't shut before four unknowns walk in.

"Hi, you must be Bryn. We've heard so much about you," a woman with braids cascading down her back says and offers me her hand. "I'm Shane's aunt, Luayne. Today's my birthday."

"Nice to meet you! Happy Birthday! It's my birthday weekend as well."

"Gemini. That means you have a crazy side. I know you're little and cute, but it had to be something else to get my nephew's attention."

Funny she should say that. Shane hasn't even seen my crazy side. It almost came out last year at brunch in LA when his little fangirl Andrea and crew were being disrespectful. Jen pulled out the knife and I was ready to throw hands. Thank God, we made it out without causing a scene.

There's another knock at the door. Auntie Luayne answers it, and then introduces me to her circle of friends, her husband Monrieka, and Shane's sister, Nika, who immediately gets comfortable in the sitting area. "Where's Shane?"

"He's in the bedroom."

The two of them bolt through the living room and barge into the bedroom, interrupting Shane and Romello. Luayne dances and sings, "It's my birthday," while Nika, at top speed, sacks him onto the bed.

"Now you see where I get it from?" Shane laughs.

"Get up, punk!" Nika play-boxes him.

It's a lot of energy for me so I decide to give them privacy and pass them to get to the bathroom.

"Where you going?" barks Shane.

"To take a shower."

"Wait, let them out first."

"They just arrived." I backpedal to the bedroom and Shane hands Romello his credit card.

"You know my size. All white," he says. Romello takes the card, bear hugs the other birthday girl, and leads them out. I follow, lock the door, and hope that they are our last visitors for a little while. I'm trying to spend some quality time with my man. Back in the room, Shane's phones are bleeping nonstop.

"Ugh, I would go crazy." I plop down on the bed.

"Whatchu mean?"

"The constant. No alone time."

"I'm used to it." Shane strokes my hair.

"I mean you are broke down and it's still nonstop."

"I come last."

"You come first for me." I kiss him on the lips.

"What about Bailey baby?"

"Okay, maybe not first. But you're the number one man in my life." I flash him a cheesy grin.

"Oh yeah?" Shane pulls me close and smacks my ass.

"Yes!" I give him a quick peck on the cheek. "Now I must shower."

Shane lays back. "Shit. Get on top. That shower can wait." He lifts his white T-shirt, exposing the top of his hard dick peeking out from the waist of his basketball shorts.

"You are so nasty." I unbutton my jeans.

"Keep dem red bottoms on."

An hour later, we're naked on the bed when I wake to more

knocking on the door.

"Get that." Shane taps my arm.

"Is this what it's going to be like all weekend?"

"Put on a robe first." Shane struggles with his basketball shorts.

Seriously? I think, tying my robe tight. *I'm going to answer the door ass naked.* I go out to answer and it's Nika and approximately twenty other people. Embarrassed that I'm answering the door in a robe and my hair disheveled, pretty much announcing to the world that we were just fucking, I discreetly run back into the room, leaving the crew to their own devices.

I hear the commotion over the running water. Someone has found the music and they're getting the party started. The door opens and closes again and someone yells, "Yo, you not ready yet? We're going to be late to dinner!"

"She's still in the bathroom," says Shane, blaming me for our tardiness. Normally, I'd take offense but since he just had me for all five courses of his meal, I'll give him a pass. He was definitely backed up. Then my anxious mind goes there. That means he's not fucking anyone else. It shouldn't even be a thought, but I can't lie, it creeps up every now and again. I shake off the negative thoughts, put my robe back on, and peek out the door.

"Can I have the room, please?"

"Get out," Shane says to DeShaun who's staring at me. Romello herds the group into the living area and closes the double doors. "Hurry up, we late." Shane hobbles to the bathroom and I grab my bags to quickly unpack.

I hang my clothes up at top speed and lotion my body down. I slip my dress on, and my perfume, all before Shane returns wearing only a cast.

"I had to take a whore's bath."

"I don't want to know what that is." I grab my make-up case and go back into the bathroom where there is water everywhere. "Shane!"

"I can't get my cast wet."

My make-up is simple. A red lip and three layers of mascara, a trick I learned from a YouTube video of Kim Kardashian. Since we're wearing all white, it's my pop of color. I'm puckering my lips when Shane hobbles in to check on me.

"You ready?" he offers me his arm.

"Let's go!" I spin around to face him and take his arm.

He kisses me on my forehead. "You look beautiful. I'm so lucky to have you."

Lovingly staring up at him, I say, "Yes. You. Are."

Shane decides he doesn't want to ride in his wheelchair tonight. Instead, he's using DeShaun and a pair of crutches. Since I know that Vegas and crutches don't mix, it's going to be an interesting commute to dinner. Our trek to the front lobby is excruciating. Between Shane's leg and my stilettos, it's a slow and agonizing lull. With relief just a few more steps ahead, I get excited, but when we're outside, we realize we can't all fit and have to wait for the truck. Both of us feel a bit deflated.

We don't wait long. And it's a quick ride to the neighboring casino, the Cosmopolitan. Shane rejects a wheelchair when we arrive, so our painful trek resumes until we reach the many escalators and ride them upstairs to STK. Inside, a group of ladies sitting at the bar watch us walk in and immediately recognize Shane. One of them actually screeches his name. He smiles and nods his head to acknowledge them. As we pass, the plastic blonde blatantly looks him up and down and I'm instantly aggravated. *So disrespectful.* I think a few people with us notice as well because Romello makes his way over to me and nudges me along. "Come on, Bryn, smile. You're with your baby."

"I know. I know." I blush. Still, it doesn't change the fact I want to smack her eyes straight. It makes me think of the story Terry once told me about Carice throwing her shoe at a woman in Vegas and almost starting a brawl. And right about now, I completely understand. These women are so disrespectful.

"It's so disrespectful," says a cousin.

"Exactly! You read my mind."

"A round of Patron shots," Shane orders with our waiter before he sits at the far end of the long table set for twenty. The table is split in thirds as conversations go. The furthest part from us is already engaged in a boisterous celebration. That's the friends' section. The middle is made up of more relatives and the few that I already know: Romello, Qmar, fake cousin Will. The final section, our section, is made up of DeShaun, Terry, me, Shane, Nika, Luayne, and her husband Monrieka.

I sip on a white wine, while everyone else is onto their third shot of tequila. I don't want to seem like the bougie one of the group, but I can't handle shots.

"You gonna loosen up tonight?" Luayne asks from across the table. "Let me order you a drink. A margarita with your strongest tequila," she tells our waiter.

"She's a lightweight," Monrieka says. "She's been nursing that same glass of wine since we sat down."

"She and Nika are lightweights!" She orders another margarita for Nika. "Get loose because we partying tonight! And I know you know how to party. I heard about them events y'all did for Shane. They was talking about them for damn near a year."

"Is that how y'all met?" asks Monrieka.

"Yes," interrupts Shane. "We broke the rules."

"What rules?" asks Luayne.

"He was my client. We worked together so we figured it would look bad."

"Me and Monrieka worked together before we got married." She looks over at him, nodding. "He was nothing but a young innocent pup back then." They rub noses." Wasn't you, babe?" She caresses his chin.

"Yup!" Monrieka starts whimpering and frowning with his chin low and eyes up staring like a homeless puppy.

"Show them, babe, show them what you do now." Luayne's face lights up.

Monrieka sits up straight and squares his shoulders. He inhales deeply and then starts barking like a dog, a very, very large dog.

"Yes, trained him up good. Now he's full grown," Luayne growls, swaying in her seat.

Jesus. "Oh, my. I—" I look to Shane for help.

"She's fifteen years older than him," says Nika, giving me some color.

"And next year is our twentieth anniversary," says Luayne proudly. "And he comes home every night."

"Every night?" asks DeShaun.

"I ain't been with no other woman since the day we met."

"That's right! See, I ain't want no full-grown dog, like you,

DeShaun."

DeShaun cups his heart with his hands and falls back against the chair.

"My ass." Luayne rolls her eyes. "I wanted a young pup I could train. Teach them the ropes. Keep 'em coming back. Feed a dog for three days and he'll remember you for three years."

Monrieka starts barking again.

"You've got to have sex everywhere. Not just in the bedroom." Luayne twirls her fork.

Monrieka nods in agreement.

"Go on, y'all go sneak off to the bathroom. Go that way," she points, "and make a quick right. That will loosen you up."

"Me? I'm loose," I assure her. The barking helped with that.

"How you gonna get loose with your arms crossed?"

I look down. I hadn't noticed. I uncross them and place my hand on Shane's thigh.

"You don't have to drink that if you don't want," says Shane.

"Nah, I'm good." Actually, my stomach is doing somersaults. This drink is disgusting. I swear it's straight gasoline with lime chaser to mask the smell.

"Here's me in the bathroom." Shane holds his phone in front of my face. It's a younger, thinner version of him, ass naked, a side view showing everything he was born with. "Freshman year in college, when I was a young pup."

Shane starts barking and Monrieka joins in.

I hold my head.

"Bryn, nothing is friendlier than a wet dog." Luayne sticks out her tongue when she laughs.

Nika nudges me. "Don't mind her. My aunt is crazy."

"Better get used to it." Luayne looks at my hand, and then proceeds to laugh loudly. "It's toast time, and we got a saying around here, don't we y'all?" She raises her glass.

"Family first!" shouts Romello.

"With me, it's always family first." Shane kisses my forehead.

16

IN DA CLUB

We're at the door as soon as Shane settles the $5,000 dinner tab. Luayne is ready to party. I practically have to beg them to wait while I visit the ladies' room. Nika goes with me and when we return, they're already out the door and we have to play catch-up.

"How was your dinner?" She's making small talk.

"Delicious. And yours?"

"It was alright." Nika rubs her stomach.

"You ready to party?"

"I'm not the biggest partier. I'm just going to keep them out of trouble." She points to Auntie and Monrieka. "They like to dry hump in public." She points. "See, look." Monrieka is grabbing Luayne from the back.

"Wow." I laugh. "They seem cool as shit though."

Nika smiles. "You know, my brother is really lucky to have you."

"Thank you. That's so sweet of you to say."

She places her hand on my shoulder. "No, he really is."

It's nice hearing that from her. It's one thing to hear it from friends, or cousins. But to hear it from his older sister kinda turns things up a notch.

Monrieka bending Luayne over the limo causes a commotion at the valet stand. Nika runs over to move them along. I wait with Shane for a second truck. Resting my head on his arm, I reach for his hand and let out a huge yawn.

"Tired? Want to go back to the room?" Shane squeezes my hand.

"No, no. I'm fine." I yawn again.

"Okay, just checking. I know you had a long flight."

"I'm fine, seriously. That just escaped. I'm sure I'll get my second wind soon."

"I don't want you sleeping in the club."

"I'm good," I assure him, rubbing his arm.

Walking into the club, Kanye's *Power* blasts through the speakers, lights flash, and everyone looks like they're moving in slow motion. They card each one of us and just like in a hot rap video, we're led though the crowd to our large section. The bass is so intense, it feels like my heartbeat keeps resetting. Shane is the first to sit and once he's settled in, perched on the back of the section with his feet on the cushions, everyone else files in. The bottles practically follow us in, filling our center table with vodka, chasers, and lots of Moet Rose. Then during the acapella section

BIANCA WILLIAMS

of the song, the haze intensifies, and single dollar bills rain from the ceilings.

The DJ skillfully mixes in *I Gotta Feeling* by the Black Eyed Peas, and when the beat drops, so does confetti. Practically everyone in the entire club is jumping up and down. "Let's do it!" Romello pops the first bottle, spilling a little onto the floor before pouring the first round. Shane declines Champagne. I use this as an opportunity to show off my bartending skills. Not too many people know that I went to school and became a licensed bartender. I can mix up about one hundred fifty cocktails from memory. I mix him up something nice and present it to him like it's a prized possession. He takes a sip and gives me a nod with the thumbs up.

Then Luayne signals she wants one as well. I hook hers up extra special. She takes a few sips and lets me know that it tastes good. Two gold stars for Bryn. Monrieka says he wants one. I'm so busy being the local bartender I miss when two groupies enter our section to say 'hi' to Shane. One of them actually bumps me out of the way. I give her the bitch-you-better-back-the-fuck-up-before-I-punch-you look. Romello catches it as well because he swings into action, snatching them both back and pushing them onto the other side of the ropes. He returns and offers me a drink. "Nah, we ain't doing that tonight." Romello fills a champagne flute, places it in my hand, and tells me to drink. "Let's dance."

Four glasses of Moet and a numbness has come over me. The next thing I know, I'm off. Dancing, jumping, and spinning like a top, like I'm high on something. I'm dancing to *Tic Tok* by Kesha as if it's the hottest track in the world. Romello doesn't care. He grabs both my hands and jumps while more cash falls from the ceiling. Then someone hands him a flickering rainbow light baton, which he passes to me. Once I hold it in my hands, it becomes my favorite new toy.

DeShaun and Romello are holding me up when the beat drops to Ushers' *OMG*. That's when I hear Shane's roar piercing my soul. "Sit down!" He points to the empty spot on the sofa between his legs. DeShaun laughs and starts taunting me. "You better go over there and sit in time-out."

I wobble to the sofa and sit, slightly irritated at Shane. He rubs my shoulders and I look back at him with tight lips.

"Just chill for a minute," barks Shane.

"It's my birthday!" I yell over the music.

"Not yet. Keep drinking and you gonna ruin your b-day. You need to drink some water." Shane signals to Romello to get me a bottled water.

"Water is going to make me have to pee."

"Well, eat some ice chips."

"Everyone is dancing except me." I look at him. "And you." I take his hands. "Will it help if I dance with you on the sofa?"

He nods yes.

"Great! Romello! Another round!" I yell, hushing Shane as he's about to speak. *Right Round* by Flo Rida drops, and I sing along. White spotlights shine in the center of the club on what looks like two thirty-foot stripper poles. A girl on each, they work their way to the top. Bills start raining from the ceiling. Romello pops another bottle of Moet and brings it over to me. By this point, I can't taste anything. It just slides right on back.

Shane taps Romello and takes my arm. I'm as loose as a rag doll.

I lean between his legs and talk into his mouth. "You want me to go down?"

"No. I mean, later. Right now my aunt and sister is watching."

That's when I start barking.

Shane scowls. "I'm ready to go!"

17

THE HANGOVER

"Bryn!"

I wince.

"Bryn!"

Opening my eyes, my vision is blurred. I blink and all I see is marble and glass.

"Bryn! Don't you hear me calling you?"

I lift my heavy head from the cold marble floor and wipe the drool from the left side of my face. "Oh shit!" When I look down, the drool I thought I was laying in is actually vomit. "Yuck." As I pull up with the assistance of the bidet, I feel an excruciating pain in my head.

"Bryn!"

Fuck. "I'm. . . I'm in the bathroom." Then I panic. *I hope he doesn't wobble in here.* I need to call maid service. But how will I get them past him? I stare down at last night's dinner mixed with white wine, vodka, and Champagne, and angrily unroll the toilet paper to clean it up.

"Bryn!" Shane calls again. "I gotta get in there."

My head starts to pound. "Umm. I'm not feeling well, honey." I cringe. "Can you manage to get to the other one?"

"Fine."

I exhale. There's no way he can see me like this. I tiptoe out of the toilet area and put the shower on. I try to clean up as much as I can with toilet paper and toss it into the waste bin and tie the bag tight. It smells like exactly what you'd think regurgitated lobster, creamed spinach, and mac and cheese would smell like. Rancid.

Of course, since I slept in it, it's also in my hair. Yuck!

I practically drown myself in the hottest water I can possibly stand. I use the entire bottle of shampoo and conditioner (since I didn't pack my own) and wash my body at least five times. The boom-chicka-boom from the base is still playing in my brain and I want to scream. I let my face run under the water and take in some to rinse my mouth. Then I gag. *Urh.*

Oh no. I jump out and run back to the bidet. I dry heave a bit. "Oh God." *Urh. Belch.*

After about ten more minutes of burping and dry heaving, I feel like it's all out of me. Now I need rest. I jump back in the shower for another cleansing, brush my teeth and tongue a thousand times (while also trying to refrain from gagging), and put on my fluffy white robe.

A cloud of fog follows me into the bedroom.

"What were you doing in there?"

"I was feeling nauseous." I wobble my way back to my side of the bed.

"Want breakfast?"

"Sure. American breakfast is fine."

Shane calls in breakfast and I crawl into bed. My side looks messy so I can only surmise that I did in fact sleep in it.

I stay quiet while Shane is on a call, then when he hangs up, the scolding begins.

"You know DeShaun almost saw you naked last night!"

I turn to Shane with a look of sheer terror. "What are you talking about?"

"I sent you to the room and when I came in, you was passed out laying in the middle of the bed ass naked. Legs wide apart."

"You sent me to the room, alone?" I try and recall. I vaguely remember a blurry hallway with crazy carpet patterns going in and out and running my hands along the walls. "Someone could have snatched me!"

"You think I would do that? Nika walked with you."

"You sent me to the room like a little kid?"

"You was trying to take my dick out in the club."

"No, I was not." Flashes of me leaning between his legs come to mind. He was elevated because he was sitting along the back of the sofa with this feet on the seat cushions. But I would never. "I'm sure I was just trying to kiss you."

"And when I kissed you, you started unzipping my pants."

My eyes widen.

"Yeah, and my auntie saw you! Good girl my ass."

"Did you tell her I was a good girl. Wait, I am a good girl."

"One who can't handle her liquor. You was giving that glow stick head on the way out the club."

"You lie, stop fucking with me."

"When I snatched it from you, you started to cry. You literally started crying like a spoiled-ass kid."

"I liked that glow stick."

"A little too much." Shane rolls his eyes.

"So back to the naked part. I was in the bed, how would DeShaun 'almost' see me?"

"My leg was hurting so I had him bring me all the way in the room. I wheeled myself in and saw you and leaped up with one leg to hit the light, and told him to get the fuck out."

I can't deny it because I don't remember. I take a moment and try to recall, but nothing. I don't even know. "I can't believe you sent me to the room. Anything could have happened to us. You could have been wheeled in here to find me murdered by some crazy serial killer."

"This hotel is safe. Wasn't no one going to snatch y'all."

I fold my arms and scowl. "I can't believe you would do that. You should have sent a man to walk with me."

"So they could try and fuck?"

"You'd rather take your chances with both of us being assaulted?"

The tension in the room is thick. Out of nowhere, I remember I need to call maid service. "Pass me the phone."

He passes the phone and reaches for the room controller to open the curtains and turn on the TV.

I shield my eyes. "Can you keep them closed? I'm still a bit hungover."

"As you wish." He continues with the TV and finds a movie that we both haven't seen yet. Then the food arrives.

I'm famished. My stomach is completely empty and although the smell makes me feel a bit sick, I scarf the food down. Maid service arrives shortly after breakfast and at the same time, Shane's phone starts to chime.

"No rest for the weary." He answers and I hear a bunch of voices at the other end. "They want us to come down to the pool."

"You go. I'm going to rest. I'll meet you down there later."

"Okay. Bet." As Shane gets ready, the entire crew shows up to our room to get him and I open the door for them. When they welcome themselves into our bedroom, Shane gets an attitude and signals for me to get under the covers. I swear he's being too much. "I literally just let them in dressed in this white robe."

The others move into the living room but DeShaun plops onto the bed, laughing. "I saw your ass last night. Little, but cute."

"Kiss my ass, no you did not."

"You're right. I didn't. But I could have. You was fucked up. I was turned on watching your show."

"My show?"

"You little freak." He laughs again. "Now I know why Shane can't get enough."

I narrow my eyes. "DeShaun, I'm not feeling well. Best you go in there with everyone else before I call Shane."

Romello runs in and plops on the bed too. He's Shane's other half and he's in protection mode. He lifts his hand for a high-five. "My girl!"

I high-five him.

"She knows how to party." He laughs. "She might not remember anything, but she got hers last night." Romello does his best impression of me at the club.

"I'm glad I could entertain."

"Why you not dressed? You don't want to hang with us today?" Romello rubs my shoulder.

"Got a slight headache." I rub my temples.

"I bet." Romello hits DeShaun, grabs him like he's got to tell him something, takes him into the living area, shutting the French doors behind him.

"Gotta love him," Shane says, returning from the bathroom. He gets dressed and joins me on the bed. "I feel bad leaving you."

"No, don't. You go right ahead. I'm going to finish this movie, repent, and hopefully get some sleep." I blow him a kiss.

"You sure?"

"I'm positive." I nod.

"Okay. Come lock the door, put the second lock on. I don't want anyone coming in here and finding you naked again." Shane offers me his hand.

"Ha, ha, ha. Very funny." I stand up and feel a little bubble in my stomach. *Ugh.* The bubbling gets worse as I walk to the door, and I begin to sweat as they all file out of the room. Shane leans in to kiss me. "Umm." I offer my cheek.

"See you later, babe."

I grin and bear it and wave him goodbye. If I don't shut the door in the next second, I fear that Luayne is going to get the worst of it. It's not my fault she forgot her phone on the table. When I try to say bye, the vomit is in my esophagus. Slamming the door, I rush into the second bathroom and it's like the exorcist up in this bitch. Cheesy eggs cover the place and the smell is downright putrid.

I'm practically gasping for air as I try to request room service for the second time. When they arrive, I apologize profusely while pulling chunks of eggs out of wet strings of my hair. He assures me that he has seen worse and cleans my bathroom spotless within minutes. I've never seen anything like it. Dressed in all black, armed with disinfectant, gloves, and air freshener, the attendant has our suite good as new.

Hours pass and I'm still confined to my bed settling for a liquid diet. My beverage of choice, a crystal blue Powerade. Just looking at it and my stomach grumbles. I'm hungry, yet scared to eat any solids. So I simply find another movie to fall asleep to.

The credits are rolling when I awake to Shane and DeShaun returning to the room. I don't say anything, just wave. Afraid of what Shane might say about me still lying in the bed, I close my eyes to appear exhausted instead of bored out of my mind. Shane looks over at me again. I cuddle in the pillows.

"You look sick. You going to be able to go out tonight?"

"My stomach is still a bit queasy, but I don't feel as lethargic. I honestly think it was a virus."

"It's called too much liquor," snaps DeShaun.

"Alright. Dinner and a show is in a few hours so you can start getting dressed."

I take what feels like my hundredth shower in the last twenty-four hours. I'm a bit longwinded getting ready since standing makes me feel a bit dizzy. When I emerge, Shane gives me a side eye as he hobbles by with just a towel around his waist, holding a roll of Saran wrap.

"Smart." I wink at him and continue into the room to pick out an outfit. I slip on a black spaghetti strap jumper I was concerned about fitting a bit snug, but after this morning I think I'm down four pounds. Slick my hair back in a neat bun, add big hoop earrings and a red lip. Perfect.

We're all dressed, matching each other's swag and ready to go when Romello and DeShaun arrive at our door. Romello takes Shane's crutches and DeShaun brings the wheelchair. "I see you finally put some clothes on," DeShaun laughs, sticking his tongue out.

"Leave her alone. She looks like she's still hungover," Romello laughs.

I don't laugh.

"I'm fucking with you. You look beautiful." Romello gives me a side hug.

"It's your fault, you know! I have a two-drink limit and you were the one getting all fancy with the spirits."

"Man, don't be too hard on yourself." Romello holds the elevator door and motions for me to enter first. "You die once, you got to live every day to the fullest."

"The room is nice and all but I would have rather chilled with y'all by the pool."

"You ain't miss nothing," barks Shane. "It was hot as fuck."

When our car pulls up, DeShaun helps Shane in. "You sure you going to be alright?"

Shane nods yes and DeShaun shuts the door.

"Just us tonight?" I ask.

"Just us."

I smile and reach for his hand. Looking out of the window as we pull away, I give the boys a wave goodbye.

18

L.O.V.E.

When we arrive at Prime Steakhouse, we're taken to a table reserved for two directly in front of the Bellagio fountains. Shane being the gentleman that he is pulls out my chair. And before I can ask about the next showing, the maître de hands Shane the wine menu and lets us know the next water performance is in ten minutes.

"This is very romantic."

"I know." Shane smiles, eyeing the menu. "I'm hungry. You know what you want?"

"I'm going to go with the soup."

"Your stomach still bothering you?"

"It's best I don't chance it."

"I feel you." Shane places the menu on the edge of the table.

"You getting the usual?"

"You know it." He takes a sip of water. "Have fun in bed today?"

"Not really. I was too busy missing you."

"Kinda missed you too."

"You're just saying that." I rub his hand.

"Na, for real. I wished you were with us today."

Our waiter interrupts with warm bread and what looks like whipped garlic butter, and then takes our order.

"Your aunt is funny." I pinch off a piece of bread. It melts in my mouth.

"Yeah, she's like my second mom. I ever tell you she helped raise me? My moms was working like two full-time jobs and going to school at night. My auntie would help my dad out 'cause he got hurt on the job. She and my oldest sister would make sure I got to all my games, practices, and stuff. My mom would sneak in for some of my games, even if it was for only fifteen minutes on her lunch break. She'd be the loudest one on the sidelines letting me know she made it." Shane smiles at the memories. "Man, she ain't miss one game. She still the queen holding it down for the family and keeping us all together. I get the credit, but she's the brains behind it all. I don't know where I'd be without her. I was determined to make it big, not necessarily for me, but I was gonna make it so I could retire her. So when I got drafted in the first round, my first check went to buying her a house and I told her she would never have to work another day in her life. She on a permanent vacation. I think she's in China visiting the Great Wall right now. I'm waiting for her to send pictures."

"That's sweet. I can't wait to meet her."

"You'll get to meet her at the wedding. She, uhhh, how do I put it. She's very over-protective of her only son. Leave it to her, I'll stay single for the rest of my life. I'm not ashamed to say that I can be somewhat of a momma's boy."

"Really?" I laugh sarcastically. "I wouldn't have guessed it."

"I love my momma. That's another reason why family is so important to me. She instilled that in us when we was young. We look out for one another, no matter what."

"So your older sister, is she with her in China?"

"Nah, she just moved to Canada with her husband. Married some Italian guy. He in the mob or some shit like that so we don't see her that much. She's pregnant now so I can't wait to be an uncle for real."

"Well, Bailey still calls you Uncle Shane."

"Nah, she my daughter. That's gonna change."

"I guess we'll tell her at the wedding too?"

"I can dig it." Shane sips his water. "I can't wait to see the look on her face. It's going to be priceless."

My eyes widen. "I bet."

We both look up when water shoots from the fountain. The lights shine warm amber as Frank Sinatra's *LOVE,* begins to play. *It must be fate. The stars are aligning.* I reach for Shane's hand and squeeze it tight and picture myself in that wedding dress and his reaction seeing me in it for the first time. I play out our entire lives together during the three-minute song. We grow old together. I could live in this moment forever. "Love," I sing when the song ends.

Shane blushes.

"Speaking of going to school at night. Did I mention that I enrolled in graduate school?" I say.

"You didn't."

"Yeah, I got a new boss. Harry, you remember Harry from the holiday party dirty dancing with his young hottie?"

"Oh yeah. I remember them."

"Well, he sold to a VC so I've got a new boss, Lee. He recommended that I get my MBA."

"That's dope. When did this happen?"

"The sale of the business happened at the beginning of the year."

"An' you just now mentioning this?"

"You were busy with the surgery and kids, so I just figured—"

"I'm never that busy."

"How is your leg by the way?"

"It's fine. I'm just ready to get this thing off so I can scratch it. I'm trying to start rehab as soon as possible so I'm ready for camp."

"When are you coming back to Baltimore?"

"When camp starts."

"That's another month. I'm going to miss you."

"Babe, we have a whole day before you leave. Let's make the most of it."

I nurse my soup as Shane devours his steak. It looks delicious but I don't want to get sick.

After dinner, we make our way to the theater to see O. We arrive just in time and because of Shane's cast, we get to sit in a handicap seat, which is located smack center. It's chilly in here so

I snuggle in close and when the lights go down and those large red curtains open, after a few people dive into the water, my eyes close and I fall asleep.

Shane taps my shoulder during the grand finale.

"You let me sleep though the entire show."

"You ain't miss nothing. I barely stayed awake." Shane motions for assistance and asks the theater attendant to get us a wheelchair. "I can't walk back to the entrance. Carry my crutches for me." We leave before the theater lets out to beat the crowd. They hand Shane off to another staff member of the casino and they take us to the back entrance and call for car service.

Romello and DeShaun are at the Aria entrance to receive us. I'm thankful, because Shane is too big for me to try and push in these heels. Romello takes the crutches and DeShaun gets him into the wheelchair.

"Did y'all have a good time?" Romello asks.

"Yeah. Did you take care of that?" Shane barks.

"Of course." Romello waves me to follow him. "You look like you need me to carry you."

"My feet do hurt. Louboutin says his shoes are like candy. They are made to stare at and to be adored. They are not made for walking Vegas blocks."

"I don't know why y'all pay all that money for a pair of shoes that you can only stand in for a couple of hours." Romello shakes his head.

"They are an acquired taste. Besides, Shane likes me to keep them on." I nudge him.

"I bet he does." Romello hands me our room key to open the door. Once inside I hit the light. There's a beautiful bouquet of exotic flowers in a glass vase next to a strawberry shortcake with *Happy Birthday Bryn* written in thin red icing.

"Aww. Thank you!" I get a little teary-eyed. I sit in Shane's lap and give him a huge hug.

"Happy birthday, beautiful," says Shane. "I love you," he whispers in my ear.

Giving him a big wet kiss on the lips, I whisper, "I love you, too!"

19

BREAKFAST IN BED

We sleep in until room service arrives. Shane gets up wearing nothing but a pair of basketball shorts and a cast and hobbles out of the room to answer the door.

"I could have gotten it!" I shout.

"Nah, it's your day."

I pull the sheets, tucking them under my arm, and fish around the bed for my clothes. Retrieving Shane's white T, I put it on and twist my hair in a high bun. I pat my face a bit, hoping I look refreshed. I slept great last night. Shane made sure of it. I'm smiling from ear to ear when he rolls in the cart and hands me my food.

"Breakfast in bed."

I love it.

"I figured we'd try again."

"No worries. I feel a million times better today."

"Tea or coffee?"

"I'll have tea, but I'll wait until I'm done eating. Come join me." I pat the bed.

"Don't mind if I do." Shane gets comfortable, grabs the remote, and channel surfs to find a movie. "Wanna watch some porn?"

I shake my head. "You kidding, right?"

"Just thought I'd ask. I'll wait." He continues to search.

"Wait until I leave." I check the time. My flight home is in five hours, which means I need to make the most of these next three hours.

"How about, *Oooh! Dear John.*" Shane hits play. "It's my favorite."

About an hour or so into the movie, I have finished both my food and tea while listening to Shane speak dialogue along with the movie. I wonder how many times he's seen it. By the end, I've practically emptied the box of tissues on the nightstand.

"I love, love," Shane says.

"This movie was so sad. All of that and they don't even end up together in the end."

"But they got something special like us. That no-matter-what kind of love. It stands the test of time. It's a love that lasts forever."

"Is that what you think about us?" I ask.

"I know you'll never leave me."

I pull my head back, distorting my face. "That sounds very

"one-sided."

"I know what we got and no matter what happens, I'll always love you."

"Now you're worrying me."

Shane pulls me in close. "Don't you worry. Now go get dressed. You have a plane to catch."

I check the time and realize I've still got to pack. I bolt out of bed and rush to the bathroom to get ready. My car will arrive at the hotel in one hour. It's bad enough I lose at least twenty minutes just getting to the hotel lobby.

Shane is silent and watches me intently as I pack.

"You alright?" I slip my shoes into their red velvet dust bag.

"Those shoes are hot. How come you haven't worn the blue ones yet?"

Because, duh, I'm saving them for our wedding. "I didn't even think to stop by your place to grab them. I could have worn them with my all white."

"We'll do something special when I get back."

"When is that again?"

"Camp starts in four weeks. I may come back a little late 'cause of rehab."

"Five weeks." I clench my teeth. "And why can't we fit something in between?" I remind him of the contract.

"I'll make up for it. Don't stress. It will go fast."

"Just because I know doesn't mean it doesn't suck."

"Speaking of suck." Shane pulls back his covers revealing a large imprint in his shorts.

"I wasn't expecting that."

"I could see your boobs while you were bending over packing.

And I've wanted to put it between them the entire time."

"Aren't you going to watch porn when I leave?" I laugh, pointing at the television.

"We can do both. Can we?"

"I just brushed my teeth so you better tap me," I threaten.

Shane is like a bull in a china shop as he scrambles, searching for the remote control buried in the sheets. "Ooh, open the blinds. I want people to watch us."

"You are such the exhibitionist."

"Well, that's part of why you love me."

I have to agree. "Good point! Hurry with your flick."

Shane fast-forwards to where a female is moaning, groaning, and having the fakest sounding orgasm I've ever heard in my life. I don't know how he watches this shit. I can tell he's getting a little too into it when he grabs my head. I hit his thigh and he lets go. Her screaming is rather distracting and is throwing my rhythm off, so I try my best to block her out. Then he taps my shoulder. "Come, reverse, cowgirl." He lifts my dress, slips my thong to the side, and pulls me onto him. My eyes roll back in my head. I lean forward as Shane grabs the back of my neck. Then I reach down and fondle his man jewels. Shane's pumps become more penetrating, leaving me breathless. My body starts to tremble. I scream, the porno lady screams, and Shane quickly pushes me off and pulls out. He lays back, coming on his stomach. I do him a favor and grab a hot washcloth and clean him up.

"Aww man, did we just do that?"

"Fuck?"

"No, come at the same time?" Shane has a huge grin on his face.

"We did." I nod.

"That was nice. Spontaneous sex."

"I think she came too." I point to the TV. The guy is now eating her out.

"I would suggest that we do that too but I know you got a flight to catch."

"I do and I think I'm going to be well rested."

"Give me a kiss."

I pucker my lips.

"I want a real kiss. I'm not going to see you for a month."

We share a passionate kiss. One that makes me climb on top of him. "Let's do what they're doing. I'll catch the next flight out."

The next flight turns out to be a red-eye. I should have looked into it before getting drawn into some last-minute birthday sex. It was just too good to walk away from. Shane and I do our best not to take those types of chances. . . especially since the miscarriage. I'm not worried though because I was just on last week. I won't be fertile for another week or so. I know my body.

When it's time to board the plane, I send Bailey a text. It's only 9 pm her time so she should still be awake. I hate leaving Shane, but I can't wait to get home to my baby. She texts me back saying that she has a surprise for me. She's so sweet. I let her know that I love her and turn my phone off.

I sleep the entire flight, only waking up when it's time to land. I pop some gum in my mouth and take a few sips of water to keep my ears from clogging as the plane descends. We're on the ground in twenty minutes and because I was in a rush to catch my flight a few days ago, I'm parked in the hourly garage. It works out because it's too early in the morning to be waiting for a shuttle.

When I'm safely on the highway, I crack the window and blast my music until I safely reach home. Bailey must have set an alarm because when I pull up, I see her bedroom light turn on. I debate whether I want to take my bags in tonight or take them in the morning, but when I see her open the front door, I pop my trunk.

She meets me halfway, jumping and giving me a huge hug. "Happy birthday, Mom!"

"Thanks babes! What are you doing still up?"

"I wanted to be up when you see your surprise." She has a weird grin on her face. "Let me take your bag." She giggles.

"Where's your Auntie Jen?"

"You'll see. Let's go downstairs."

"Okay." I hit the hallway light.

"No." She turns it off. "It's a surprise. Just hold onto the railing."

When we reach the family room, Bailey takes my hand and stands me in the center. She lets go of my hands and walks away. "Ready?"

"Now or never!"

Bailey hits the lights and on my wall is the largest television I've ever seen in my life. "It's eighty inches! And listen to this!" She turns it on and *High School Musical* plays. I feel like I'm on the basketball court with them. "Surround sound!" She starts pointing to the speakers in the ceiling and a subwoofer in the corner. "And there's one in your room too!"

"There's an eighty-inch TV in my room?" I scream, and pray that there isn't.

"No, that one is only fifty inches. Mine is forty inches!"

"Wow! Okay. I'm not sure how to react right now. Where did

you say Jen was?"

"She's in your room watching a movie. There's another surprise in there too!"

"Was this your idea?"

"Yes. Shane said anything I wanted to get for both of our birthdays, since he missed mine this year."

"Wow, and he got it done really fast."

"I know. It was so cool. It was the same guys that did the theater at his house."

"Well, I love it. Let's go check out the rest of them." When we get upstairs, Jen is sprawled on my bed with her mouth wide open snoring to her favorite movie *The Holiday* playing on my new television. And curled up next to her is a tiny furry thing. *What is that?* I hit Jen with a pillow, waking her up. "What do you have in my bed?"

"You mean your new son?" She rubs her eyes and fishes for her eyeglasses from the nightstand. "Meet King."

Bailey jumps on the bed to rub him. "He's a Morkie. A Maltase Yorkie and he's all mine."

"I'm going to kill him." Bailey hands me the puppy. He weighs about two pounds. Cute, fuzzy little thing. "It's like holding a newborn. I'm afraid he's going to break." I hand him to Jen.

"How was your trip?"

"It had a rough start but it turned out okay. And I mean, I come home to state-of-the-art televisions, and a puppy, my goodness."

"Tell me about it. You better be lucky he's hired me to watch it for y'all during the day. I wasn't expecting that!"

"I certainly wasn't expecting this." I give Bailey a hug and kiss goodnight. "We can discuss over tea. I'm actually wide-awake now. And bring the pooch."

"Sure, why not. Goodnight Bailey." Jen waves her goodbye.

I follow Bailey into her room to check out her new TV. I swear it's half the size of the wall. "Bailey!"

"It was his idea. Go big or go home."

"Please don't stay up all night, your eyes give you enough trouble. Remember to back up."

"I know, Mom." She climbs back into bed. "I hope you like yours."

"I do and I appreciate it."

"Uncle Shane said when he comes back we're going to have movie night downstairs. He also said the games are going to be so much better to watch at home."

"Can't wait. Love you. Get some rest, you still have two weeks of school left."

"A week and a half."

"Same thing." I give her a kiss on the forehead and close her bedroom door on my way out. Downstairs, Jen has started making the tea.

"English breakfast or mint?"

"Mint, I'm not trying to be up all night. I mean I do have to work in the morning." I pick up King and pet him.

"Well, start talking about your trip."

"There isn't much to say because I don't remember. I drank so much the first night I was there, I just remember waking up like Stu in *The Hangover*. I was on the bathroom floor drooling on myself and half of my head was in vomit. I'm so thankful I didn't choke and die. I literally woke up to Shane screaming my name from the bedroom. I don't know how long I was in there and I don't remember how I even got to the bidet. But other than that, I got to meet his family, we had some alone time, breakfast in bed, and last but certainly not least, some great birthday sex."

"Well that's to be expected."

"I don't think Shane would have it any other way. It's what bonds us." I laugh so hard I almost spit my tea. "No, seriously. Remember I told you I love having dinners with him?"

Jen nods.

"It's because it's quiet and I learn so much about him. That's when he really opens up. We had a very intimate dinner in front of the Bellagio fountains. Oh, I almost forgot. You're not going to believe which song played first."

"Try me."

"*Love*, by Frank Sinatra. It's meant to be, girl."

"I don't know, the universe might be involved in this one."

"Can you believe it? I think we're finally getting it right."

"Crazy, right."

"I feel a bit relieved. Like I can finally exhale. I'm not looking over my shoulder constantly. Carice is an issue but not really anymore. In fact, I don't think her name came up one time. I'm so happy right now. This is it. He's doing and saying all the right things. Third time's a charm, I guess."

"Think it was the contract?"

"No, it feels like it's something that he's just committed to." I look at the puppy. "He's so darn cute."

"I know. Well, if you're happy, I'm ecstatic. I'm glad it all worked out. I know deep down inside Shane is a good guy and I use the term 'good' very loosely. I know he loves you. I hope nothing but the best for the two of you. I'm just impatiently waiting to plan the wedding."

I jump up to grab my phone. "I just realized I haven't sent Shane a text to let him know that I made it home safely." I shoot him a quick text. "Jen, if you're impatient, just imagine how I feel."

20

GAME DAY

It's officially game day! So, Bailey is super-excited when I tell her
to get dressed and that I'm on my way to get her from her dad's.

"I wanted to go to the game today!" She hops in the car,
sweaty, hair flying everywhere. "Can we go home so I can change
into my jersey?"

"Yes, we're going to go to the house because I have to get
dressed as well." I take another look at her. "Have you showered?"

"Yes! We were playing a dance game." Bailey turns up the
music. I turn it back down.

"Did you have a good time with your dad? How is he? How's
the family?"

"Yeah, it was fun. We had like other family over and we had

game night. What did you do?"

"I had schoolwork. And work-work, and Platinum Events work. Busy as usual."

"You work too much." Bailey turns the music back up and bops her head to the beat. "Oh, I need ballet tights for class tomorrow."

"How do you suppose you get those tights? I have to work to earn a living so that I can take care of you." Bailey just looks at me. "Whatever. That's fine. I have to go to Walmart and pick up a few things for the house." She has no idea. "You should be able to get a pair from there. In fact, when are we supposed to hear back about your auditions?"

"Any day now."

"I'm nervous. Aren't you?"

"I'm confident. I gave it my best and I believe I'm getting in."

"Good. I'm glad to hear I haven't wasted my time or money." Bailey has been taking ballet classes since the age of four. I'm hoping it pays off. A college scholarship would do wonders.

"Mom, why are you complaining? You're rich."

"Is that what you think? I'm not. A hundred thousand dollars a year is not rich. You'll realize that when you get older."

"That's what my cousin Shanice said. She asked about you."

"Wow, I haven't seen her in years. How old is she now?"

"I think she's nineteen. She looks completely different. She was there when you dropped me off. She really just wanted to know who bought you this car."

Ummm. Her little ass was always a bit grown for my taste.

"She asked me if Uncle Shane had a girlfriend."

"Is that right?"

"Yeah, she said she needed a new purse."

I gasp and have to clear my throat. "What is wrong with her?"

"She plans to have a baby by an athlete so she can get child support. She says she wants to be the next Kim Kardashian. I'm not surprised. A lot of girls in my school say the same thing."

"IN ELEMENTARY SCHOOL?"

"Yeah, in my dance class. They say if they don't make it as a dancer, they want to be strippers or make a sex tape."

"IN ELEMENTARY SCHOOL?"

"Why do you keep saying that? Yes. They want a glamorous life. The boys too!"

"I'm sick. You just really made my stomach queasy by sharing that. Well, let me tell you the not-so-glamorous side of the story to share with your little dancer friends. What they don't tell you is that the strip clubs are located a few blocks away from the jailhouse. At least the ones in Baltimore are. And you know what else? All those guys who just came home with a dollar in their pocket?" I look over at Bailey and her face is distorted. "They will have to split their butt cheeks and more for that filthy single dollar bill. Not so glamorous, is it?"

"That is gross." Bailey turns her nose up.

"I got a five-dollar bill one day and it had written on it, 'Stay in school. I had to do something strange for this. Stay in school.'"

Bailey looks like she's smelled something awful. "What are you looking at me like that for? I don't want to be a stripper."

"I'm just saying." I nod with one eyebrow raised.

"Mom, let's go. You're tripping."

"Elementary school, my mind is blown."

"Why did I even say anything?" Bailey shakes her head and

tries to open the door before I can put the car in park.

"Listen, Ms. Sassyfrass."

"What, what did I say?" she whines.

"Watch your tone and keep your hands on your head. Comprende?"

"Si."

"Great, now let's run in here and get out so we have time to rest before the game."

I can never run into Walmart to grab just one thing or spend less than $50. There must be subliminal messaging playing though the loudspeakers. An hour and a cart full later, I'm loading a ton of bags into my trunk.

Bailey's feelings are still a little hurt from being checked earlier, so she decides to plug in her earbuds and listen to her own music. That's fine with me. If I don't check her now, she'll be on someone's pole later on. Besides, it's a short ride home and I could use some silence.

As I arrive home, a car catches my eye, because it's parked on the right side of the road with its front lights facing me. It takes a lot of effort to park that way. Besides, it's unfamiliar. With one eye on the car, I make a right in my driveway. I could be overreacting. Technically, it could be a visitor for one of my neighbors, but then I'd ask why they are parked like this? So I wait a few moments, dancing along with Bailey. She's in no rush. This is one of her favorite songs.

When the song ends, I pop the trunk, exit my car, and stretch. The windows in that car are so dark, I can't tell if anyone is inside. Still, I survey my surroundings as I take out my keys and proceed to the trunk to grab a few bags. We take as many as we can into the house. I go out a second time and grab a few more bags. Bailey trails seconds behind. I take a few more bags into the house and run them to the kitchen table. That's when I hear Bailey talking. My entire body fills with fear and I rush to the door to find Bailey standing at my trunk with the remaining bags, in time to see the car screeching off.

"Who were you talking to?"

"There was a man in the car. He rolled his window down and yelled, 'Smile!' and took a picture of me."

"Get in the house!" I rush back into the house and grab my keys, back out of my driveway like a bat out of hell, screaming all the while I'm searching for the car. "Motherfucker! When I find him. Fucking pervert! What the fuck?" When I get to the intersection, I make a left and drive until I hit the main road. He's nowhere in sight. I turn around and drive down a few roads and residential cul-de-sacs to see if he's hiding someplace else.

After hunting the neighborhood, I return home raging and Bailey is totally freaked out as I search the house for a baseball bat or some other weapon to ward off our stalker. I don't know why a stranger is waiting out in front of my house and apparently taking pictures. My initial thought is that it's definitely Carice having me followed, but then again, why would he approach Bailey? It all seems too strange.

"Mom, I'm going to get into the shower and get dressed."

"That's fine." I'm fuming as I put the groceries away. "Fucking pissed." It's been some time since I've had a full-blown panic attack and since I don't want to visit the emergency room, I take a few deep breaths, and have a glass of wine to calm down. Today was supposed to be a good day.

Once Bailey is dressed, she joins me downstairs in the living room. "Umm, why aren't you dressed?" She throws her hands on her hips.

"You're right." I get up and go to my room. I haven't seen my man in months, and even though he isn't playing today, I still need to look cute.

When Jen arrives, we all look at each other and laugh. We look like triplets with all three of us wearing Smith Nighthawks jerseys and black jeans. Jen and Bailey are wearing tennis. As for me, I'm wearing a pair of my new black boots Shane sent to me, just because.

It feels like it's been forever since we've been to a game. Usually, I only like going when the weather is nice. As soon as it gets cold, I'd rather watch from home. Tonight, Shane invited us out so I'll be there to support.

It's a long line at the will call window designated for the Nighthawk players' family and friends. Bailey is passionately retelling Jen the events from earlier when I hear someone call my name. It's Terry, a few people in front of us. He calls for Jen and Bailey, pointing with his lanky arms. The line continues to move forward so after he gets his tickets, he stops over to give me a hug. "How are y'all?" He's beaming.

"Terry! How's life?" Jen gives him a huge hug.

"It's good, man. It's good. I'm seeing somebody now. It's serious." Terry smiles, clapping his hands. "Finally!" He puts his hands together in prayer. "I don't know. . ."

"Congratulations!" I give him another hug.

"I think she's the one." He grins. "In fact, I met her that night in Vegas at the club."

"Terry, that weekend was a blur."

"Right, right, 'cause you was—"

Jen cuts him off. "Oh, Terry. I see not much has changed since I've last seen you." She laughs and points to Bailey. "But you look good! Clean as can be. I see you," Jen teases.

"My bad. But nah, I mean, we are going strong. She's talking about moving to Baltimore. I'm already thinking about buying a house for when she gets here."

"Oh, it's *that* serious," says Jen.

I reach the front of the line and excuse myself. "Hi, I'm here for three tickets for Bryn Charles."

"Player's name?" asks the customer service representative.

"Shane Smith."

She flips through a bunch of envelopes. "Three tickets?"

"Yes."

"Sign here." She hands me a pen.

"Thank you." I get our tickets and slowly walk to the entrance with Terry. It's when we reach security, I realize we're sitting in a different section. "We're seated in a few sections to the left," I say to Terry.

"I miss y'all. Man, we need to do another event."

"Tell Shane!" laughs Jen.

Bailey gives Terry a hug and I wave him goodbye as we walk our separate ways.

We eventually find our seats, a few sections over from where Terry is. It reminds me of the very first game we attended when Terry met us at our seats and made sure we had everything we needed. Although he sat a few sections over, he checked on us and made us feel welcome. It's crazy how time flies. It feels like yesterday, but so much has changed. I find myself looking back over my shoulder in his direction.

That's when I see Terry with Shane's kids, and a woman who looks like it could be. . . Carice.

21

IT'S ALL GOOD

It's the longest, most aggravating game ever. Does he really have both of us at the game? *He wouldn't.* I don't have cell service, so I can't get a call through. I don't think he's allowed to have his phone on the sideline anyway. But that doesn't keep me from trying.

"What are you pouting about?" Jen gives me a side eye.

I shake my head no. "It's all good."

"If you say so." Jen doesn't believe me. She looks where I look to see if she can figure it out. Meanwhile, I can't wait to leave.

When I get to the car, I finally have reception and hit the send button on my phone and drive home with purpose. I'm angry, but I wrestle with wondering if I have the right to be. I mean, who else is going to bring a four and a two-year-old to a football game? The nanny? Then again, I guess he could have one. But one that looks like Carice? I let my rambling thoughts get the better of me and while Jen and Bailey are celebrating a Nighthawk season opener win, I'm stewing in a bit of jealousy.

I fake the funk and put on a half-smile for Bailey as we go into the house, and tell her to get ready for bed. To sweeten the deal, I tell her she can watch a movie when she gets out of the shower. As for me, I immediately shower and change into something comfortable. In bed, I check the time and give him a call. "Hey!"

"What's up? I'm finishing up dinner with a few of my teammates. You want me to bring you anything?"

For a moment, I consider. I'm PMS'ing and craving something sweet. But I decline. "Nah, I'm good."

"I'll be there, leave the door unlocked."

Shane likes to walk in on me unexpectedly, especially when I'm taking a shower. It reminds me of some psycho shit, but anything to keep things spicy. However, after today's bullshit, I'll be sitting right in this living room waiting for him to show up. "I can't. Just call me when you get here."

"Why not? What's going on?"

"We'll talk about that when you get here."

"What now?"

"I'll see you when you get here."

"That's wack."

It's an hour later when Shane knocks on the door. It startles me. I must have dozed off, so when I hear him knock again, I toss the Grace Ormonde magazine under the throw and rush to the door. "What time is it?" I rub my eyes.

"That's why I said to leave the door unlocked."

"I couldn't. Apparently, we have a stalker."

"You for real?" Shane takes off his pullover sweater and kicks off his Nikes. He straightens his stark white t-shirt and adjusts the drawstring on his grey sweats.

"I am," I reply, momentarily concentrating on his visible bulge. "I mean. . ." I shake my head. *Keep to the script, Bryn.* "I was flipping out. That car wasn't following Jen, it's following me." Shane follows me into the living room and sits next me on the couch, directly on top of my magazine. He lifts the throw and grabs it before I'm able to snatch it away.

"What is this?"

"A magazine."

"It's a wedding magazine." All the color seems to leave his face as he swallows hard.

"Oh my goodness," I toss it by the front door. "Back to what I was saying, I should have gotten the tags." Trying to give him a visual, I'm talking with my hands. "I knew it looked weird the way it was parked. I waited to see if there was any movement in the car, but nothing. So I went into the house with some bags. Bailey and I had just come from Walmart. And then when I came out for like the second round, Bailey said that the car pulled up behind mine and told her to smile for the camera! And took a picture of her. I lost it! I jumped in my car and tried to catch him, but he was gone."

Shane rubs my leg. "Yeah, that sounds like some fuck shit. I'd be pissed too. But let me ease your mind." He slumps back onto the sofa and rubs his temples. "It's probably Carice."

"What the fuck!"

"I swear I can't make this shit up." He scratches his brow. "She's got a PI on me again."

"What the fuck?"

"She don't like you."

"I don't necessarily like her either. I mean. She's got people at my house. What is wrong with her? In fact, don't answer that question. I feel my blood pressure rising."

"She wants to make sure I don't have the kids around you. I had them today at the game. I guess she sent her guy here to make sure I didn't bring them over."

"So. . ." my heart beats a little bit faster. "She wasn't there today?"

"Hell no!"

"I thought I saw her."

"You saw her cousin."

"So does this mean I'm never going to meet your kids. I mean, you are around Bailey all the time but it's a crime for your kids to be around me?"

"Until I get custody back, I mean. Nah. I mean, what do you want me to do? I can't."

"Oh, my goodness. This could go on forever. I need a drink. And let's change the subject," I say, trailing off into the kitchen to open a bottle of wine. I'm relieved it wasn't her. For a moment, I thought we were done.

Shane creeps up behind me. "Where's Bailey?" he whispers.

"In her bed."

Shane's eyes light up. "Let's go downstairs."

"Don't even think about it."

Shane chuckles, throwing his head back. "But you have to

show me the TVs."

I cross my arms. "You've seen TVs before. You have them in every room of your house."

He laughs even harder and reaches for me.

I swat his hand. "I'm not playing. You just gonna have to wait until you see me again."

"But why?"

"Because I said so."

"That ain't a good enough reason. Don't tell me you going to start holding out and only giving me ass on special occasions. Or like only suck my dick for my birthday and shit like that."

I burst out laughing. "Don't give me any ideas."

"I wouldn't allow it. Speaking of my birthday, it's coming up and I want to do something special. I'm thinking a hot-ass party. I want it to be real classy. On the level of TGS's shit. I'm thinking some suit and tie shit. Niggas in Paris. Hot, ain't it? I'm thinking airplanes and shit."

"Hmmm. Let me think. Actually, I've got something even better. How about The Most Interesting Man in The World?"

"That's fire! You never cease to amaze me."

"That's why you pay me the big bucks." I smile.

"What if I told you I have a surprise for you?"

"Humor me." I pour another glass of wine. "What is Shane the Great going to surprise me with?"

"Are you drunk?" Shane takes the bottle and puts the cork back in, placing it in the cabinet.

"Just a wee bit tipsy." I sashay back into the living room. I feel Shane's eyes on my ass. I lay across the ottoman like I'm posing for a centerfold.

"I feel like sexing you, right here, right now."

"Why don't you tell me how you really feel? Don't try to change the subject. What's my surprise?"

"Not even like a quickie?"

"What if Bailey comes downstairs? How do I explain that?"

"Let's go into the bathroom!"

"Oh, my goodness!"

Shane kisses my neck, lifting me at the same time. I throw my head back, laughing. "You don't listen, do you?"

"I told you I get hit in the head a lot."

"You are rehabbing so you haven't gotten hit in a long time."

"It's all the same." Shane carries me down the stairs and opens the bathroom with his foot. "This is a small-ass bathroom. How the hell we gonna do this?" Shane sets me on the sink. Then I think about his first party, and the bill to fix the detached sink when the lead singer of TGS took a girl in the bathroom. I slide down, not wanting to explain to my handyman why I need a new sink.

"You sit down." I point to the toilet.

"Oh shit, you getting on top?"

I roll my eyes. "What is my surprise? You can't just come over here, get some, and then roll out."

"I like the sound of that." Shane licks his lips and tugs on my shorts.

My mind is telling me to stay strong. But my body knows what it wants. Slipping me out of my silky shorts and lifting me onto his shoulders with ease, Shane hits the light switch.

"This better not be my surprise," I say, caressing his head.

"Oh, it's not." Shane whips out his hard dick. "This is better than the surprise."

I jump up and ask again.

"Okay! Okay! Carice and I go to court on Tuesday. I'm going to get custody of my kids back and then we can do us." Shane hugs me tight. "We're fourth and goal."

My smile could light up the sky. "Well, what are you waiting for?" I leap into his arms.

And that's when we hear someone try the door.

"What the fuck?" spits Shane.

In the darkness and in full panic, Shane puts me down and I wrangle back into my shorts and smooth out my hair. "You stay in here. And be silent," I whisper. I flush the toilet and wash my hands, let out a huge yawn and hit the switch, sneaking out as slowly as possible. Tiptoeing out, I look around for any signs of Bailey. Then I hear the front door. I back track and peek out my window to find Jen.

I wave Shane out and he rushes to the sofa, sweating and trying to catch his breath.

"It was the front door."

"Whew! That was close."

I shake my head and open the door for Jen and let her in.

"Excuse me, am I interrupting? I didn't realize you had company. I didn't see Shane's truck out front."

"I'm parked down the street."

I turn to him with a raised brow. "Why are you parked down the street?"

Shane gives me a dumbfounded look, reminding me that I know why, and then greets Jen. "What brings you here on this lovely evening?"

"I was coming to speak with Bryn. How about yourself?"

"I mentioned to Bryn an event I need y'all to plan."

Jen eyes widen and a grin creeps across her face. I see her eyes dart to the Grace Ormonde magazine I threw earlier and shake my head no. She deflates a bit. "What type of event?" she responds with less enthusiasm.

"Yeah, not that event," laughs Shane. "My birthday."

"Okay. What did you have in mind?"

"I want it to be some top-shelf shit. I'm going to be 'The Most Interesting Man in The World'. You got six weeks."

"Shane! You still don't respect my time." She huffs, leans on her hip, then shifts her weight to the other as he stammers, trying to explain that he always comes first. "What's up with you only giving us a few weeks to plan an event? And what's your budget?"

"There you go. Don't I always take care of y'all?"

Jen purses her lips. "Platinum Events is growing and I have a larger staff."

"Just you and Bryn on this one, maybe Bailey. I'll pay her separately."

Jen looks appalled.

"Shawty, that last girl you had around y'all showed up at my house with TGS and offered to suck my dick."

"What the fuck! Why am I just hearing about this?" Jen is yelling so I signal her to hush.

"She was drunk."

"Do you mean the one that Terry used to date? The short one?"

"You know she used to strip?" Shane starts dancing, gyrating his hips and sticking out his tongue.

Jen gasps loudly.

"You need to do a better job of screening your staff. That ho is a trending topic in the locker room."

Jen holds her head and her heart. "Oh my God. That's why she was so helpful. She brought me soup and orange juice when I was sick. She let me borrow luggage when mine was lost. . ."

"She also knows we're together," I interrupt.

"These hos don't care. Besides, she ain't got nothing on you." Shane grabs me and pulls me in for a side hug.

I give Jen a stern look. "Just me and you."

"You think you know a person. . . I don't know what to say." Jen shakes her head back and forth. "Sasha is the only other person we can ever have working with us. I mean it this time."

"Great! Now that that's settled. . ." Shane stands and stretches. "Can you leave so I can get a quickie?"

"Shane!" I hit him on his arm.

Shane grins and rushes Jen out the door.

22

<u>BLACK MONDAY</u>

Shane lies. A quickie? *Please.* I don't think we've ever truly had one. After we snuck downstairs and he pinned me against the wall and whispered in my ear that the wait was finally over, I couldn't keep my hands off of him. The sex was glorious. We covered every inch of that basement and I swear we set a new record time. Shane is a complete lover. Always has been since day one. He's a patient lover, making sure the whole of me is completely satisfied. When we're together it's like nothing else matters. It's perfect and it feels so good that I literally cry tears of joy. It's borderline spiritual. I've been thinking about it all morning and that is why I'm all smiles dropping Bailey off at school and King to doggie daycare.

I'm so ready for this new life with Shane. And with Carice out of the picture, I'm giddy at the thought. She's the only thing keeping us from ruling the world. Seriously. He and I complement each other in so many ways and I feel like there's nothing we couldn't accomplish together. A real power couple. Lord knows it will be refreshing to truly let my guard down and not feel like I have to solve all the problems and save the day. As black women in America, we are expected to be superwomen. It would be nice to sit back and lean on my superman. Or Hulk, as he likes to refer to himself. On my way to work, I listen to nothing but love songs. I'm singing *Is This Love* by Corinne Bailey Rae when Jen calls.

"Morning!" I sing.

"Good morning to you as well. I *heard* you had a great night."

"From who?"

"YOU!"

"How, when you're just calling me?"

"Like I said, I heard you had a great night through the walls."

"You lie." I giggle. "He and I, we were made for each other. I'm so comfortable with him. You would think after all this time, it would have started getting boring or that we would be used to each other, but it feels like we're just getting started. We're so perfect together. He's the only man I desire, and that's the honest-to-God truth."

"You mean to tell me Nick can't get any?"

"I can't even imagine being with someone else."

"Wow! And that's why I'm calling that wrong number back, today. The wait is over."

"You are crazy. Does wrong number have a name?"

"I'll let you know if he gets invited over a second time."

"Oh, it's like that?"

"Listen, I'll be thirty in November. Time waits for no one."

"Girl, I know. That's why I'm so excited that my time has finally come. I'm sooo ready. It's like it's okay to be excited now. I can finally think about forever with him and not feel so afraid. I want the dress, I want the big wedding. I'm more ready than ever. He has court tomorrow! Finally! I feel like my life at this moment couldn't be more perfect."

"I'm happy for you. Seriously. Y'all look good together. You were literally glowing last night."

"I know. He does that to me. I just can't believe it. I finally know what bliss feels like."

"I can't wait to join that club. But I'm sincerely happy that everything is working itself out. The two of you seem like y'all are good."

"We are more than good. It feels like it took us forever to get here."

"Well, all right now. There may be wedding bells for you yet."

"I've been planning in my mind all morning. I'm thinking I want a spring wedding. Small, intimate wedding in a tent, reciting our vows under the moonlight. Single long table with a runner of peonies down the center."

"Oh, now you're talking."

I laugh. "I've been so afraid to dream about it. It felt like if I talked about it, something bad would happen. But I'm telling you, we are so there, I can feel it. Anyway, I just pulled up to the office so I gotta go." I hang up with her, park my car, and practically skip into the office. I pass Mandy's office.

"You look happy!" shouts Reba.

"You bet I am." I continue down the hall, passing Lee's office.

His door is closed. I make a right down the hall and in my office sits Lisette and Mandy. "Morning ladies!"

Mandy stands and hands me a piece of paper. "I put in my resignation today!"

"Mandy!" I give her a hug. "You can't."

"I did. Don't worry. I got a new job doing what I love."

"Spying on people?"

"Yes!"

"For real?" I back up and look at Lisette. She's nodding her head.

"Man, I started looking a while ago and something finally came through. It's with this security company out of D.C. They just opened a satellite office in Annapolis. I'm going to be a private detective, girl!" She slaps her knee and laughs.

"Well, I'm so proud that you are following your dreams."

"Yeah, I'm done with the place. Y'all got me for two weeks, but since it's not a conflict of interest, I've already started working with them. It's so cool. I have access to all of this information. Girl!" she squeals.

"You're like in information heaven, aren't you?"

"Yes! But I have more news."

"Good, I hope." I brace myself.

"I'm taking Reba with me."

"It hasn't even been a year!"

"She said this job would be too boring without me. So I got her a job in their contracts department! My parting gift to you is the radio from our old office. And if I'm correct, it's country day." Mandy turns on Keith Urban and starts line dancing in the center of our tiny little office.

"I'm shocked about Reba." I hold my head.

"Actually, I have news as well," says Lisette.

"Nope, you can't quit." I turn my back and start my computer.

"It's not that. Josh and I are engaged."

"Congratulations! What the hell? Mandy is a private eye, Reba is quitting, and you're getting married? You must allow me to plan the wedding!" The last twenty-four hours have been full of surprises. It's obvious that we aren't going to get any work done today. Reba joins us in our office and our laughter fills the halls, so I'm not surprised when Lee stops by.

"Why, aren't you ladies a sight for sore eyes."

"Good morning, Lee." I smile.

"Bryn, can I see you in my office for a minute?"

"Sure." I reach for a pen and pad.

"You won't need all of that."

"Okay." I look back at the girls and follow Lee out. In his office is Harry sitting in the far corner. Lee offers me a seat across from Harry and Lee sits at his desk.

"I'm sure you've heard that Mandy and Reba have turned in their notices. We have two weeks to do some information gathering from the two of them so that we can transition their work to their replacements. Harry and I have discussed this in great detail, and we're looking to you to get this done. Build your team and do whatever you feel needs to be done. We know you just got promoted less than a year ago, and although we want to offer you a new position, it's not just because they're leaving, it's because you deserve it. You have proven yourself to be a leader at Pearsons." Lee turns to Harry.

Harry flips over a piece of paper and hands it to me. "We're promoting you to Director of Finance. You'll be over all of accounting and finance."

I take the letter and read it.

"As you can see, it also comes with a significant pay increase. We hope you accept."

"Yes, thank you. I'll take care of it."

"We're confident you will. Do you have any further questions for us?"

"Can we wait until a later date to announce this? Mandy isn't just a co-worker, she is my friend. I know she'd hoped for something like this, but I'm glad she's finding happiness elsewhere."

"I think we can agree to that."

"But I'll take the pay increase immediately." We all laugh. I stand and give them both a handshake and head back to my office, which is empty when I return. I use the silence as an opportunity to call an old friend.

"Hello? Michael speaking."

"You still looking for a job? I'm in need of a controller."

"Hey, stranger! How are you? What number are you calling me from?"

"I called you from my office phone. This is a business call. I'm trying to recruit you." I haven't spoken with Michael in what feels like a year.

"I might have to. You paying top dollar? I'm going to need it. I'm having a baby!"

"What? Mike the great having kids before marriage? I thought you were a forever bachelor."

"Yeah, well she got me."

"You got trapped, or are you going to put a ring on it?"

"Not so fast. Not so fast. She didn't trap me. We planned it. But let her pop this baby out first, then I'll think about getting down on one knee."

"You are sick. You are the only man I know who waits until they're sixty to have their first kid."

"You got jokes. You talk about me, when are you getting married?"

"Keep an eye on your mailbox for an invite."

"Scandalous! Who's the lucky suitor?"

My phone alerts me to a text message.

`Nick says he's in for Shane's party`

Yes! I silently cheer.

"What? Bryn, who's the lucky guy?"

"Wouldn't you like to know," I whisper.

"Is it one of your Hollywood friends?" Michael starts cackling.

I pause for a moment and decide if I'm finally ready to share. What do I have to lose? "Shane. Shane and I are an item."

"I thought he was still with his baby momma. Didn't they have some drama lately?"

"They always have drama but all that is coming to an end tomorrow. Tomorrow is the first day of the rest of my life."

"Bryn, I can't say I'm surprised. I kind of had a feeling when you passed out a few years back at your ProBowl party when he mentioned he was engaged. I hope it works out this time."

"Oh, it will. He signed a contract and he's not going to break it." I laugh.

"He signed a contract?"

"It was the only way that I would take him back. I told him I was getting older and I was tired of the games. I want the dream."

"If you get with the wrong guy, that dream can easily turn into a nightmare. But if he signed it, I guess he's serious. I would never sign a contract. He's a celebrity, what was he thinking? I just don't understand people these days."

"It's not for you to understand. Just be happy for me." I hear Mandy coming down the hall. "Alright, Michael. Let me know if you're interested. I'll email you the job description and benefits package. I already know you're qualified. I'll give you a call later this week."

I hang up right as the girls return to the office.

"What did Lee want?"

"He asked me to do your work."

"That sucks, but I'll have everything cleaned up to make it easy on you." Mandy gives me a hug. "I'm gonna miss you, girlie."

"Same here."

While Lisette walks down the hall towards Mandy's office, I get back to checking my email. I notice one that I don't recognize but the email address ends in '.edu'. As I read it, I can't believe my eyes. It's an email of acceptance from the director of dance of the performing arts magnet school Bailey auditioned for. This day feels like it's too good to be true. If I didn't know any better, I would think the world was coming to an end.

23

SIDELINED

Something is definitely up. I haven't spoken with Shane since Sunday. His court date is today, and thanks to the skills Mandy's acquired over the years, I know that they were scheduled on today's docket at 9 am. Even though I knew, I made sure not to call or text him. It was important to give him space. When 7 pm rolls around, I'm a little concerned, but instead of sitting around and worrying, I run myself a hot bath and light some candles to relax my nerves. Also, just in case he calls or comes by, I'll be looking and feeling refreshed.

I toss in a bath bomb as an extra treat. I haven't used one of these in a very long time. I even put on a playlist that Shane sent me a while ago. Almost immediately, I'm totally relaxed. This is exactly what I need to keep from allowing my mind to go down a certain path for no reason. When my thoughts do drift to something crazy, I dismiss them and bring myself back to the present. Living in the past or the future only causes depression and anxiety. I hear the sweet melodies of the music, smell the lavender in the water, and feel my soft skin. I'm totally at peace.

After about twenty minutes, I have to get out. The water is still very hot and if I stay in any longer, I may pass out. Wrapping my bath towel around my body, I lie on the bed and doze. A text from Shane wakes me.

`I need to see you`

I send a quick reply, leap out of the bed, and slip into something cute. Then again, I could surprise him and answer the door in just my towel. I actually like that idea better. We are at a critical period in our relationship. Anything can happen. I keep my hair pulled up and don't apply make-up, simply adding a touch of gloss.

He's only minutes away so when I'm done, I look out the window. His truck is in my driveway with the lights still on. *Why is he just sitting there?* Either way, I go to the front door, unlock it, and wait for him to come inside. When he opens the door, I let my hair down, tossing it to the side. Shane closes the door behind him and right before I drop the towel, he holds his hand up. I stop mid reveal.

"We need to talk," he says to me but he's looking at the floor. "Where's Bailey?"

"With her dad. He picks her up from school on Tuesdays. Are you alright?" He looks haggard, as if he hasn't slept in days.

"No. I need you to sit." Shane removes his shoes at the door. He keeps his baseball cap on and pulled down low. "You should get dressed first."

"Okay. . . well, let me go get cute."

"Nah, don't get cute."

I don't know what it's about, but whatever. I leave him downstairs and change into a pair of cute pajamas just in case he changes his mind. When I return, Shane looks distressed.

"Come sit with me."

I purposely skip over to him in the living room to lighten the mood and sit on the floor next to him. "Ahh, there, there." I rub his strong shoulder. What's troubling you, my love?" I know it's something to do with court. He's probably going to tell me he needs more time. What he doesn't realize is that I would wait a lifetime. He has nothing to worry about. "Babe, it's okay."

"It's not." He sits with his back against the sofa, his knees bent, rocking them back and forth and biting his lip. I can see something is *really* wrong with him.

Did someone die? Oh no, someone died, and I put on these itty-bitty shorts trying to seduce him. I feel a bit ashamed. "I'm so sorry." I lay my head on his shoulder.

He remains silent, looking defeated. Meanwhile, my stomach starts to feel like an empty pit.

After what seems like an eternity, he finally looks up at me, eyes swollen, wet, and bloodshot.

"Is it the kids? Did something happen?"

Shane parts his mouth to speak and squeezes his eyes shut, then holds his hand over his eyes to keep the tears from falling.

Oh my god! I've never seen him like this. I lean my head on his shoulder and rub his leg. King, who was quietly sleeping in his crate, starts to whimper. I get up to let him out and return to Shane's side. King trots behind me, trying his hardest to climb onto Shane's foot.

Shane exhales loudly and looks towards the ceiling. "I don't know how to say it." He looks at me with watery eyes.

"Say what?" My voice is warm, consoling. "You can trust me with anything!"

For a moment, he's silent. Then a tear starts to fall.

I take his hand. "I'm here for you," I assure him.

"You're perfect. . ." He swallows a few tears and his eyes burn red in anguish. "You're perfect, your daughter is perfect, even your little dog is perfect." King gnaws on Shane's sock, trying to pull it off. Shane swipes his face with his hands, sending his tears flying. I wish I could save him from this apparent torture. "I don't want to hurt you." He takes my hand.

I try to brace myself for what's coming next.

He lowers his head and begins to speak. "I. . ." he swallows hard. "I ugh. . ." His solemn face breaks. "I can never see you again."

Time stops. I'm sure of it because I'm irrationally calm and momentarily deafened. I can see Shane's mouth moving but a deafening ring drowns his words out. At the same time, a knowing from deep within me rises up. I can't hold it in. "You're going to marry her!"

Shane's taken aback, giving me a surprised look. "I NEVER said that!"

I stare at him. "You didn't say no!"

Shane wipes a few tears from his cheeks. "It's not about her. I mean." He goes momentarily silent. "I don't hate her," he whispers. "She is the mother of my kids." He searches for some type of justification that I'm supposed to accept. "I have to give it—" he chokes on his words, "a chance. For my kids."

I can only offer silence. My mind is blank. In a situation like this, I would have imagined I'd be screaming and crying. Do I even believe it? Is he really going to leave me? Does our story really end like this? "You're going back to her?"

Shane turns to me. "I love you."

Nothing comes out. Instead, I look up at him and feel my eyes start to swell.

"Carice knows it too." Another tear escapes his eye, then another, before he wipes his face. His vulnerability is killing me. "I don't want to leave you. It pains me to do this. I didn't even want to come in here. Taking the easy way out crossed my mind. I considered doing something really fucked up to you so you'd hate me. But you deserve better. You deserve a real man. Someone who is going to love you like you deserve to be loved. Someone who can be with you every day without conditions. Someone who checks all the boxes on your list and more. I can't." He wipes his tears. "You made exceptions for me." He pauses. "I don't deserve you. I never did."

I gasp. How. . ." I catch my breath. "How can you say these things? Why are you saying this to me?" I cry out. "That's what love does. It isn't perfect. If you really love me, we figure this out."

"My chickens have come home to roost. I have to face this like a man."

Numbness overcomes me as I stare at him, willing him to look up at me. He can't. Instead, he looks down at the floor and fidgets with his hands.

"I told her I would never see you again." He finally looks up. "I thought about how I could do it, you know, still see you. But you shouldn't have to compromise any longer. It isn't fair." He lowers his head again and King lunges at him and nips his finger. "I like him," he chuckles, pointing to King.

Good boy. Bite him again.

"He's protecting his mommy. I thought we were going to make it this time. I really thought we would."

"I wanted us to. But Riley called me this week crying, telling me that she missed me and begging me to come home. I mean, what if that were Bailey? You get to have Bailey every day. You don't know what it's like to share. What if she lived with her dad, and you only got to see her every other weekend? You would understand."

"There isn't anything that I wouldn't do for my daughter."

"Exactly. That's what I'm saying. I've got to give them a chance. They ain't have one. . . because I met you."

I'm left speechless yet again. He can't be trying to Jedi mind-trick me, at least I hope not. But what can I say to this? I sit in silence.

"Bryn, say something."

I toughen up. "I understand. I'm going to miss you." My bottom lip quivers.

"I'll miss you more."

"Will you?" My heart finally starts to break, and I feel an ugly cry brewing. I cover my face and run to the bathroom so he won't see me like this. I imagine I look desperate because I certainly feel it. When I return, he's standing with his keys in his hands as if he's ready to go. I can't accept this fate. As I walk towards him, our fondest memories flip through my mind. We're holding hands walking through the Christmas tree park in D.C. as the snow starts to fall. He turns and smiles at me in the Polar Express 4D ride. He caresses my face and tells me his promise. That morning I believed that we were made for each other. The memories start to fade, and the tear in my heart grows deeper. The thought of life without him in it becomes too much to bear. I literally gasp for air.

Shane wraps his arms around me. "I guess this is goodbye."

"I'd hoped we were forever. . ." He watches me slip the ring from my finger. My hand shakes as I place it into his. Squeezing his closed fist tightly, I start to wail.

"Bryn, you're killing me."

"I can't believe this is happening!" I cry out. "I can't give you up."

Shane hugs me, squeezing me tightly. "I'm still in love with you, but you have to understand, if I stay, I'm going to lose my children."

I can't bring myself to tell him to leave them, so I ugly cry into his shirt. What type of human would I be if I begged him to stay? A selfish one. He'd blame me forever. Instead, I'll bear the brunt of the disappointment. All I can do is sob.

King starts barking and whining and clawing at my ankles for me to pick him up.

"Is this really the end?" Catching my breath between sobs, I cry out, "I love you, Shane!" Wrapping my arms around him, I scream, pressing my face to his chest hoping he'll change his mind.

BIANCA WILLIAMS

"Don't cry." Shane kisses the top of my head. "Come on. Come on." He rubs my back. It's impossible. I can't be consoled. I can't let go. My heart is breaking into a million little pieces. When his arms release me, I start to panic. My legs buckle and I feel like I'm going to collapse onto the floor and die.

Just as I let go, he walks out of the door and out of my life.

24

DOOMED-ACCORDING TO SHANE

I can't look back.

There's a special place in hell for me.

25

DAY 1/DENIAL

It's when I'm able to pick myself off of the floor that I'm able to locate my phone and call Jen. When she answers, I just come right out with it. "Shane just broke up with me." Then I start laughing hysterically and before long, it turns into a loud cry.

"WHAT? I'm sorry, excuse me. I'll be right back."

I hear a lot of commotion. She must be out and about. "I know, right?" I gasp for air. "Crazy!" I nod, wipe my face, grab a paper towel to blow my nose. Tissue wasn't made for this type of outpouring. "I'm sure it's only temporary," I say. "Until he works things out, I'm sure." I pace in circles, barefoot in my living room, wearing my sexy pajama set that I was originally hoping was going to be removed.

"You can't be serious."

"Oh yes I am!" I scream. "He just left. Yup! It's finished. Finito. He's got some drama. He says he's going to give him and Carice an honest try. He's got to do it for his kids. Yeah, I'd like to see how that turns out." I burst into another fit of laughter.

"You sound unstable. It could be shock or you could be on the verge of a mental breakdown. Either way, I'm coming over." She hangs up on me. I try to sit but I've got too much wild energy coursing through me, so I unlock the door and go and grab my robe. When I return, Jen's in my kitchen filling the teakettle with water. "I was not expecting you to call me and say that. I need to hear everything." She pauses, looking at me.

"Yeah! It was rather shocking to me as well. I thought someone had died! But no. . . this one kinda came out of left field. I swear, I didn't see it coming. I mean, it doesn't even make any sense. They don't get along. They're not going to make it! Besides! He loves me! He's still in love with me!"

Jen just stares at me.

"He'll be back. Two weeks. You'll see. I don't want tea. I need drugs."

"I brought vodka for you. I'm making tea for myself. Do you think you can start from the beginning? I want to try and make sense of it. I need to understand how you go from almost being his fiancée, to him getting back with his ex in a matter of twenty-four hours. It's not like y'all have been fighting. Things have been going pretty well, even if I say so myself. I mean, it was just two days ago y'all were practically coming though the walls into my house."

I take three shots of vodka back to back. When I feel the burn,

I'm able to share more details. "Well, remember, he had court today. I suspect that this is a product of the judge's ruling. That's why I don't think it's real. This is one of Carice's games, I'm sure." I chuckle. "And I guess he's just given up." My bottom lip quivers. "I'm sorry, I need to get some fresh air." I rush out of the house into the warm fall air, feeling like I'm falling apart. I look at the starless sky searching for a sign. Nothing. Just silence. Our story can't end like this. Not us. No, no, no. Shane and I were made for each other. We were on our way to forever. I can't wrap my brain around this. That's when I start blaming myself. I should have stopped him. I should have continued to fight. Was it my pride that kept me from pleading with him? How could he do this to me? I can't accept this. I'm a complete mess. I wish I hadn't let him leave. He said he wasn't choosing her over me, but it doesn't change the fact that he's going back.

I go back inside. "I think he's tired of fighting her, I guess. But one thing I do know, and it's that he loves me."

"You sure you sure?"

"I'm positive. I mean, the man was in tears. He probably looked how I look right now. Seeing him cry like that." I shake my head. "I cried watching him cry."

"Shane cried?" Jen freezes.

I exhale after realizing I've been holding my breath. "I know. It was surprising to me as well. I had the same reaction. That's why I believe him. I know what is at the root of his decision. It's just that I don't understand how someone can accept being so miserable."

"So, he just comes over and says, 'I'm getting back with Carice, for the kids'?"

"Pretty much. Logically, everything he said made sense. At the end of the day, he wants to see them full time. He used Bailey and me as an example so, I mean, what could I say in response? Stay with me and give up your kids? I mean, that's fucked up. I'm not like that."

"How did he say it? Like, was that the first thing he said?" Jen takes a seat at my dining room table.

"He walked in and told me to have a seat. That was when I knew for sure something was going on, but I still wasn't expecting him to drop that bomb."

"But what did he say exactly?"

"Exactly? It's kind of a blur. I didn't write it down and honestly, I figured I'd never forget. Now, I only remember him sitting down next to me looking really bad. He looked like he just got jumped by a gang and got his ass handed to him. I mean, I've never seen him look so downtrodden. He looked lost. As soon as he sat down on the floor next to me, he broke down and started to cry."

"Like real tears?"

"Real tears. Yes, I was shocked. I've NEVER seen him cry. EVER. He was just overcome with emotion. I didn't know he was capable. I read that narcissists don't feel emotion. Or at least they're oblivious to it. That's why he had my undivided attention. At that point I knew we were dealing with something serious, and I honestly thought he was going to tell me someone had died, never thinking that a breakup was about to occur. Then he said it. 'We can never see each other again,' just like that." My laughing turns into a loud cackle.

Jen stares at me with her mouth wide open.

"I know. That was my reaction. I was surprised and confused at the same time. You know that deafening sound you get in your ears? Tinnitus? That happened. Then he said that he loved me. He loved Bailey. I was perfect. Bailey was perfect. King was perfect." I pick him up out of his bed. "Good doggie." I pet him. "He bit him. Hard too." I laugh. "He was protecting me."

"So he tells you that you're perfect and breaks up with you."

"Yes, he said, 'It's not you, it's me.' Yeah, that happened. But you know what's the craziest? It actually came to my mind that he's going to marry Carice—"

"Really?" Jen's eyes widen. "God, I hope not."

"I straight up asked him. Shit! I wanted to know. He said NEVER! That's why I said that I give them two weeks. At the same time, he was like, we can never see each other again. Like never never. He said we can't be friends. He wouldn't be able to give his family a fair chance if I was still in the picture. So, not only am I losing the love of my life, I'm losing my best friend. No offense."

"None taken, but this is just awful. I wouldn't wish this on my worst enemy. Well, there is this one person. . ."

"It's pretty shitty. I've never ever been through any shit like this. I mean, we could have tried to be friends. But we both know that there's too much history between us for that. Besides, Carice fucking hates me. Part of me wants to sit back and watch this play out. The other part is like, just wait, he'll be back. He and I have way too much between us."

"Did you give the ring back?"

"I did. I don't want it if I can't have him. It would have just been a terrible reminder. I want to give him the benefit of the doubt."

Jen raises her brow.

"Hear me out. He came over here and broke up with me. So technically, he did right by me. I mean, he said that he didn't want to face me, he thought about doing something really fucked up so that I would never forgive him or speak to him again."

"And he doesn't think this is that very thing?"

"I guess not. I don't remember. My mind's getting foggy."

"I feel you, but you would take him back?"

"Ugh. I hate this. He made it very clear that he's not choosing her over me. He's choosing his kids and I have to respect that. I don't like it, but I have to respect it." I look away into the distance. "I didn't want him to leave, Jen. Selfishly, I wanted to tell him that we'd have children one day, but I couldn't. I had to let him go. And now, she wins. She is finally getting what she's always wanted. This shit sucks."

"But I think there is more to this story that he isn't sharing. If they were at odds the way you tell it, give it time, it will come out. But for now, I think you should let Bailey stay with her dad for the rest of the week. I think you need time to process."

"It just doesn't make sense. Why now? We were so right there." I think of my something blue and realize it's still in his closet. My hands start to tremble uncontrollably. "This can't be real. He's got to come back."

"I don't know, Bryn, I think it's finally run its course."

"I won't accept that." I dial Shane's number and pace the kitchen, but he doesn't answer. It breaks me as I know there'll be no more goodnights.

"As much as it pains me to tell you this. . . I must say it. You don't have the choice."

26

DAY 14/ANGER

Fourteen days. No calls. No texts. No email. No Shane. This breakup was supposed to be like all the others. We fight and then we make up. Even Carrie and Big had three major breakups before they finally got married. Except it's day fourteen and not one word from Shane. I guess he really meant what he said.

This is happening.

He's really gone.

I peel myself out of the bed and schlep my way into the bathroom. I stare at the dark circles around my eyes and my tangled hair, wondering how I'm going to pull myself together to go into the office. No amount of make-up that I own can fix this. I look haggard. But if I don't get back to work, they are going to think I'm dying. The flu excuse worked the first week, but I have a feeling after day fourteen, they'll want a doctor's note. I can't lose my man and my job. I stand up straight and accept my fate. *We didn't make it, and Shane has dumped me for good.* Then I start to cry.

What an asshole. He could at least call and check to see how I'm managing. Or not. I'm sure it would hurt him to know that all I've been doing is crying. Except he'll never know. My phone doesn't ring. It feels like he's not even thinking of me. How could that be? Is it possible that he's not hurting just as much as I am? It doesn't make any sense. Nothing is making sense anymore. I scream. I miss him so much. And just like that, I feel another piece of my heart chip, breaking into a million little pieces.

Mending my broken heart is useless. My crying never ceases. Morning, noon, and night, I leave a trail of snotty tissues from the kitchen to my bedroom. They are everywhere. As for Bailey, she's between her dad and my mom, Joan. Don't want her 'catching the flu' is my go-to excuse, but my mom knows the truth. I could never let Bailey see me like this. That's what's pissing me off. He's off happy in his new life and has left me to grieve this breakup alone. It isn't fair. Fuck-that-selfish-bitch-ass-nigga!

When I arrive at the office, I place my shades on so no one can see I've been crying. And unfortunately for me, when I sit down at my computer, staring back at me is my screensaver, a photo of us dancing at the holiday party. *Shit.* I forgot I even set this, and I don't know how to change it. Instead of calling the IT department, I imagine running into him. We're in a nightclub; I walk right up to him with a bottle in my hand and hit him over the head. Then I'm at the grocery store and he walks out with an armful of bags. I slam on the gas and strike him with my car at top speed. Then I'm at Chick-fil-A grabbing lunch. He's walking out as I'm walking in. I hit his hand, knocking his food and drinks all over him. "Yeah, I better not see that fucker in the streets."

I look at the photo again and this time the breakup starts playing like a movie on replay in my mind. *What have I done?* I shouldn't have let him leave, or at least I should have made it harder for him. I let him off a bit easy. Instead of understanding, I *should have begged him not to leave*. I should have made a complete fool of myself, throwing myself down at his feet, latching onto his leg, and pleading for him not to go. I shake my head, hoping to rid my mind of its memories. Perhaps I should have grabbed him, kissed him. I know, trapped him. I'm sure I could have gotten pregnant again that night. Then right about now, I'd be calling him and telling him the news. *This is ludicrous.*

If only I had known it was the last night I would ever see him, I would have done things differently. But I didn't know, he did, and he robbed me of that. *Why?* Why did things have to end suddenly? It was so unexpected. I wish I knew so that I could have planned for it. Protected my heart. I feel so exposed. It's becoming hard to breathe again. I shut my eyes tight and count backwards from twenty.

"Good morning, Bryn." Lisette walks into our dark office and places a muffin from Panera Bread on my desk. "I wasn't sure if you'd eaten today."

She's so kind.

"Would you like some hot tea?"

I nod yes. When she returns, I turn my chair around to face her and nibble at my muffin. "I appreciate this."

"Whatever it is, it will pass. I know this." She turns her chair to face me. "Difficulties seem like they will never get better. But just think about your life five years ago and where you were. You've overcome so much. Imagine what the next five years will be like. It will be great." Lisette sits across from me with her hands folded in her lap. "This too shall pass."

"He said he could never see me again, and he meant it." Covering my face with both hands, I take a deep breath, trying to fight back a tidal wave of emotions. "He doesn't love her. He's still in love with me! He's trying to do what's best for him right now and I get that. I do. But I miss him. And not talking to him is killing me."

Lisette gives me a hug. "Oh no, Bryn."

"I want to tell him." I grab my phone. "I'll call him."

Lisette places her hand firmly on mine. "He knows. Trust me, he knows."

"What if he marries her?" I cry, clenching my phone. "My heart can't take it. I will die, I'm sure of it. I can't breathe."

"I am so so so so sorry, Bryn."

Lisette is giving me a hug when Harry arrives at our office wearing an official Shane Smith jersey. "Don't let me interrupt," he jokes.

If I weren't wearing these shades, the look I'm giving him would surely get me fired.

Lisette hands me the box of tissues before addressing Harry. "Is there something I can help you with? Bryn isn't feeling good today. She's going to be taking the afternoon off."

"Nah, just getting ready for the big game. Did you go to the game last Sunday, Bryn?"

"No."

"Man, tell Shane I said thanks. He came over to my section and autographed some stuff. He even pointed up at me. It was freaking awesome! I got it on video. Want to see it?"

"Okay," Lisette says. "Excuse me, Harry, but Bryn needs to leave for the day. You don't want this flu bug. I'm going to see her to her car." Lisette gets my muffin, purse, keys, and helps me with my coat. When we reach my car, she gives me a concerned look. "Are you sure you don't want me to drive you?"

"I got here. I'll be fine."

It's not like I'm going to run him over with the car he bought me. Not that I haven't thought about it. I will crash into his Range Rover if I see him on my way home. It's in his best interests not to drive down my street or anywhere near it. "I hate him for this."

"Do you want to call Jen?" Lisette unlocks the door and helps me in. "I think you should call someone. I don't feel safe with you on the road like this. Just whatever you do, don't call Shane. Call me if you have to. Just don't call him."

"If I call him, it's only to curse him out for hurting me. Bastard!" *What if he doesn't answer?* "I hate him." I hate that I start to cry. Pulling my door shut, I put my car in reverse and wave goodbye to Lisette. All I know is, he's going to regret the day he met me.

Jen calls me on my way home and instructs me to come directly to her house. It's not like I have anywhere else to be, so I listen and instead of going into my house and crawling under the covers, I go to her house and plop down on her comfy sofa. "I hate him."

She hands me a drink. "Let me preface this by telling you that

Shane is a *horrible,* heinous individual." Jen downs her drink and pours another. Turning her back to me, I hear her mumbling to herself, "Rip the Band-Aid. Just rip it."

"He's actually trying to make it work with her. Well guess what, Sherlock, it won't." I laugh. "I can't believe he's trying. Oh, my bad. It's not you, it's me. Really?" I purse my lips. "Excuses! Whatever! I should egg his house. Then again, I may run him over with my car on sight. I'm soooo angry I could burst!"

Jen spins to face me. "I know, and that's why I was going to call over the cavalry."

"For?" I shrug and knock back my drink. "Thanks, I needed that." I slam the glass on her table and slouch back in her chair. "I think I can take him on my own. I feel like I have the strength of a thousand men. I can feel it tingling in my toes. If I had a gun right about now, I would shoot him. In his foot, of course."

"Thank God you aren't a gun owner."

"Thank you, Jesus." Tears begin to fall again.

"Bryn. . ."

"I'll be okay. It will pass. He'll call. I know him. We've got something special."

"Oh Bryn." Jen's stern look softens. "I'm so sorry. I got a call today."

"Yep!" I kick my feet up, close my eyes, and exhale loudly. "My phone didn't ring. Fourteen days and that fucker hasn't sent a kite, a raven, or a fucking fart in the wind. Nope, nada, nothing. And you want to know the saddest part? I almost fucking texted him today, ya know. Why today of all days, I don't know." I can't stop the tears from falling. "I just want to tell him that I love him and miss him dearly."

"Shane's getting married!" she blurts.

I sit in her chair, not moving.

"Bryn. I need you to breathe. Bryn?" Jen claps her hands together.

"What did you just say? Shane's getting married? When?"

"Right now."

"What!" I leap out of the chair. "Where?"

"I don't know." Jen runs after me.

"How do you know this?"

Jen grabs my hand. "I got a call from Mandy saying she came across a marriage license filed two weeks ago. I told you then that there was more to the story. Your intuition was right. I didn't know what to do and I wanted to confirm so I called Qmar. For what it's worth, he told me to tell you that out of everyone, you were always his favorite. You were his choice for Shane."

"His favorite? What the hell am I supposed to do with that? I need to be Shane's choice."

"He also said Shane and Carice are getting married, tonight. He's on his way to the wedding."

"Right now?"

Jen stands motionless staring back at me.

Tears shower my cheeks. "Jen, like right now?" I feel breathless and slightly lightheaded.

"Right before you walked through the door."

I shake my head no. "Call every church in the state of Maryland! The city of Baltimore. In fact, start in Baltimore County." I grab my phone, not knowing where to start, and just start Googling 'Shane Smith wedding location', as if it's going to give it to me.

"Bryn! What's the point! It's too late. This is happening whether you believe it or not."

"It can't, Jen! I can't live without him."

"What are you going to do? Run and stop him?"

This is my worst nightmare becoming a reality before my eyes. I let that man walk out of my house, I can't let him walk down that aisle. "Jen, please help me, I've got to try!"

27

DAY 30/BARGAINING

I think a lot, especially at night when I'm in my room and the house is quiet. I can still feel him. His presence is here with me. Not only can I not get the vivid memories of him out of my mind, he's very much still in my bed. It's hard to sleep. He meets me in my dreams. It's pure agony. Mornings are even worse, because it's a new day knowing Shane is no longer a part of my life. It's so painful I feel like I'm going to die. My heartbeat feels faint and my breathing is shallow. My next breath may be my very last. I know it's irrational to think that I'm going to die, but there is nothing indicating otherwise. I inhale deeply, holding my breath for ten seconds and exhaling out of my mouth. I repeat again, and again, but it's of no use. I'm unable to quiet my mind. The worst thoughts won't go away.

But the reality for me is that he is the walking dead. While he is still very much alive to everyone else, Bailey, Jen, and I are all in constant mourning. The space that he once occupied in each of us is now a void. I liken it to a deep grave.

I prepare for the day, as usual, and get Bailey to school. She finally found out about the breakup and Shane's marriage to Carice. She caught me crying one evening when I was refreshing my messages, hoping that one would come through. I was thinking 'how many weeks are going to pass without him saying a single word?' It was three weeks since our breakup and I was so furious I threw my phone against the wall so hard that the screen cracked. When Bailey retrieved it and brought it to my room later that night, she told me that she read through my text messages and understood why Uncle Shane hadn't returned any of her calls. When I heard that, I immediately dialed his number and found out it was no longer in service.

My mental and emotional health are at an all-time low. My days are filled with misery and I just sit in it, unable to free myself of its grip. It's a lonely, dark, and dreary place. It gets so dark it terrifies me, and still, I don't have the strength to fight it. Instead of looking to God to pull me out, I sink deeper, blabbing about Shane to anyone who will listen.

At work, Lisette has taken the day off so I bury myself in work. At the end of the day, Harry stops by to check on me so it's his turn to hear my woes. After I've been talking non-stop for about fifteen minutes, he finally gets the chance to speak.

"Bryn, you're such a great catch," Harry tries to convince me, "I mean, you're young, beautiful, director of a multi-million-dollar company. He's nuts! Man, if I had a woman like you, I'd—"

"He definitely had a lapse in judgment. I mean, who marries a so-called crazy woman? A so-called crazy woman who you *claim* not to love."

"Well, believe it or not Bryn, men love crazy women."

"So, are you telling me the key to keeping Shane was to act crazy? You should have shared that man-code with me months ago. Maybe I wouldn't have been so accepting. When he tried to break up with me, I could have gut-punched him and told him he wasn't going anywhere." I karate chop the air.

"Wouldn't have hurt to have tried. It's something about crazy women that men love. We know they're bad for us, but we're drawn to them like bees to honey."

"You've met Carice, remember? You know that girl was wild."

"Oh, I'll never forget. That one was definitely a firecracker. On sports radio this morning they called it a shotgun wedding."

"I wouldn't be surprised if she held a gun to his head. I just wish he could have been honest with me when I asked him. I knew it!" I ball my fists. "It was like I could read his mind. As soon as he said he was going back, I knew it was ending in marriage. I didn't want to believe it, but I felt it in my gut. It's just that he convinced me otherwise, so I wasn't prepared for this. He let it go off like a bomb in my face."

"No way he was going to tell you that to your face." Harry leans back in his chair.

"He owed me that. He could have followed up with a call or a text. I shouldn't have found out from anyone but him. Two weeks! Two weeks, Harry. He'd already filed for a marriage license when he broke things off with me. If Mandy hadn't told my best friend, I wouldn't have had *any* warning."

"Wow! Mandy?"

"If it weren't for her, I would have found out from the local newspaper. That fucking picture is everywhere. 'Shane marries his best friend'. What a fucking joke. Even he knows it's a lie."

"Did you read the line from his publicist?"

"Most definitely. He did not come up with those words. They were so forced. I know the real Shane and he didn't write that shit. Besides, I know he doesn't love her."

"He'll never forget you. Trust me."

"From the looks of it, he already has. I swear, my mind just won't stop trying to figure out what I could have done differently. I've analyzed this thing a million ways and I now know I'm second guessing everything. Maybe he never really loved me. Love is an action word and love wouldn't have let him do this to me. Not like this."

"We lie to the ones we love." Harry rocks back in his chair. "And what about the love for his kids? Sounds like he was forced to make a choice."

My eyes get teary. "Thanks for letting me vent."

"Anytime. I was rooting for y'all. I think he's going to be calling you again one day."

"He won't be calling. That's not his style. But I give them two years, if that."

"Want to make it official?" Harry pulls out a dollar and pins it to his board. "Dollar bet."

"I'm going to take your money." I chuckle for the first time in a month. I didn't realize it was still possible. It feels kinda good. "Thanks for listening."

"You'll get through this. The important thing is to talk about it. You don't want to hold it in."

"I appreciate it. Thanks for caring."

"Goodnight, Bryn."

I wave Harry goodnight and pack up my things to leave the office. I get into my car and search the station for something upbeat. It's of no use, I still feel so alone. I decide to call my mom. "Hey there."

"Hey, hey, hey."

"Today was another rough one."

"Did you talk to Shane?"

"Hell no! Why would you ask me that?" I instantly get an attitude and want to hang up on her.

"Well, I heard some news. I spoke to my girlfriend Charmaine. You know the one who's ex works down at the courthouse?"

"Not really, but go ahead. What about her?" My heart starts to race.

"Well, she said that her ex was working the day. The day, you know, Shane went to court. He said the wife won full custody and she was outside the courtroom telling Shane she was moving to Toronto."

"So, she essentially was leaving the country? Wow, another threat to get what she wanted. Well, hats off to her. It finally worked. I mean, I've got to get off this merry-go-round. I still need to function so I can keep my job and finish grad school."

"How's that going, school?"

"I want to write another paper like I want another hole in my heart."

"You'll be alright."

"Maybe. But she's officially Carice Smith now. Whether she forced him or not is a moot point. Besides, he's not a puppet. He does have a brain. At the end of the day, he agreed to it. Honestly, I've been trying not to look. The wedding pictures alone damn near took me out. The only thing that was somewhat satisfying was that her dress was ugly, and he looked miserable."

Once I get home, I don't have the willpower not to look at what my mom was speaking about. I Google 'Shane Smith married' and get hundreds of results. Article after article, I read each and every one. Some have more details than others. Most include extra commentary surrounding the same set of facts. Shane and Carice got married after an argument involving their kids. The story doesn't change. Shane's wedding photos made it to every newspaper, sports website, and gossip website. There's even a photo of them kissing.

I turn my phone off and pull the covers over my head. The pain is as real today as it was yesterday. It seems endless. It hurts so bad and I know that only God can end it. I attempt to pray but I'm emotionally empty, filled with a deep sadness. I'm so sorrowful that the burden is simply too much to bear. I feel hopeless.

I'm never going to recover from this.

"Lord, if you take this pain away, I promise I will never go back to him."

28

12 MONTHS/DEPRESSION

Funnily enough, today it's officially three hundred and sixty-five days since the Shane debacle, and still no call. Even though I've made some progress on my journey to healing, I'm still counting the days. My therapist says I'm in the fourth stage of grief. At first, I denied that I was depressed. She informed me depressed people are not aware that they are depressed. Makes sense, right? While working with her, I've also learned that I bury pain and then walk around smiling saying I'm alright. The problem is, it's showing up elsewhere, such as in sleepless nights, weight gain, and adult acne. They are all a byproduct of this traumatic incident.

These days, my therapist and I have been focusing on forgiveness. I don't know how that's even possible since Shane never apologized. How on earth do you forgive someone who isn't sorry? She says it's possible and then reminds me that the forgiveness isn't for him, it's for me. She claims this forgiveness will allow me to truly accept the circumstances and let him go. Only problem is, I think I've got this vice grip because I still love him.

Jen's trying her best to encourage me to move on. It's easier said than done. Her new beau, David, says the best way to get over Shane is to get under someone else, so he's been trying to send his friends my way, but I have no interest. That's why I'm stalling to fly to meet them in New Orleans. Jen's once nameless athlete is a retired Saint. Somehow, they've convinced me to come and visit them this weekend and against my better judgment, I agreed. If I'm honest, the only reason I said yes is because I found out that the Nighthawks are playing the Saints on Sunday and I've bought a ticket. Yes, it seems desperate but if I'm being honest, that's where I'm at these days.

Now I need to figure out if I'm wearing black and gold or black and blue. I should probably wear neutral colors, but I pack my Smith jersey just in case I feel warm and fuzzy. I'm ashamed that I still even have it. Still, I tuck it neatly in a side pocket of my bag. No one else needs to know. Once I'm all packed, I call for Bailey. She's eleven now and too cool to hang out with her nana while I'm out of town, so I drop her off at her cousin's house for the weekend and head to the airport.

It's a short sunny ride, and since I arrive early and want to save some money, I park in the long-term parking lot. I take out my phone to check in via the mobile app and let all of my friends know I'm headed to New Orleans. Immediately, I get an alert. It's

Qmar. He's heading to New Orleans as well. I decide to send him a message.

```
Hey! Hit me up when you get down there.
Maybe we can meet and have drinks
```

I wonder if he'll respond. Then my phone chirps.

```
Okay cool! I know Shane would love to
see you
```

Shane would love to see me? My heart races as I read his message over and over and over again. I sit in my car with my mouth wide open. Why would Shane love to see me? I thought he wasn't allowed to see me or talk to me or even acknowledge that I exist! *What? This doesn't make any sense.*

My mind is racing a million miles a minute. Flustered, I start tossing everything around in my car to gather my things, but then drop it all when trying to open the car door. *Breathe, Bryn.* I take a deep breath and try again. When I get the door open, it slams shut in a huge gust of wind. I look up at the sky through my front windshield and see an enormous black cloud rolling in at top speed. My instincts kick in and I look for the nearest shuttle before it starts to pour. Jumping out of the car, I struggle against the wind to get my bag out of the trunk, then run. The last thing I want to do is sit on a plane for over three hours in soaking wet clothes.

I make it onto the shuttle before the sky opens up. It's like something from a movie. Everyone looks out of the window, making comments about the torrential rain. It's not until we reach the overhang at the airport that we get some relief from the rain pounding on the bus. It doesn't help my state of mind. I hate flying, but I *really* hate flying when it's raining. However, I suspect that my flight is going to be delayed. Inside the terminal, I go over to a kiosk to check in my bag.

Kiosk after kiosk is down. The chatter in the airport escalates. Then a voice comes over the loudspeaker announcing that a blackout has affected the entire airport. All flights have been canceled.

Everyone looks around at one another. *Did they just say what I thought they said?*

I ask an employee mopping up a spill, "Excuse me, the entire airport is out of power?"

"This has NEVER happened before. We can't believe it."

I'm shocked. "How long has it been down?"

"It just went out less than ten minutes ago."

Ten minutes ago, I was in my car. I think. "Hmmm."

"Do you believe in signs?" he continues.

"I do." That's when guilt sets in and my stomach drops and starts to churn.

"Then I wouldn't be flying today."

"I agree." I make my way back to the shuttle station. The rain has subsided, so it's quiet enough for me to give Jen a call. "You will not believe it. There is a blackout at BWI."

"A blackout?"

"The entire airport is out of power. No flights. In fact, I need to call Southwest because I think I can get a full refund. Crazy, right? So y'all are just going to have to have fun without me."

"Man, that sucks. I really wanted you to come down. We're having a wonderful time."

"It's best. Girl, enjoy. It's your time to shine. Post pictures on Facebook. I'll see them."

"My smile is so big."

"I know it is." We laugh and she knows why. Meanwhile, back at the long-term parking lot, when I exit the shuttle and walk to my car, the dark clouds part, revealing a vibrant blue sky. Sunlight shines through. Someone yells from the shuttle to get back on. The power is restored.

For a moment, I contemplate returning to the airport, thinking of a plethora of 'what if' scenarios. Then I recall the promise I made to God: if he would take away my dark pain, I wouldn't go back to him. I don't know what I would have done if I'd seen Shane, but I'm going to accept that it was a sign. I'm going to take my ass home. On my way there, I get a call from Mandy. I haven't spoken to her in months.

"Hey, girlie! What are you doing?"

"Hey, stranger! Leaving the airport. How are you?"

"Girl, where you coming from?"

"Nowhere. I was supposed to meet Jen in New Orleans."

"For the game?"

"Hell no, but I can't lie. I was going to sneak off to it. But then a storm came and knocked all the power out, so I'm taking it as a sign that God doesn't want me to go. I don't know what I would have done. My crazy ass might have jumped onto the field and run after Shane." I giggle. "Or worse, ended up at his hotel room, or Shane at mine. It would have been a recipe for disaster. It all worked out. I'm not ready to see him. I've got to lose some weight. I've put on twelve pounds. I'm the heaviest I've ever been."

"You know they're not together, right?"

"No! How would I know that? I haven't spoken to him. How do you know? OMG!"

"There's so much we need to catch up on. I was calling to see if you wanted to meet for drinks? I could use one."

"I think I need one as well. Meet me down in Canton. In fact, I know the perfect place." I hang up with Mandy and can't keep my mind from trying to put two and two together. Maybe that's why Qmar said what he said. They aren't together? I Google it and according to Wikipedia, they are still very much together. It's all so crazy. I turn on the radio as a distraction and *Best Thing I Never Had* by Beyoncé starts playing. *Another sign?*

Mandy is waiting when I pull into the lot. I almost don't recognize her in the cherry-red convertible Lexus, but when I see a pair of binoculars hanging from the rearview mirror, it's a sure sign that it's her. Mandy jumps out of the car, swinging her short blonde bob.

"Well, you just got a total makeover, didn't you?"

"Girl, me and Jimmy are divorced! I wear it well, don't I?"

"What?" I put my hand on my heart. This is too much in one day! "Come on, let's get that drink first." Mandy and I walk to a bar I haven't visited in years. Nick's bar. It's not crowded yet so we're able to get two seats at the main bar. Happy hour doesn't start for a few more hours, but the bartender offers us specials anyhow. "You hungry? You want to get a couple of appetizers?"

"As long as they're healthy," Mandy says.

"Who are you?"

"Girlfriend, this divorce changed me. As soon as I left, you know, around the time I found the license?" She places her hand on my knee. "I'm sorry. I just couldn't call you with that news."

"It's okay. Everything happens for a reason. Sharing bad news with a close friend is never a fun thing. I appreciate you telling Jen. It was probably best that way."

"It messed me up. It was right after that I found out Jimmy was cheating. Her name's Karen and she's a freaking bartender with a bunch of tattoos. After investigating, in other words hacking into his Facebook account, I found out they went to high school together. They reconnected on Facebook. I was done. I wanted to ruin him, but I thought about the kid. So I left him. Well, he left and bought a new house down the street so we can still parent together. It works. It changed me, Bryn."

"It looks like it was for the best. You look great. As for me, it's been a year and I'm still struggling." We order a few cocktails and when they arrive, I say to the bartender, "Is Nick around? Tell him Bryn is asking." Bold move, but why not? I take a few sips. "I'm still hoping for a miracle. I had a bit of hope today and then the whole blackout thing scared the shit out of me. He's no good for me, obviously, he's someone else's husband. But it still doesn't seem like it's real. That's my Shane." I shake my head at the thought of them being together. "I can't lie. I still love him."

"That's the first step. You have to be honest with yourself."

"Who are you?"

We laugh and finish our first round of drinks. When the bartender brings our second round, he lets us know that Nick says they are on the house.

"Ooh! Thanks!" Mandy gets excited. "So much has happened this past year. I mean, I got a new job, a new haircut, a new therapist, new meds, and a new man."

"Did I hear that right, new man?"

"Yes. We're keeping it light. I'm not ready for anything serious. I call him when I want three hots and a cot."

"You are still so silly. I miss you, girl."

"I know, I miss you too. I wish I'd been there for you when it all happened. I talked to Lisette and she told me about you being a hot mess at work."

"Yeah, she and Lee would come in and just give me hugs. It was awful because all I would do was cry. In fact, I was crying this morning. I literally cry every day. Seriously, every freaking day."

"I know it seems impossible, but it will stop."

"I'm still a mess. It's probably best I didn't see him this weekend. I sent his cousin a message. He said that Shane would love to see me."

"Oh right. Girl, him and that crazy girl are separated. I don't know why he would love to see you because he's with someone else."

"Really?" I feel a knot in my throat. I wave for a second round of drinks. "He's seeing someone else and I'm still crying. What the fuck?"

"Men replace."

"How did you find out?"

"His social media. I still stalk him."

"Wow! I wonder what happened. . . that didn't last long. I guess he just said fuck it. Wow. I'm shocked. And I'm even more surprised he didn't call me."

"He was probably ashamed. He married that girl, it was all over the news. It was a mess. He's most likely embarrassed."

"Wow. Life stopped for me. This is truly a reality check. I really need to put this shit behind me. I'm working on this whole forgiveness thing and it's so hard."

"It is, it took me months to forgive Jimmy."

"Shane isn't sorry. And if he and Carice aren't together, he really has no excuse not to apologize. I guess he thinks he's off the hook because he technically broke things off with me. But you don't get married two weeks later and never call or anything to say, 'my bad, sorry about that'. That is just beyond fucked up."

"You can free yourself by forgiving him. You'd be surprised how you can actually forgive someone who hasn't said they're sorry."

"I can't even imagine." I sit silent for a moment with all my feelings. That awful night is on repeat. "I'm still far away from forgiveness. I'm still yo-yoing between loving him and busting the windows out of his car." I laugh.

The bar music turns up and *Party Rock* by LMFAO booms through the speakers. "That's my song." Mandy slides down the bar stool and starts dancing. "Remember us in the office?"

"How could I forget?"

29

2 YEARS/ACCEPTANCE

Two years ago today was the last time I saw Shane. Even though I'm still keeping track of the days, today is the first morning that I've opened my eyes and they're dry. It's a small victory, but a victory all the same. I don't know if it's because I'm truly over him or because I'm super-excited about my upcoming flight to Dubai. Either way, I'm counting it as a win.

It's so refreshing. Today feels like the beginning of the rest of my life. Feeling like this has been a long time coming. I make my bed as soon as I get up then head into the bathroom to brush my teeth and shower. My travel clothes, leggings, a tank top, and a long-sleeve floor-length cashmere sweater, are laid out on my chair. Once dressed, I style my hair in a messy high bun for the flight. Diamonds, bracelets, oversized Gucci sunglasses, and my lip gloss and I feel so *Sex and the City*. I blow my reflection a kiss, and she responds with 'no more tears'. I receive it and head out on my newest journey.

Jen's more excited than I am. I've barely made it to my front door when I hear her squealing goodbyes to David. She's been trying to get to the United Arab Emirates for a while now. As for me, I originally wanted to go with Shane, but life doesn't always give you what you want. Sometimes, it actually has something better in store.

The shuttle drops us off at the airport just in time for our red-eye to Dubai. After check-in, since we missed access to the Emirates lounge, our flight attendant is kind enough to walk us through their famous first-class cabin to our seats located in business class. Unfortunately, all of the pods are occupied, and I can't see inside. More importantly, I can't see who is sitting in them. Those seats are at least $20,000, the price of a car. What kind of job do you need to afford something like that?

We don't have pods, but business class isn't shabby at all. Jen and I are grinning from ear to ear as we settle in our seats. They are big and roomy and there is a compartment to hold everything. Our seats come equipped with storage, personal bar, eye mask, and designer toiletry bag.

"Did I tell you I'm never flying coach again?" Jen reclines her seat and the attendant hands her a hot lemon-scented hand towel. "I'm already impressed."

I laugh at her. "Want to meet at the bar after dinner?" I point behind us.

Jen's eyes widen as she pops her head up to look back. "I

thought that was only for first class."

"You're thinking of the shower. We have access to the bar."

"Oh yes, wake me." Jen pulls her eye mask down and gets ready for takeoff. We both have our pre-flight rituals, especially flights that cross a large body of water. Lots of prayer.

I doze off a bit but come wide-awake when my table tray is turned into a white cloth dinner table with real china and silver. "Thank you." I smile as if I'm a pro at this. Unlike Jen, I'm containing my excitement.

"Ms. Charles, would you like turndown service after dinner?"

Turndown service? "Why yes, please." I hear Jen thanking the Lord. This time I can't hold in my laughter. She is being so extra.

Dinner is delicious, and when we finish, Jen and I go to the back of the plane for a drink while our seats are being converted to beds. "Bryn, this is so unreal. I never want to forget this." Jen holds up her champagne glass. "Take a picture."

"It's pretty awesome." I take out my phone and snap a few photos.

"Would you like to come behind the bar for a photo?" the flight attendant asks.

I can count all of Jen's teeth as she nods wildly and hands over her phone. When she finishes, she joins me on the bench. "We've come a long way."

"We have." We clink glasses. I look around the lounge and take it all in.

"We worked hard for this. We deserve it. And most importantly, we did it on our own."

"I can't lie. I'm looking forward to seeing what the United Arab Emirates has in store for me." I finish my Champagne and return to my seat, which is now a bed. It's unbelievable that I'm lying completely flat. There's no turbulence. I look over at Jen, who's starting a movie. Since we've got at least nine more hours of flying time, I reach into my compartment and pull out my worn-out copy of *The Alchemist*. I learn something new every time I read it.

After a full day of travel, we finally arrive at our hotel in Abu Dhabi. As soon as we step out of our car, we're greeted by the call to prayer. It's kind of surreal and I'm oddly intrigued.

"I wish I knew what they were saying," says Jen.

"I know, but please don't ask." I discreetly discourage her from asking our driver.

"How do you say 'thank you' in Arabic?" she asks him instead.

"Shukraan."

Jen attempts to repeat this and hands him a tip.

"Obama. We love Obama," he says, as he pockets the dirham.

"Obama! Yes. We love him too! We're from Maryland!"

"Nighthawks?"

"Yes!" Jen screeches! "Nighthawks!"

Unbelievable. I've flown across the world and my driver knows about the Nighthawks. What are the odds?

Hours later, Jen calls me down to meet her by our hotel pool. Since I've already noticed that in Abu Dhabi, everyone dresses in traditional garb, in other words, completely covered up, I change into the most conservative dress I can find. I even wear a scarf. I'm not worried about covering my head, but I definitely want to cover my shoulders. Downstairs, I find Jen sitting poolside in a draped white cabana. She's lying back with her feet up, sipping on a cup of tea. "You must try some." She pours. "It's Moroccan tea, so sweet and absolutely delicious. I've never tasted dates this good either." She holds one up for me to try.

"I don't really like dates."

"You're missing out." She pops one in her mouth. "Can you believe this, Bryn? We are in freaking Abu Dhabi and we'll be in Dubai in a couple of days. We did the darn thing. A toast to the graduate." She raises her glass. "To dreams coming true. To living our lives not having to depend on a man."

"Alright now." I look around at all the Emirati men dressed in their white robes and headdresses smoking hookahs. "Girl, these men are so fine. I'm scared to look. I'm not trying to go to jail. But riddle me this? They are ultra-conservative and can't date women, but they can smoke? I mean, everyone in here is smoking."

Jen delivers the best 'chile please' look on cue. "I've already downloaded a dating app. And I've already received a proposal from a man who's giving me directions to the nail salon."

"What on earth? What did he say?"

"Will you marriage me?" Jen giggles.

I laugh so hard. "What about David?"

"What about him? I don't have a ring on my finger. And, are you blind?" Jen starts looking around.

"Okay, playa playa." I get comfortable on the bed, leaning back against the pillows.

"Do you want to try some? It's called shisha." She waves over our waiter.

"Why not. When in Rome, do as the Romans do."

When our flavored shisha and a second round of Moroccan

tea arrives, Jen proposes a toast. "To all of our accomplishments and not letting anything get in our way. Not to bring this up, but you know we were supposed to go to Hawaii and Dubai with Shane? I'm just saying."

"Say it."

"We are on a first-class five-star trip to the United Arab Emirates and we'll be in Hawaii in a couple of months for Christmas. Won't HE do it? And you did this without him. You did this with hard work and determination. Shane might be winning, but girl, you haven't missed a beat. The end game doesn't have to be getting the man. The end game is being happy and your whole self."

"Amen. Speaking of which, I didn't tell you, did I?"

"Tell me what?"

"I didn't cry today. Well, yesterday, since we're already into tomorrow. Two days, tear free, since two years ago. It feels amazing! I don't feel sorry for myself. I don't feel lost. I don't feel like I'm in a deep hole looking up at the light screaming for help. I feel like a weight has been lifted off of my shoulders. I'm afraid to claim it, but I think I've been delivered!"

"You know I'm claiming this victory."

We raise our tiny teacups and indulge in some Abu Dhabi shisha.

I'm so excited for today's excursion, I skip the breakfast buffet and get something light to eat that I can carry with me to visit the Sheikh Zayed Mosque. Our driver keeps stressing the rules for this visit to the point I'm scared to go in. But then he shares amazing stories about Sheikh Zayed that are simply unbelievable.

"Did you know he went to America to get a surgery?"

"No," Jen and I say in unison.

"The people prayed for him. It was a success. When he returned, it was a huge celebration. He got rid of all bills and all debt and no work. He loved the people. He did so much for the people. He loved the Emirates."

"That's amazing." We pass by a humongous billboard the size of an office building. It's a picture of the sheikh with 'our father' written in Arabic – so our driver tells us.

I stare out the window looking at all of the greenery, forgetting that I'm in the desert. But I'm reminded when a random camel is about the cross the street. Our driver hits his brakes. "It's illegal to hit or kill a camel. They are sacred."

"Really?"

"Yes, if you hit a camel, you have to pay the owner ten thousand dirham."

"But I thought I read about camel burgers?"

"Those are the old ones that have lived their life."

I make a face.

"If you can eat shark, you can eat camel," Jen reasons.

"I'll think about it."

As we inch our way closer, we see the magnificent white mosque. There is a lot of traffic, tour buses everywhere. When we finally park and exit the car, I feel like I'm going to pass out. I'm covered head to toe in all black and it's about a hundred twenty degrees in dry heat outside. Breathing is almost impossible.

"Remember, you will have to go through security and they will inspect you. I will be sitting here when you get out."

I take a deep breath and we walk to the first set of security guards.

"Calm down, nervous Nancy. I can see the stress all over your face." Jen nudges me along.

Absolutely no one is speaking English, and I feel so American and out of place. But when I reach security, the man who is collecting the tickets looks like he was personally carved and created by Allah and sent down from the heavens. Starting with his complexion, he was kissed by the sun. His hair is curly, thick, and dark. His eyes, my goodness, are intense. His smile could light up the world. I'm smitten and unfortunately, it's written all over my face. Jen closes my mouth for me and guides my hand to give him my passport.

"Stop drooling." She kicks me.

I'm speechless. *Loving You* by Minnie Riperton plays in my mind as he returns my passport. Jen pushes me out of the way.

"As you know, I love Jesus, but some of these men are so fine. I hear they can marry Christians. I think as long as you believe in God. . ."

"The kids have to be raised in Islam."

"What if I don't have any kids?"

"They want kids. You'd have to be like the first wife or something and the younger wives would have the kids."

"For that man, I don't know. I'd consider marrying for papers."

"He doesn't want to come to America. Everything is actually better here. Americans want to come to the UAE."

"I see why they're super-strict and have to cover up. They're so beautiful, if they didn't, it would be debauchery in the streets. How could anyone contain himself or herself?"

Jen starts laughing. "Okay, fix your thoughts before we go in."

"You're right." I remove my shoes and place them in a cubby.

"Don't worry," an older woman says to me. "They will be here when you return. No one wants to get their hand chopped off for a pair of Chanel sandals."

"Thank you." I smile and clear my mind then take my first step onto the hand-woven Persian rug. I'm truly in awe of this mosque. The intricacy of the décor and architecture is breathtaking. This house of worship is beyond anything I've ever seen or even imagined. I'm truly amazed at the reverence they give to God. I take my time and walk through the temple, amazed at its beauty.

At the end of the tour, I have a moment's silence and take in the experience. I meditate on today and bring myself into the present. For a second, Shane comes to mind and then quickly vanishes. I release all the pain, worry, and stress. I'm okay. I accept today, I accept my life the way that it is. And my life is great without him in it. I open my eyes and take one last look at the mosque. "This place was built for God. How divine."

Upon exiting, I'm quickly reminded that I'm in the desert and the sun is at its peak. I need water and a biscuit. Jen and I snap a few pictures, but in all of them, my face is twisted in irritation. Underneath my abaya I'm drenched in sweat. I must find our driver.

He's waving us down with two bottles of water in his hand. "Thank you, Jesus!" I shout, speed-walking to him. "Oh no, was I allowed to say that?"

"I need the air on as high as possible," Jen tells the driver. She jumps in the passenger seat and rips the scarf off of her head.

"I'm melting. Good thing we booked the beach club for today. Please, take us straight to Yas Island."

I fall asleep from the heat and Jen wakes me when we arrive at our destination. The private beach club is everything we could imagine and more. It's so sexy and chic, I'm lost for words. And since it's private, we don't have to worry about covering up. We reserved a cabana by the pool, which is fully stocked with an ice bucket filled with sparkling water and Champagne. Our waiter is waiting to take our order. It's perfect because we're starving.

Jen is taking forever to decide on what she wants to eat, so while she's looking though the menu for the fifth time, I'm trying to take the perfect selfie. Hat on. Hat off. Sunglasses on. Sunglasses off. Hair up. Hair down. Smile. Serious. After about twenty-five takes, I finally settle on the one I accidentally took and upload it to Facebook. I must have drawn some attention to us because when I'm done, we get a visitor. He doesn't look familiar, but we can tell he's American.

"I had to get a closer look." He removes his shades. "I remember y'all. It was that party in Baltimore in that high-rise a couple of years ago. I'd never forget because I've traveled all over the world and the stuff y'all did in Baltimore was lit. Y'all still doing events like that?"

"Hi, I'm Jen. My business partner Bryn. Yes, we still do events. We're here on vacation though. Bryn just got her MBA, so we're celebrating." Jen brings that fact up on the fly.

"Congrats!" He waves. "What parties y'all planning on going to?"

"We're not sure yet. Do you have any recommendations?" Jen takes out her phone to take notes.

"Not here, that's for sure. Abu Dhabi is old school. Y'all going to Dubai?"

"We leave to go there in the morning."

"Alright, that's where I'm staying. I was just here for a business meeting. Kobe is out here doing his basketball initiative. Take my number."

Jen taps away on her phone. "What's your name?"

"Mac."

"You have a last name?"

"I just go by Mac." He smiles and takes Jen's phone and enters his number. "Hit me up when y'all get to Dubai. I know of a few hot parties y'all should come out to. Especially since I know how y'all get down."

Jen and I laugh.

"Oh, and y'all be safe out here. It's not a lot of us in the UAE. They think black women are either English teachers or prostitutes."

"Glad to know, thank you." Jen and I clutch our non-existent pearls.

"I mean, y'all cool here because this is private and a lot of Americans and Europeans chill here. But when y'all are out in the streets here and in Dubai, remember that." Mac bids us farewell with a peace sign.

We finally place our food order and while we wait, I take a dip in the infinity pool. The water is body temperature. Staring out at the Arabian Sea from the pool's edge is simply stunning. My life right now feels perfect. I push away from the edge and float on my back until our food arrives.

"I can't believe we're on the other side of the world." I look at the sky and it's turning a shade of burnt orange.

"I don't want to go home," says Jen.

"I'm not there yet. But I haven't thought of home." I take the last bite of my salad and steal a few fries off of Jen's plate.

"You should have ordered your own." She swats my hand when I go back for more.

"I'm back down to my normal weight and I'm trying to keep it off."

"I hate to bring up Voldemort during this lovely moment but what were the odds of running into someone who was at his party? That was four years ago! Not only did he remember the party, he remembered us."

"That's pretty coincidental. But don't worry about saying his name. I don't have a reaction. Like in the past you would say his name and I would just start with the waterworks. Now it's nothing. I truly wish him happiness wherever he is. It's day three. No tears."

"I can't tell you how happy I am to finally hear those words." Jen gets up and grabs her camera. "Come, let's walk down to the beach. I want to take some pictures by the Arabian Sea during this sunset for David."

I get my wrap, my hat, and my phone, and follow her down to the private beach. After what feels like a thousand shots, Jen is finally happy with two. I hand her the camera and walk along the beach getting my feet wet. On cue, the sun starts disappearing into the sea. I couldn't have planned a better first day.

30

ARAB MONEY

On our way to Dubai, our driver takes the scenic route down some famous street where all of the royal family members have estates. Directly across the street are the homes of the royal household. From the looks of these four-thousand-plus-square-foot homes, they live better than most Americans. We can't believe the wealth. It's insane. As he drives down the long road, he continues to tell us that the UAE have enough oil to last the next hundred and fifty years. Gas is cheap and that's why half of the population drives exotic vehicles. The lower the tag numbers the better. And last but certainly not least the United Arab Emirates have the best, tallest, strongest, and largest of everything in the world.

By now, Jen and I are already sold on coming back. In fact,

when we arrive in Dubai and see that's it's more relaxed than Abu Dhabi, we start confirming dates. But as for today, we have a full agenda. The first item on our list is visiting the Dubai Mall and going to the top of the tallest building in the world, the Burj Khalifa.

We make the right decision to wear tennis shoes. Trekking through this mall in heels would be a nightmare. It's the largest mall in the world at over twelve million square feet, complete with an indoor aquarium. At the main entrance, we don't know whether to go left, right, or straight. To our left is a group of Emirati men checking out a white on white on white Tesla. To our right is Hermès, flooded with women, their nannies, and their three-plus small children. Their men are also with them. We're told Saturdays are family days.

"I want to check out a watch." Jen grabs a map.

"You know where I want to go." I search the map for my favorite footwear boutique. "I know they're going to have some sick ones here."

"It's on the ground floor. I think we're on the first or second." Jen looks around.

"Let's just start walking straight. Where there are stairs, I'm sure elevators and escalators aren't far."

It takes us about an hour to find the boutique. Besides the mall being ginormous, there are people everywhere. I sit down the first chance I get. Jen on the other hand walks up to the sales rep. "Oh my goodness, you are so stylish. Did you dress yourself?" Jen asks. He's tall, Asian, and dressed to the nines in all white. "You make chic look so simple."

He smiles and tosses his long hair back. "How are you ladies?"

he asks in what sounds like a British accent.

"We are doing great. My best friend is looking for the hottest selling shoe that we can't find in the States."

"I've got the perfect pair. They just came in this morning. I can't keep them on the shelves. What size do you need?"

"Thirty-eight please."

Jen starts dancing and looking at a pair on the wall. "Not only would my knees give out, I think my arch would break trying to get my foot in those." She shows me a spiky platform. "They are hot though." Jen continues to prance around the store watching other people try them on. "Those look gorgeous on your feet," she says to a young lady trying on a pair from the Strass Line.

The sales rep returns. "My very last pair." He takes them out and hands me a stocking so I can try them on.

I slip my foot into the red and black ombre pump and they are like candy. I stand and spin in front of the mirror a few times. "These are so sexy. I've seen them before but only in the So Kate Line, which you need a high instep to wear. They actually feel good. In fact, I'm going to wear them out tonight."

Jen raises her eyebrows. "Okay."

"I'll get these." I place them back in the box and reach into my cross-body bag to retrieve my credit card and hand it over to him with the shoes.

"Would you like anything else?"

"No, thank you. These are fine."

"How many pair do you have now?"

"Well, these will be the first pair I've bought myself. I think this might be lucky number six."

"Bryn, did you just hear what you said?"

My eyes shift, trying to figure out what she's getting at. I shake my head.

"You are buying your own Louboutins." She nods her head. "Man. You're a changed woman. A man isn't going to be able to tell you anything. Even though you-know-who is out of your life, not much has changed for you. Like you are still doing it up big. That is a big deal and you should celebrate it."

"I haven't given it much thought. I'm just happy he doesn't come to mind every second of the day. So, best friend, if you don't mind, stop bringing him up."

"My bad."

The sales guy returns with my shoes, credit card, and two small bottles of water. "You ladies enjoy the rest of the day."

"Thank you." I put my card away and check the time. "I think by the time we finish finding this watch store, it'll be our turn to visit the Burj so let's try not to get lost."

Hours later after walking through this maze of a mall, we never find the watch store, but we do end up in the wing where we can get to the Burj Khalifa.

I look at Jen wild-eyed as we check in. "I can't believe we're doing this." We're both terrified of heights. The elevator ride alone is longer than a minute. "You sure you want to do this?" My heart beats wildly in my chest as we're taken to a small room to wait for our tour guide. The elegant room is adorned with lush seating and exotic flower arrangements, and another small group of people also waiting. There is hot tea being served in real china, and dates for days.

Jen and I try to hide our excitement and have our own little photo shoot while we wait. It's not until our guide arrives and we speed past the crazy long lines that I look at our tickets to see that we booked a VIP tour. "We can't do anything regular, can we?" Jen and I laugh.

Arriving at the elevator, I stare at the countdown display on each door. The wait is over, and I get cold feet. "Jen, I think I'm going to vomit." The doors open and our tour guide takes the lead inside. *I can't look*. I close my eyes and fish for someone or anyone's hand. I'm not the only one who's scared shitless.

"We'll be visiting the hundred forty-eighth floor," I hear someone say.

"I thought it was only a hundred twenty-four?" I immediately panic and want to get off, but it's too late. I feel the pull of elevation and take a deep breath. Our tour guide continues to talk as the lights go dim. The interior of the elevator is like a movie screen. It's an interactive educational tour on Dubai and the construction of the tower. Even though we can't see, I know we are very high because my ears are starting to pop. When the lights come back on, the doors open, and we're at the top of the world.

Jen and I tiptoe out onto the observation deck. I think all of the blood has left my extremities. A photographer is trying to get us to smile for a photo, except he's only able to capture pure terror. "I'm going back inside. I need a minute." Jen and I take pictures inside and enjoy a fruity drink and hors d'oeuvres. "I can't come all the way to the top and not get a fabulous professional picture," I say. "We've got to face our fears and do it." After much convincing, we finally muster up the nerve to walk out and get our photos done. The photographer suggests that we sit, and it makes all the difference.

Back downstairs and in the mall, Jen and I are pumped up on

pure adrenalin. There's nothing we think we can't do. Jen even walks up to a fine-ass Emirati dressed in full garb and asks him and his equally fine friend for a selfie. He can't speak a bit of English, but he knows the word selfie. Who knew it was universal? We get our picture. After they leave and we look at it, we see that our eyes are practically shut from smiling so hard.

"I'm trying to meet a sheik." Jen sashays through the mall. "I don't want to go home."

"Girl, you crazy. Don't be out here getting locked up. Remember what happened to Samantha in *Sex in the City*. She was facing jail time. In fact, I think you can still get lashes here." I make a whipping sound.

"Please stop. I've been trying to get here forever. Like this is my dream trip."

"I agree. It's a beautiful trip so far."

We continue to walk the mall until dinner. Since our internal clocks are still messed up, we have a late dinner reservation. The restaurant isn't too far from the Burj Khalifa. From the outside, at night, it's lit up in all its glory. It's so big, it's impossible to get a picture of it in its entirety.

Jen made the reservation at Bice Mare, an upscale Italian restaurant. So, when we're taken to our table, a small table for two on the terrace in front of the Dubai fountains, memories of my last trip to Vegas with Shane flood back to my mind. Jen notices because she asks me if I'm okay. I won't lie. I have a mind to bring that night up with Jen, but then I decide not to dwell on it. Shane is two years in my past and thousands of miles away. Today, on the other side of the world, we've had such a fun-filled day and it's of no use allowing something like that to put a damper on it.

Over drinks, I think my thoughts, feel my feelings, and move on. It's okay. And when the Arabian music starts to play and the fountains dance along, all is well with my soul.

I'm ready to call it a night except Jen gets a text from Mac asking if we've made it to Dubai.

"He wants us to come to a hot party tonight. He said he put our names on the list."

"You really want to party tonight?

"Hell yeah! I didn't fly all the way to Dubai to stay in my room." Jen's flagging our waiter down for the check. "Just throw on a dress. You just bought a pair of hot shoes. Ya look cute. Let's make it happen."

"When in Rome. . ."

"When in Dubai!"

We rush out of the restaurant and head onto the main road to find a taxi. Apparently, we walked out of the wrong entrance, so it takes forever for one to stop for us and luckily, it's right before Jen's feet give out on her. That still doesn't stop her from wanting to hang out. We agree to meet back in the lobby in one hour, dressed and ready to go. Since it doesn't take me that long to get ready, I spend the first twenty minutes talking to Bailey and checking up on her and King. They are both doing great, so I give myself permission to go out on the town and have a bit of fun.

Despite wanting to call it a night, I'm actually glad Jen pushed me to go because the party is lit. There's a good ratio of men to women, unlike in the States. It's usually a thousand women looking at the same man. Here, there are plenty of men to go around. To drink or not to drink, is the question of the night. I heard that drinking isn't permitted in Dubai except in certain places. But still, I don't know if it's worth it. I'm going to rely on my winning personality to get a bit loose.

We are smashed like sardines in a can and it's nearly impossible to get to Mac, so Jen and I settle where we get stuck. It's not a bad view. Everywhere I look, there's another fine man. They aren't dressed in their traditional attire. Here, everyone is dressed more relaxed in skinny jeans and either a t-shirt or a collar shirt. Not only is it filled with Emirati men, there are also a lot of Africans, Russians, and my admirer just happens to be from Poland. He begs me in broken English to meet him at the beach tomorrow.

Jen's all smiles, while I'm shaking my head no. I've got an appointment at Talise Spa in the Burj Al Arab that I'm not missing for anyone. He eventually tires of me and moves on.

"What was he saying?" Jen yells over the music.

"We don't have a future, so it's no use talking about it." I laugh.

The DJ starts playing *Arab Money* by DJ Khaled, and Jen goes crazy. She's dancing and dropping it low in her already too short red dress. She gets a lot of attention. A group of people in the VIP section right in front of us invites us in. And there he is. Our eyes glisten with glee. Sitting quietly in the corner of the section with a top bun on his head is a man so beautiful I swear I can hear the angels sing. Jen looks at me. We're sporting the same crazy grin. We celebrate and telepathically tell each other that this is our new beginning, jumping and dancing and singing along with the song.

31

THE ALCHEMIST

Standing barefoot atop a sand dune with my feet sinking into the sand, I can only think of two things: a desert creature biting my toes and a book that I read on the flight over here, *The Alchemist* by Paulo Coelho. It's such a fascinating read about love and one's personal journey. It's profound and spiritual, and it speaks to my soul every time I read it. For some strange reason, at this very moment it's falling on my heart to buy a copy for Shane.

I don't know why and more importantly if I do it, I don't know how he's going to receive it.

For some time, I've been on my own personal journey to reach my highest potential. It took two years of hard work and searching inward to find out that the strength was in me all along.

There's a moment in the novel where it speaks of the boy having to turn himself into the wind. His life depends on it. He speaks to the desert, the winds, and the sun. It isn't until he makes his silent plea to the one Creator, that he realizes the one who created everything is also in him and he too can perform miracles.

It might seem insignificant to others, but forgiving Shane was a miracle. I read countless books, went to therapy, and tried every remedy under the sun to figure out how to truly free myself from the failed relationship. I sought freedom from the memories, both good and bad. Unraveling from the bonds of unrequited love. I needed to rid myself of the burden of pain that I'd carried for so long. It was nothing but God's grace and mercy that gave me the strength to continue to fight. And on the other side of that dark pain I was feeling love and forgiveness. It was there that I found my peace. My eyes have been dry for four days and God gets all the glory.

Maybe that's it. Shane needs peace. It's not for me to figure out right now, but I'll give it some thought when I return home. In the meanwhile, it's time to get back onto the camel and head to our campgrounds for dinner, music, and live entertainment.

32

<u>FATIMA</u>

Looking back, these past four months have been the best yet. Instead of sitting around analyzing if this great love affair even happened or wondering if Shane was lying to me all along, I've accepted things as they've happened and chalked it up as part of my life's journey. Since my trip to Dubai, I've been refocusing on me and finding things that bring me happiness, and travel is one of them.

As I prepare our bags for our flight to Hawaii, I see on my bookshelf the book I purchased for Shane when I returned from Dubai. I think about mailing it before we depart so he can get it for Christmas. Hopefully that way it doesn't seem so strange and random. Either way, I'm sure he'll still find it very strange and random. So, I dismiss the thought and pack the final contents in our bags.

"You're going to love what I got for you this year." Bailey walks into my room and taps her carry-on backpack.

"I love what you get for me every year."

"I didn't get pajamas this time."

"But I love pajamas."

"Mom, it's time to get out of the house." She puts her hands on her hips and reprimands me.

"What are you talking about? We're on our way to Hawaii! You've always wanted to go and we're finally going."

"This trip doesn't count. I want you to find a husband. I don't want you to be alone when I go away to college."

"What are you talking about? I'm so happy my face hurts from smiling." I give Bailey a hug. "Please don't think that just because I'm single, I'm not happy. I've got peace. Always remember that peace of mind is priceless. I'm alone but I'm far from lonely. Besides, I've got plenty of time before you go off to college."

The Alchemist crosses my mind again. *I'll have to mail it,* I think, looking off into the distance. An immense feeling of grief follows the thought. Then an overwhelming sadness overtakes me. My inner peace is replaced by what feels like a huge weight. I've got to get this monkey off my back. So, it happens. I search for Shane on Facebook. Even I can't believe it's happening. When I find his page, it's filled with movie quotes and a few old pictures of him, Carice, and the kids. It comes as a shock that I don't feel any warm and fuzzies. *Okay, this might not be bad.*

I hit the button and draft him a message.

Hey you! This is actually more shocking to me than to you but. . . I was packing for Hawaii when I felt an overwhelming sense of grief thinking of you. The last time this happened (the day of your wedding) I listened to a friend (not Jen) and didn't reach out to you and I've regretted that decision ever since. Now, it happens to be two years later. . . I'm saying all of this just to say. . . I sincerely hope that you are well and that my worries and concerns about you are amiss. With your permission I'd like to give you something I picked up for you. I can mail it or sneak it into your mailbox in the middle of the night, like Santa. I just don't want to impose. Either way, Happy Holidays and take care.

What have I done? I slam my laptop shut. He's going to read that message and think I've lost my mind. I know it. Reaching out to him out of the blue. This is ludicrous.

"Mom, are you alright?"

"I'm fine. Got a lot on my mind."

"Okay, well, Taylor is over Jen's so I'm going next door to help her repack. Jen says her suitcase is overweight."

"Have fun!" When she leaves, my heart starts to race, and I reopen my laptop and log onto Facebook. One new message in my inbox. I hold my breath as I open it. It's from Shane.

I don't know what to say. . . I'm speechless in every sense of the word. Umm, don't know if I'm okay, but I'm a little happier than I was. . . However, I hope all is well with you. Pretty sure Bailey is a shining star. You can drop it off.

Now, I gotta call Jen. She's not going to believe this.

"Hey," she answers. "I was just about to come by. Bailey says you're mumbling to yourself."

"Yeah, you should come."

"Should I bring a bottle?"

"It isn't necessary, but it won't hurt."

"On my way." When Jen walks in with two bottles of wine, I'm standing behind a chair at my dining room table. I manage to stay quiet as she enters the kitchen.

"How's David?"

"You *are* being weird. You never ask about David. But since you've asked, he's fine. I was trying to get some, but Taylor showed up early and blocked. But. . ." She squints her eyes. "I know this look. What have you done?"

"I want you to read something." I slide my laptop towards her.

"I'm going to pour a couple of glasses first." Jen searches the drawers for the wine opener. "It's written all over your face." She joins me at the table with two glasses. "What do you need to show me?"

I point over her shoulder to my computer screen. "Start here."

Jen's mouth drops open. "I read fast. What does 'don't know if I'm okay, but I'm a little happier than I was' mean?"

"I don't know. I felt all this sadness about him, and so I reached out to him and this is what he said. I'm still connected to that joker."

"That's so crazy. After all this time, you still feel what he feels."

"Right! I know."

"Maybe y'all do have something special."

"Had," I point out. "Don't go there."

"Where is this book? Are you going to drop it off? I mean, our flight leaves in a few hours."

"Can you ride with me really quick to drop it off?"

"Make it quick."

I inscribe the book with a message: *Shane, look to God in your time of need. You're going to be alright. You've got that something special. I hope you find your Fatima.* I wrap it in a textured silver paper complete with a blue bow (as fate would have it, I just happened to have his favorite color bow).

"It's gorgeous." Jen smiles while examining the packing. "Bryn, it's a beautiful gift. I wouldn't leave this anywhere except for in his hands."

"I'm putting it in his mailbox. Let's go."

Jen hops in the passenger seat like any best friend would and rides with me to drop off Shane's gift. When we pull up, his entire house is adorned in blue lights. At the front of his long driveway is his mailbox. I pull up and get out and place it inside. "Should I put this thing up?"

"I mean, that's just letting the mailman know he has a pickup."

"What time is it?"

"It's 7 pm."

"Well, mail should have been dropped off already. I'll put it up." I jump back in the car. "Package delivered."

"Why are you out of breath?"

"I want to hurry and leave. I don't want anyone coming out. Especially him."

"It's been real, now take me home."

Back home, Jen leaves and I go into the house to send Shane a new message letting him know that I placed it into his mailbox. He replies immediately.

Shane: Which house did you take it to?

Bryn: The one with the blue lights.

Shane: Nothing was in there. . .

Bryn: OMG.

Shane: Maybe you should have knocked on the door. . .

Bryn: I didn't see any cars. That sucks. Did anyone in the house get it for you?

Shane: Was it big or small?

Bryn: Small, with a big blue bow.

Shane: Guess I wasn't meant to have it.

Bryn: Did the mailman steal it? Was there mail in your box?

Shane: No mail at all.

Bryn: Hopefully it will turn up. It would be too weird for it not to. If the mailman thought it was for him, after he reads it he will realize it's not and return it. Hopefully. LOL.

Shane: Hope so.

33

<u>OVER HIM</u>

All year, not a word from Shane. But today, at work, six months after I left that book in his mailbox on the eve of my birthday weekend, I get a Facebook message from him.

Shane: Why The Alchemist?

Bryn: You finally got it? Did you read the front inside flap?

Shane: I will take a look. I lost my Fatima a long time ago.

Bryn: I know the feeling. You will find love again. Pure unadulterated love. You've got something special (like the alchemist) and it shines through.

Shane: Honestly I think I'm done with the love thing. I'm fine with being alone!

Bryn: Well, I hope you are okay. I hope the surprise message and gift wasn't intrusive. I wanted you to have it. I mean it.

Shane: Not intruding at all. Can I see you?

I pause. Wow. What do I say? It would be nice to see him again. Since I don't feel like there's any harm, I continue with a response.

Bryn: Sure! I'd love to catch up. Are you in town? It's my birthday weekend though. I don't know if I want to chance you messing it up.

Shane: I got traded. I'm in Arizona now. But they have this new invention called airplanes. They're really cool. Can take you from one side of the country to the other. Really neat stuff.

Bryn: Bwahahahahah you are so funny. You got jokes. You know my DoB. Book a flight.

And surprisingly, within a few hours of our messaging, I get a text message to check email for my flight confirmation.

The rest of my workday is going to be unproductive, so I leave to go home and pack. I've been staring into my closet for over an hour, searching for something that he didn't purchase. The last thing I want is to be sentimental when he sees me wearing a dress that he bought. Nope. I continue to slide through the dresses until I land on a nude Hervé Leger dress I purchased myself for Valentine's Day this year. I'm sure when he sees me in it, he'll be asking or at least wondering who bought it.

It's empowering to still maintain a certain lifestyle without a man. It's interesting because I never 'needed' Shane for anything anyway. Still, he made me feel special when he did think of me. Who doesn't like to feel special every now and again?

"Mom!" yells Bailey. I hear her shut the door and run upstairs.

"I'm here!" I yell back from inside my closet.

"Where are you going?"

"Away. . . for a surprise birthday trip."

"With who?"

"Myself." Technically, I am traveling alone.

"Oh well, have fun."

"Thank you. I asked Jen if you could stay here instead of going to Nana's."

"Bet." Bailey skips out of my room.

I figured she'd prefer to stay home. She's only got two weeks of school left. Then she will officially be an eighth-grader. Time flies whether you are having fun or not.

Once I'm finished packing, I prepare dinner and go over a list of dos and don'ts with Bailey. She's able to get away with murder these days. I think it's because I wasn't the only one who was hurting. Bailey didn't mind reminding me that Shane didn't just walk out of my life. As much as he may have wanted to maintain that relationship, he knew it would lead right back to me. Anyhow, I've been keeping an eye on her progress and I've had a family therapist on redial just in case. Since she's been spending half the week with her father and his new wife over the last few years, I don't see the need to make any sudden moves.

She nods her head and agrees to all of my stipulations. No company unless Jen is here, walk her little brother, and keep my room free and clear of dirty dishes.

"Anything else, Mother?" she says in a sassy tone.

"Just be safe."

"I'm officially a tween." Rolling her eyes, she slips the baby a piece of chicken before clearing the table.

"And walk him on the main road. Don't cut through the woods."

She picks up King, our pampered pooch, who's now fully grown at five pounds, and hands him to me. "Give him a kiss goodbye."

"I'm going to miss you, pudding." I let him lick me on my nose which is his version of giving me kisses. "Be nice to your big sister."

"Technically he's your grandson. He's my dog."

"Right. Who takes care of him?"

"Whatever." Bailey takes King out of my arms and talks baby talk to him on the way upstairs.

I load the dishwasher, start it, and turn the light out.

Then I get a call from Jen. "I can't believe you're going!"

"I know, weird right?"

"Where will you be staying?"

"I know he isn't that crazy to think I'm going to stay with him. I'll ask to be sure and I'll text you." My mind starts to wander. *He wouldn't. . .*

"Good. I pray that you don't have any setbacks."

"I'm good and I'm not going backwards. I need to do this. Trust me, I'm over him.

34

FORGIVENESS

A black SUV is waiting for me. The driver collects my luggage and takes off. I don't know where we're headed. All I know is a ride through the city eventually turns into endless views of red rock mountains and it's breathtaking.

He pulls up to one of the many resort properties and the doorman greets us, takes my bags, and leads me to the front counter for check-in.

"Welcome to the Fairmount Princess."

I look around, smiling. Shane wouldn't tell me where I'd be staying.

"Name on the reservation?"

"Bryn, maybe. Bryn Charles."

The rep types away but then has a puzzled look. "No, I don't see a Ms. Charles. Would it be under another name?"

"Smith, Shane?"

"Ah, yes! My apologies. You're already checked in. I have your key right here. We have you in one of our corner king suites overlooking the pool." He opens a sealed envelope and hands me the key.

"Sounds lovely."

"It is." He smiles and waves the doorman over and hands him a paper. "Please take Mr. Smith's guest to her room please."

"Si." He nods to me and takes my bags again, leading the way.

We walk through the lobby and the first thing I see is a vast cobblestone courtyard with a blue-lit fountain in its center. And around it, secluded fire pits and lounge seating. Once through the courtyard we enter the building and take the elevator to level four. A quick ride up and my room is directly to the right.

The doorman gives me a tour of my suite, starting with the view from the balcony. "You can have breakfast on your terrace in the morning. Just give us a call and we will set it up for you." Next, he opens double French doors to the master king bedroom fully equipped with a master bath and walk-in closet. He sets my bags in there. Then he shows me the minibar fully stocked with liquor and snacks. "Ms. Smith. Thank you and please let us know if there is anything you need."

"Thank you," I walk him out and secure the door with the security bar lock. I backtrack to the balcony to look out onto the pool. They're hoisting a large movie screen and people are paddling out to its center on floats. "This is so sweet." I look up and see a bright full moon over the dark mountains. It's glorious.

I close my eyes and take it all in.

Back inside, I check my phone and see that Shane has text me and wants to meet for dinner. The next text reads that he's on his way. I drop my phone, quickly unpack, and rush to get ready. Once I'm dressed, I give Jen a call and talk to her on speaker while I apply my make-up.

"I'm at the Fairmont Princess in Scottsdale. My room is gorgeous. It's a lot of room for just me," I say, putting on a second layer of mascara. "I hope he doesn't get any ideas." As soon as those words fall from my lips, I hear a bang that startles me. "What the fuck! Hold on."

I rush out of the bathroom and see my front door ajar, Shane's foot and a sliver of his hat through the crack! "Oh, my God!" I run to the door with my blush brush still in hand, close it, remove the security bar, and open it. It's really Shane standing in front of me, much slimmer and more muscular than ever before. He's even sporting new designer stubble. "Hi," I whisper.

"Hello, gorgeous." He reaches out and pulls me in for a sweet embrace.

I'm nervous. "I, uh, actually." I step back. "I'm not finished getting ready." I hurry back to the bathroom and hang up on Jen.

"Don't rush for me. You can finish putting on your make-up."

Butterflies! My stomach gets a bit squeamish. I haven't seen him in forever. *Holy crap,* I mouth at the mirror. "I'm almost done!" I yell while applying a dark lip color. When I walk out to find him, he's in the bedroom snooping around in the closet. "I see you've got more red bottoms since I last saw you."

I smile.

Shane looks me up and down. "I like the ones you got on."

"Oh, I got these in Dubai."

"Dubai?" He seems shocked.

"Yup, I went to Dubai and Abu Dhabi."

"Wow. I guess we have plenty to catch up on. You hungry?"

"Sure!" I blush. "It was a long flight."

"Great. I made us reservations at this spot I found that has live music tonight." Shane leads the way to the car and all he keeps saying on repeat is, "WOW. I can't believe it. I can't believe you're here. I called the crew and told them. Even they can't believe it."

"I can't believe it either. It feels familiar but still very strange."

Shane nods in agreement. "I feel you." He helps me into his truck and acts the little chatty kathy on the way to the restaurant. "How are you?"

"I'm good!" I nod. "I'm great actually."

"You look great! How's Bailey?"

"She's a tween now! She's officially twelve."

"Is she still dancing?"

"Every day. She attends a performing arts magnet school."

Shane covers his mouth. "She's going to make it. She's got that star quality. The it factor. She's going to do big things. I know it. I never stopped thinking about her. I wanted to call her. I was afraid though."

"You should be." I tighten my lips and nod my head.

"For real?"

"Yup. She made sure she told me that you left her too!"

"Aww, man. That hurt." He places his hand on his chest. "I mean if I call her, she's going to lay me out, isn't she?"

"I can guarantee it." I grin.

"You going to lay me out too? I know. I want you to get it out now."

For a moment, I consider letting him sit in his discomfort but when I see he's about to break out in a sweat, I give him a reprieve. "I know this may surprise you but I'm not mad at you any longer."

Shane looks confused as he pulls into the lot of the restaurant and into the first open parking space. "I thought you were going to curse me out and scream and hit on me."

"Isn't two years of crying enough pain to endure?"

Shane's eyes widen and he clenches his jaw. "I deserve to be hit. If it helps, these last two years have been the worst times of my life."

"Listen, let's not go there just yet. There will be no hitting of any kind happening tonight." I smile.

"You right. I wanna hear all about all the good stuff you've been doing. I'm trying to hear about Dubai. Wasn't I supposed to send y'all to Dubai for Jen's birthday or something?" He perks up a bit, jumps out of his truck, and rushes to my door to open it.

I laugh on the inside. I let him keep his pride and don't remind him that it was one of many promises he broke.

He offers me his arm and we enter the restaurant. Inside, it's an awesome vibe. There's a live jazz band playing and our hostess seats us not too far away. It's perfect timing because the singer starts off with one of my favorite songs, *Choux Pastry Heart* by Corinne Bailey Rae. Her voice is like liquid. Shane is clearly happy with his choice.

"You like it, don't you?"

"Nice choice. Very mature. Didn't think this type of place was your thing." I nod and give him a polite smile.

His chest puffs up. "I've grown." He orders a bottle of red

wine but waits for the singer to finish the tune before he speaks. "Well, before I say anything, I want you to know that. . . it was the hardest and the worst decision I ever made in my entire life."

"Understood."

"I knew I shouldn't have done it, but I was feeling the pressure. All I could think about was my kids and my career. She was going to take it all away."

"Wow." I take a sip of wine.

"You know we're getting a divorce?"

I choke. "I've heard rumors."

"Yeah. Last time she went psycho, I stayed calm and just took a video. I started keeping receipts on her. She wasn't catching me off guard in court again. When I had enough, she started begging for us to see a marriage counselor. It was too late. I finally saw for myself what she had been doing all these years. I just had to break it to the kids. Daddy is here for you whenever you need me, but I couldn't be around her anymore. Then I got traded, so, I'm away now anyway."

"Well, you *seem* happy."

"I'm better. . . but you! You look beautiful. I mean. You are like glowing. I see you made out just fine without me. I always knew you would."

"It's called peace of mind." My eyes water a bit. I quickly blink them dry. "It's priceless."

"It looks good on you. Maybe that's my problem." He takes a huge gulp of wine.

"Did you ever read that book I bought you? *The Alchemist.*"

"Nah. But I carry it with me whenever I travel."

"Okay. . . you want to elaborate?"

"I don't know. It's like I want to read it, but I'm scared to. Qmar saw it in my bag once and said, 'Whoever bought you that book really loves you.'"

"And that scares you?"

"I'm afraid of what it might do to me."

"It's not like it's hoodoo."

The waitress politely interrupts and asks if we're ready to order. We quickly place our orders. I want to hear more about why he's scared to read a book. "I mean it is life-changing, if that's what you're afraid of," I say, handing off my menu.

"Exactly. That's what scares me."

"Are you afraid to change?"

"It depends on the change."

"Well, someone once told me the book impacts everyone differently. It all depends on what you have going on in your life when you read it. Read it when you're ready."

"I will. Until then, it will continue to travel with me. I took it to Europe."

"Nice."

"Yeah, me and the crew hit up London, Paris, and Italy."

"Wow! Look at you! International traveler."

"London is expensive as fuck."

I laugh.

"Nah, for real. And Will got locked up."

Part of me wants to laugh. "Oh no!" I say, trying to sound concerned even though I could actually care less.

"His dumb ass had Ecstasy in his carry-on."

"He traveled with illegal narcotics to another country?"

"He said the bag was borrowed and he didn't realize it was in there when he started packing. They kept him for like a week."

"Oh shit!" Now I'm shocked.

"Yeah, it was wild as shit. He kept calling me to fix it, but it was nothing I could do. They didn't care who I was over there."

"Yikes."

"I called him a lawyer but after that, it was out of my hands."

"Y'all sure keep things interesting."

"Terry is married!" he blurts.

"You lie!"

"Yup." Shane nods. "He met her your birthday weekend in Vegas and the next thing years later we're flying to Antigua for his wedding."

"Oh, my goodness! I'm so happy for him." I genuinely mean it. "He got his happy ending."

"Yeah, yeah."

"How's Qmar?"

"Why does everyone always ask about him?" Shane frowns.

"Because he's the sweet one of the group," I laugh.

"He got everybody fooled. He's the one who taught us the game."

"Qmar is innocent. Don't talk about him like that."

Shane rolls his eyes. "He's here. He said he's going to meet us later."

I clap and cheer in my seat. "I miss him."

"But you don't miss me?"

"Nah." I won't give Shane the satisfaction. I laugh to myself, hoping it punched him in the gut.

"You're right." He can't even look me in the eyes. "I deserve the worst."

We close out the restaurant, but Shane isn't ready to take me back to the hotel. "Do you smoke hookah?"

"I tried shisha in Abu Dhabi. It was cool."

"Good." He makes a U-turn in the middle of the road and stops in a little shopping center in Scottsdale with a tiny hole-in-the wall bar hookah place.

We grab two sets at the bar and Shane orders like he's a regular. He also orders a couple of vodka shots.

"Trying to get me drunk?"

His eyebrows rise. "No. Just a little loose."

"You think I'm being uptight?"

"No, but every time I look at you, I feel guilty."

"Babe, you've got to let that go." I rub his leg. "I'm fine. You're just not used to seeing me this happy without you." He's used to seeing me fawning over him. Boy, does the truth hurt. I smile and take a sip of my drink. A group of loud guys come rushing in and over to us.

"Qmar!" He gives me a big hug, almost picking me up. "Romello!"

"Boy, am I glad to see you. He couldn't stop talking about you." Romello slaps Shane's back.

"Really?" I laugh. He sure fooled me.

"You know he loves you." Romello rubs my back.

I'm speechless.

The guys are really loud, so the bartender cranks up the music. *Burn* by Usher starts playing and I almost spit when Shane turns to face me, grabs my legs, and starts singing the hook to me.

"Are you drunk already?" I try to laugh it off, feeling slightly embarrassed.

"No, never that. You've never seen me drunk."

"You're right. I haven't. You don't even drink for real."

"I've been drinking. Like every day."

I frown. "Why?"

"I think I'm depressed."

"Depressed people don't know they are depressed so I doubt it."

"I need a drink just to start my day."

"Then you should probably see someone about it. Seriously."

"I will. How are you so radiant?"

"I stopped punishing myself for your mistakes. The anger and frustration no longer reside in my heart. It wasn't easy but I managed. It only took me two years." I try and laugh it off.

"You really cried for two years?"

"I did." My eyes water at the thought. "You never told me you were getting married."

Shane downs his drink. "Fuck, man."

I blink my eyes dry. "We don't have to talk about this. Let's enjoy the now."

"I couldn't. I couldn't tell you." Shane looks away. "There's a special place in hell for me."

"That's a rather harsh thing to say."

"I never stopped thinking about you. Believe that."

"Well, I wanted to stop thinking about you. But it happened when it was supposed to happen, I guess."

"We weren't supposed to marry, I swear. But breaking things off with you wasn't enough. She found the copy of the contract in my office. She knew you were the one. She hated it. I could be with her and fuck my ex-fiancée and any other bitch in the world and she wouldn't give a fuck, but you, it was different. She didn't believe that I would never see you again so the only way she was willing to stay was to get married. It was the only way I could get custody. I had nothing left."

"Oh well, it's water under the bridge. And now y'all are separated. I can't say I didn't see that coming. In fact, my boss now owes me a dollar."

"Everyone saw it coming. Now I just want her out of my life. She can have everything. Just let me see my kids and I want my last name back."

"Mmm." I start nodding my head to the music. I don't know what to say to him. I take a huge draw of the hookah. "I should have sued you."

"Sued me?" Shane reaches for the pipe and sniffs it. "They must have put something in here 'cause you talking crazy. Sued me for what?"

"For breaking your contract." I stick my tongue out at him and dance in my seat.

"Yeah, I'm definitely going to hell."

35

BET ON US

When I open my eyes, I thank the heavens that I'm in the bed alone. For a moment, I was sure I was going to let Shane in when he walked me to my room. His hand dropped a bit low on the hug. If I'd let him in, my God, I think we both knew what would have happened. *Whew, dodged that bullet.* Day one down, two more to go.

I turn on the television and the news is reporting record heat for today and warning everyone to stay indoors. It works for me because I did not pack for this kind of heat. It may be a while before I hear from Shane, since we stayed out late, so I order breakfast to my room. My American breakfast and French press black tea arrives in twenty minutes and I have room service set everything up on the terrace. It's so lovely. I stare out at the mountains and enjoy my cup of tea but after thirty minutes, I feel like I'm going to pass out. I drag myself indoors and lay on the sofa to cool off.

I think I must have had a touch of heat stroke because I wake up hours later to my room phone ringing over and over again. "Hello?"

"I've been calling you all day. I'm in the lobby waiting."

"You'll have to come up. I'm not ready. I'll leave the door open."

"I have a key."

"Let yourself in." I hurry and get in the shower even though my head is hurting. I take the fastest shower on earth. I need to be in clothes by the time he walks from the lobby. That means I've got about seven minutes.

I'm in the living area strapping my shoes when he walks in.

"Where do you want to go tonight?"

"I was hoping to watch a movie by the pool."

"I didn't bring my swim trunks." He walks over and takes a seat on the sofa next to me. "It's nice in here. Why do you have it so dark?"

"I had breakfast on the balcony this morning. It was so romantic and then I gave myself heat stroke and passed out. I've been laying on the sofa all day."

Shane huffs. "You should have called. I would have chilled with you. We could have gone to the movies or something."

"I was unconscious. I had no idea it was this hot here."

"Yeah, it's best to be out after the sun goes down. Alright, let's get out of here."

"Where to?"

"I'll figure it out when we get into the truck." He stands up and walks ahead of me. I follow Shane as he wanders the resort, briefly stopping by an outdoor bar, a fire pit, and eventually his truck parked in the entryway. "Alright, I know where."

"Where?"

"The casino."

"As long as they have air conditioning."

Shane's unusually quiet as we drive to the casino. I decide not to poke the bear and let him be. I'm sure we both have a lot on our minds. Either way, I want to make the most of this time that we have together.

At the entrance to the casino, the valet attendant is convinced I'm from his country of Ethiopia, to the point that Shane starts yelling at him. I'm slightly embarrassed, so I apologize on his behalf and explain to the man that anything is possible since most black people in America are descended from Africa, but I have no knowledge of any immediate family. This isn't the first time it's happened to me so I go with it. Shane ignores us and goes inside.

I catch back up with him at the cashier where he's exchanging cash for chips. "What do you want to play?" I ask him. "I only know how to play blackjack."

Shane walks through a sea of tables trying to find one with two empty seats together. Right when he looks like he's about to give up, someone leaves a table, which opens up two for us. "Perfect timing." I smile, trying to brighten his mood.

Our table is full. There are two older white trucker-looking guys to my left. Shane is to my right and two younger guys are on

Shane's right.

"Alright! We got a full table," shouts one of the guys.

Shane places his bet. "Place your bet," he says to me.

I place a $20 chip down and watch the dealer place the cards on the table. I peek under my second card. I hold at twenty. The dealer busts and the table wins. It happens again and again. Everyone at our table is excited! We're all winning. When we get a few spectators, someone comes and switches out our dealer. Five rounds with our new dealer and we're still hot. A floor manager comes over with a few sets of new cards.

"They're going to think you're counting cards." Shane chuckles.

"She's hot!" says one of the guys to my left.

"I know. He keeps forgetting," I joke with them.

"Man, you better treat her good tonight. Honey, what you drinking? Anything you want," another guy asks while we wait for our newest dealer to get situated.

"I'm fine, thank you." I nudge Shane with my elbow. "See, you should have bet on us."

"Jackpot, huh?" he looks over his shoulder and flashes a short smile. "Do you regret ever giving me a chance?"

"No."

"Not even after what I've done?"

I raise my brows. "Well, do you think we had a fair chance?" I look at my cards. I have twenty-one. "Honestly?"

"No." Shane lays down his losing cards and grabs his remaining chips from the table. "Come on, let's go."

"I'm winning." I smile and gather my chips.

"I'm losing. Seems like I've been doing that a lot these days."

I follow him through the crowd and to the cashiers' desk. Shane leans against it and looks me up and down as the clerk cashes us out.

"I poked the bear, didn't I?"

"Yeah, you did." Shane can't even look me in the face. "I lost you. I lost my kids. I lost my team. I'm saying, a person can take, but so much loss. . ."

"From the outside it looks like you're winning. I've seen your Facebook page, remember."

He chuckles.

"Mm hmmm. I saw your little party. And let me just add. It was tacky. Balloons?" I put my hands on my hips. "And the next time you hire someone in my city to do a party for you, it's on."

Shane drops his head. "That was Terry and Carice. How was I going to call you and ask you to do a party?"

"If the price was right, Carice and I would have been besties."

"Oh, it's like that now. Purely transactional?"

"I'm just saying. A party at a nightclub was not Platinum Events approved."

"They wanted a surprise location." Shane takes his cash and shoves it in his pocket.

I laugh. "It was a surprise alright."

"You just mad. How did you know anyway?"

"The internet."

"Not everything on the internet is true."

"Does that include your new girlfriend?"

"She's not my girlfriend."

"Are we really going to do this? After all this time?" I purse my lips.

"You're right. Well, she's what you would consider a girlfriend."

"I don't know what that means. Just admit that y'all are together."

"I can't. Not to you." He reaches for my hand. We walk hand and hand through the casino and out the front door. We're silent as we wait for his car.

"Where to?" he asks, opening the passenger door for me.

"Your place."

"For real?" Shane slams the door and runs to the driver's side.

I burst into laughter. "Wait a minute, cowpoke. I just want to see it. I heard you bought a $5,000,000 house. I've never seen one before."

"How did you hear that?"

"The internet."

"Is anything private these days?"

"No." I pause. "I wasn't going to say anything but let me just say this."

"What did I do now?"

"I put you on to Louboutins. How the fuck are you going to be out here lacing some other chick down in red bottoms?"

Shane rubs his neck. "You right. You right. But can we not talk about her?"

"It's okay. I'm just fucking with you. I'm truly happy for you. I'm happy for the two of you. She can have you and all your madness."

"Wow!" Shane nods his head. I can tell his ego is slightly bruised. He turns the music up a bit and raps along. When the song ends, he turns the volume back down. "I think I'm going to take you back to the hotel. My house is really romantic. It's too late at night and I don't want you doing anything you'll regret in the morning."

"I'm good. Trust."

"My house was built to be a panty dropper."

"Oh, don't you worry. I have no interest in going there. The last thing I want is to have an amazing night with you and then have to fly back home in a few days and start crying for two years all over again. If I can't have you, then I'm good."

"But you can."

"No, I don't want you for one night. I'm not going back to that. You have someone and you should honor that."

"I'm saying, the D is here if you want it."

"I'll pass but thanks for the offer."

"How long has it been?"

"I haven't been with anyone else."

"For real?"

I don't respond.

"My bad. I just never met anyone who would not be with anyone else."

"It's a choice."

"I'm definitely taking you back to the hotel. I can't have that guilt on my hands." Shane makes an abrupt U-turn at the intersection and takes an exit onto the highway. "I'll come get you in the morning. You can come visit in the daytime. It's safer that way."

"You're mighty confident."

"I am. I know you."

"And I know you."

"So you know I get my way when I really want something."

I don't respond again because I know he's right. That's one bet I'm not trying to lose tonight. "You are a hot mess." I nudge his shoulder. "I'm going to leave that alone."

"So, why did you come?"

"Come here? To visit you?"

"Yeah."

"Honestly. Hmm. Well, you invited me. And. . . I wanted to see you again. I won't lie about that. I felt like we had some unfinished business."

"We'll always have unfinished business." Shane turns the music back up. He sings along and drums his steering wheel. I can see he's in his feelings.

We arrive at the hotel and he jumps out. "I'll walk you to your room. I wouldn't want you to be kidnapped while you are out here visiting me. I need to get you home in one piece."

"I appreciate it."

He reaches for my hand and we stroll through the courtyard. We take the longest path to my room. When we finally reach my door, Shane leans down to hug me. "I thought of you every day." His hand touches my thigh. "I swear. I should have bet on us." He kisses me on my cheek and walks away. "I'll see you tomorrow. Sleep well."

I stand speechless and watch him walk down the long hall and around the corner. As soon as he's out of sight, I burst into my room and begin to wail. I drop my purse and kick my shoes off at the door, run into the room and flop on the bed. Kicking and screaming the entire time, I reminisce about the old days with Shane and I just want to crumble.

When I'm able, I search the bed for my phone and text him.

`I love you`

He responds immediately.

`I'll love you always`

"Aghhhhhhhhhhh!" I scream, sob, and dial Jen. "Oh my GOD!" I scream at the top of my lungs.

"Bryn, are you okay?" Jen sounds panicked.

"No!!!!" I cry.

"Oh my God, what happened? Are you safe? Where's Shane?"

"He. . . just. . . dropped. . . me. . . off." I sound like a kid that just got a beating and their parents start asking questions.

"Soooo, you are okay. Just not. . ."

"I love him." Tears stream down my face.

"I know you do. I know you do. Lord knows I know you do. If no one knows, rest assured, I do. I swear I do."

"But we can't be together!"

"Lord knows, I know that too."

"We had this amazing night." I stop to blow my nose. "I mean, it started off kind of rocky but then it was like. . . he was so honest. It was so refreshing!" I scream.

"What did he say?"

"Enough. But I'm happy!" I cry.

"Awww."

"I text him telling him that I love him."

"I'm sorry."

"He replied he'll love me always."

"My heart is breaking for you, Bryn."

"I know!" I fall back onto the bed crying and wailing. "Why,

Lord?"

"You got to get it out. You've been holding this in. I've been anticipating this for a long time."

Jen listens to me cry it out and when my tears finally dry up, I'm left with a splitting headache.

"Okay, I'm going to get into the shower. One more day to go." I hang up and undress in the master bedroom and walk naked into the bathroom and damn near scare myself. My face is black with running mascara and my hair is one big poofball. I turn on the hot water and stand underneath it and release some more, letting my tears run down the drain.

36

THESE THREE WORDS

Shane picks me up at dusk. He chooses to wait in the truck and calls for me to come down instead of walking up to my room. Maybe last night was a bit much for him. Hell, it was definitely too much for me. Now that I'm all cried out, I feel like a million bucks. It was one of those cathartic cries. I didn't realize I was still holding so much in. I'll have to let my therapist know that I've finally released. So tonight, I'm not going to talk about the past. Now, it's all about the future. I just want our last night together to be filled with fun. I even forgo the dress I planned on wearing and dress casual, with some skinny jeans, a cute top, and a pair of flat sandals.

"Hey!" I say, struggling to climb into his truck.

"You are so short." He laughs.

"I'm wearing flats tonight."

"I see. How was your day?"

"It was good. I tried to go outside for a walk. I made it halfway around a pond and thought I was going to die. This sun is treacherous." I yank the door shut.

Shane turns his music up. "Did you eat?"

"I did. I wasn't sure what the plans were today, so I ordered an early dinner to the room. I can always do dessert later."

Shane nods.

"Where are we off to?"

"You said you wanted to see my place, right?"

"Oh yeah! I get a grand tour? Did you clean all your girlfriend's stuff out?" Almost immediately I regret saying that out loud.

Shane shakes his head. "Nah, she don't live with me."

"Ha, ha! I thought she wasn't your girlfriend." I can tell he's not in a playful mood so I kind of leave it there. I pull down the visor and look in the mirror to fix my hair and apply more lip gloss. "Well, I can't wait to see your home."

Shane pulls into his five-car garage, and the first thing I notice is a rack of women's clothing. I bite my lip, say nothing, and follow him inside.

We start in his chef's kitchen and step down into a grand room with floor-to-ceiling windows. "This view is amazing. Oh, my goodness, the sun is setting, perfect timing."

"You should see it from upstairs." We skip the rest of the rooms and I follow Shane up a spiral staircase to the second floor and out onto a balcony, which is right off of his bedroom.

"This view is insane!" I scream. "I could sit and watch this every day and never get tired of it."

"It's alright," he jokes.

"You're right. This is romantic!" *Definitely a panty dropper.* As the sun continues its descent, the sky turns from a bluish purple to various shades of pink.

"I was thinking about last night." Shane leans on the balcony next to me.

"What about it? I said so much." I laugh.

"You still love me after what I've done?"

"Shane, I love hard. And I loved you deeply, so that will never cease. I'm free because I've forgiven you. Therefore, I can love you and not be with you."

"Your love always scared me. It was like, no matter what, you loved me. There wasn't any kind of agenda or ulterior motive." Shane looks up. "I never deserved you." He wipes his face with both hands. "I can't seem to forgive myself." He lowers his eyes to the floor. He is the complete opposite of the happy-go-lucky guy I first saw when we reunited. I don't know if it's because he knows I'm about to leave, or if this entire weekend has just opened up an old wound.

"Maybe that's why the scales were unbalanced. You could never give me your whole heart."

"How can I give you something I don't have?" He lays his hand on his chest. "My heart is fucked up."

I'm drawn to comfort him, but I pull my phone out to capture a picture instead. We both know how easy it is for us to go there and how hard it is to pull away. The panoramic views of the sunset from his bedroom don't help one bit. I fight to keep my mind focused.

After snapping a few photos, and the sun makes its final descent behind the mountain, I turn to him. "Where your treasure is, there will your heart be also. Look to God for healing your heart. And pray that HE can help you forgive yourself. There is freedom in forgiveness. I pray that you find it." I pat his chest and return to looking out at the mountain range. "But for the record, I must say, this view would never get old. It's magnificent. I would sit right here every night waiting for the sun to set." I laugh.

"I told you."

"Your home is absolutely beautiful. You should be proud." I pull open the floor-to-ceiling glass door and enter his bedroom.

"Thanks. I was debating if I was going to bring you. This is my private sanctuary. I come here to get away from all the noise. The only people allowed over here is my moms and my kids."

"Not your new girlfriend?" I tease. I can't help myself.

"Nope."

"So I'm special?"

"Yeah." He rubs his neck.

I laugh in his face. "Yeah, right. You lie!" I look at his bed. "That's why your sheets are all messy now. Y'all was getting it in last night, weren't you?"

Shane dismisses me. "What do I got to lie for? Look." He walks towards the bathroom and points to his right. "You see the closet is empty."

"I saw a rack of women's dresses when we pulled into the driveway."

"That's wardrobe for videos. Me and the crew are working on some new music."

"Yeah, okay. You were probably cleaning up like a crazy person. That's why you were late picking me up." I lean against his back, laughing.

"Ha ha. Very funny." Shane pulls away. "Want to watch a movie?" He turns on the TV mounted over his fireplace. "Then again, we should go into the theater. I wouldn't want you to get weak or do anything you might regret." Shane adjusts his dick in his basketball shorts, moving it from left to right. It's so unnecessary. As if I forgot he's built like a stallion.

"You are so full of yourself."

"I just know you ain't had none in a while, that's all." He strokes his chin.

"Remember, it's by choice. Finding dick is easy."

"Yeah, yeah. I don't want to hear about you finding any dick. I was only offering mine."

"If that's all you're offering, I'll pass."

"You sure about that? It's your last chance." Shane flashes a devilish smile.

"Boy, bye. Let's go to the theater." I push him in the chest.

He laughs and waves me to follow him into his theater room and motions for me to have a seat. I sit in one of his plush leather theater seats next to what I can tell is his spot. He flips the heat and massage button on my chair.

"Fancy."

He laughs and grabs his tablet and a blanket and gets comfortable. He proceeds to scroll through a ton of movies and lands on *Aladdin*. He turns to smile at me. "Yeah?"

"Sure, why not. It's our last night together. Let's make it a memorable one."

"Let's do it." He hits the button, the lights go low, and the music begins.

I wake up with my head resting on Shane's shoulder and the credits rolling on the screen. I'm not surprised that I fell asleep considering I pretty much didn't sleep last night.

Shane strokes my head. "Want to get a birthday drink?"

"Sure."

"There's this spot I want to take you to. Let me change real quick."

I take his hand and he helps me up. I wait for him in his kitchen. He returns dressed in a collar shirt and long pants and his infamous baseball cap pulled down low and to the side. We exit out a different door than the one we came in. He shows me his collection of cars and decides to drive a familiar one. His shiny black Range. "Remember this one?"

"How could I forget?" When he opens the door for me, I'm instantly taken back to 2008 when he first picked Jen and me up from my house to go to the club. He sang TGS's hit *Girl You Know You Want This* the entire way to D.C. I have a feeling it's going to be another long night filled with tears. I've become such a softy. The hard cast I placed around my heart is gone.

"We did it in here, didn't we?" He puffs out his chest.

"No, that was in the back of your Hummer."

"You right. Those were the good ol' days. It was real tight back there."

"You still have that one?"

"Nope, it's Carice's now."

"Yikes." I manage to keep a straight face but I'm dying laughing on the inside. I clear my throat to keep from choking.

"Change the subject."

As we ride to our destination, a full moon shines brightly. I stare out the window and take in all of the picturesque Arizona views. We take the windy road up the mountain and pull up into the valet at the Phoenician. "You're going to love it here." We take the elevators to the top floor to J&G Steakhouse.

Shane offers me his arm as we exit the elevator into the restaurant and leads me outside onto the balcony. We can see all of downtown. It's spectacular. Then I hear this big boom. Fireworks light up the sky. "I arranged that, you know."

"Are you serious?"

"Yes, what's better than fireworks for your birthday?"

My mouth drops open.

"Just kidding, they do this every now and again for special occasions. You can close your mouth now."

"I was about to say." I nudge him.

"Would you have given me some if I did?"

"I'm ignoring you. Stop offering me your dick. I just might take it and leave a stack of ones on the nightstand." I laugh.

"That's what I'm hoping for."

I roll my eyes. "You are so silly." We enjoy the fireworks then take a seat at one of the tables adjacent to the fire pits.

Our waitress comes over and asks for our drink order. "A bottle of your best Champagne, please."

"Celebrating tonight?"

"It's her birthday!"

"Happy birthday!" she says.

"Thank you."

"My pleasure, I'll bring one of our favorites."

Shane thanks the waitress and just stares across the table at me. We sit and enjoy the atmosphere. It's lovely. I can't believe this is Shane's new home. "Do you like it here?" I ask, breaking the silence.

"I do. I've adjusted."

"I know they're going to miss you in Baltimore. I don't think the Nighthawks will ever be the same without you.

"That chapter is closed. The Cardinals are my new family."

"I thought you'd retire a Nighthawk."

Shane takes a deep breath. "Yeah, me too. But all great things must come to an end."

"Yeah, just like us." It slips from my lips.

"Whoa, I wasn't ready for that. Can I have a drink before we start that?" Shane clears his throat.

"I don't know why we could never seem to get it right." I look up at the stars. "I mean, how do you not call me? It's been two years. I mean, we were friends before anything."

"For real? I was angry. Confused, really. I made this huge life-changing sacrifice and that shit was supposed to work. I was faithful. I even agreed to counseling in the beginning. I did my part and the marriage just fucking burned to the ground. So I was like, fuck it. I turned to the first thing that came my way. Whether that was the best thing to do. . ." Shane shrugs, tightening his lips. "Whether she was good for me or not, it didn't matter."

"She was there."

He nods yes. "She was there."

Our waitress returns with a bottle of Champagne on ice and our glasses. I take out my phone to get a picture when she opens the bottle. Without making a mess, she pours our glasses.

I take a sip. "As long as you're happy."

"I always choose the wrong girl. I don't know what is wrong with me. For real though, I couldn't face you." Shane nods in silence. "I got a lot of contracts with a lot of people. I didn't know if I was coming or going. I couldn't bring that type of instability to you. That's why I just felt it was best to keep my distance."

"I understand, but it's me. Not any random chick."

"Didn't think you'd forgiven me."

"Not only have I forgiven you, since then, I've wished you nothing short of complete happiness." My eyes start to tear up. I stare off into the distance and get lost in the twinkling lights. "I think I held on for so long because I thought we had forever."

"I know, so did I." Shane's eyes drop down to the table. "You were always too good for me. I live every day with regrets." He turns to me with teary eyes. "I didn't marry the woman I loved the most."

I exhale, not expecting to hear that, and blink my eyes dry. "Whelp, know the plays, or get sidelined." I force a laugh hoping to bring levity.

"What?"

"Know the plays or get sidelined. I should have paid attention more and perhaps I could have seen it coming and avoided it altogether."

"I disagree. Even I was blindsided."

I shrug my shoulders. "I don't know. I saw it coming from the beginning, I just didn't want to believe it." I laugh, shaking my head. "But I see clearly now, that's for sure. My days of being sidelined are over." I take another sip. "Friends, again?"

"Look at us. We can never be friends. We will always have too much between us for that to work. Honestly, I fantasized about being with you before you arrived. It took everything in me not to try to undress you as soon as you opened the door the first night. We got a connection that goes beyond friendship. We could never 'just be friends'. And we could never 'just have sex'. You don't want that, I don't, and for real, I ain't trying to hurt you again." Shane shrugs his shoulders. "If we get close, we going to fuck. And I'm in a fucked-up situation. Shit, I'm still a married man."

"I hear you and I can respect that."

"I'm already not sleeping at night." Shane shakes his head.

"Thank you for this weekend. We needed to have these conversations. Besides, I'm glad I got the chance to see you face to face again." I raise my glass. "To us in another lifetime." I smile and we clink glasses as I blink back tears.

"Definitely next lifetime." Shane pauses and looks up at the stars in the sky. It's a full moon and it's brilliant.

Our waitress returns, placing in front of me a chocolate lava cake with a lit candle and 'happy birthday' written in icing.

"It's lovely, thank you." I wipe away a tear that's escaped.

The waitress smiles, says happy birthday again, and briskly walks away.

Shane starts to sing happy birthday. Offbeat and off key and I don't care, it's music to my ears. "Make a wish," he says.

I close my eyes and think about how perfect the night is. How amazing this weekend has been. How I'm filled with complete joy. Shane and I once shared something so beautiful and I will never ever forget it. We were in each other's lives when we needed each other the most. Right now, today, in this moment, I am happy and finally at peace with letting him go. My heart races as I squeeze my eyes tight and wish for closure. In my mind, I embrace Shane, wrap around him an abundance of love, cut the ties that bind, and release him. I blow out my candle and when I open my eyes, Shane stares back tearfully.

"I'm sorry, Bryn."

I finally hear those three words I've longed for.

Thank you! Your support is greatly appreciated.

If you enjoyed Sidelined: The Contract, the third installment of the Sidelined Series, please consider writing a review on **Amazon** or **Goodreads**. It really does make a difference.

Visit www.biancawilliamsbooks.com to join our email list for updates regarding upcoming projects.

INSPIRED BY TRUE EVENTS

BIANCA WILLIAMS

KNOW THE PLAYS, OR
GET SIDELINED.

sidelined

(v) cause (a player) to be unable to play on a team or in a game.

the draft

1

THE PLAY

As soon as he reaches for the pen, my stomach starts to churn. *Oh Lord.* I take a deep breath. Vomiting on the table would not only be a terrible first impression, but a long-lasting one. Still, my leg rocks, my heart races, and my eyes are wet with anticipation. And while countless scenarios of me losing consciousness play out in my mind, I fight to stay alert with a forced smile throughout the execution.

"There." He tosses the ballpoint onto the mahogany table, and when he stands, almost hits his head on the wrought-iron chandelier. I try not to laugh but he's clumsy *and* freakishly large. According to Wikipedia, the infamous Shane Smith is six-foot five and weighs two hundred sixty pounds. The day Jen, my best friend and event planner extraordinaire, bragged about pitching him, I Googled the NFL superstar. Initially, I shrugged it off as another one of her pipe dreams, yet here we are two weeks later in her dining room and he's signing her contract.

"I guess I owe you a deposit." He digs into the front pocket of his oversized jeans and whips out a wad of crisp $100 bills. After placing the stack of cash on the newly signed agreement, he reaches into his other pocket. "Three tickets to tonight's game."

"Really?" Jen, wide-eyed and flashing all thirty-two teeth, takes them from him.

"Bryn, there's one for you and your daughter."

"Wow!" I place my hand on my heart as a gesture of appreciation but also to make sure it's still beating. "That's so thoughtful of you."

He tries to keep from blushing. "It's cool. I mean. You know." He glances sideways.

Awww. I smile. *He's nervous.* I think it's kinda cute.

"I'm saying." He squares his shoulders and looks me in the eye. "I want you to come see me play tonight."

I stare at him confused.

"Yeah," he says, grinning and sizing me up.

"Actually." I turn to Jen for help. "I think we have work to do."

"Do we?" questions Jen, obviously ignoring my plea.

"Don't tell me y'all are *all* business? What's the pleasure in that?" He rubs his left arm, which I can't help but notice is dark, muscular, and littered with tattoos, and then flexes it.

Have mercy.

"Come on. It will be fun." He purses his lips then licks them like LL Cool J. "I guarantee it."

I give up. "Excuse me." I leave them and grab a bottle of water from the pantry. I can't drink it fast enough.

Jen laughs at my reaction.

Shane blushes.

"Alright ladies. I should go. But I really hope you make it out. I'll be looking for you in my section." He tugs on the brim of his hat, hikes up his pants, and initiates a fist bump.

"Can't wait!" Jen shoots me a smile before walking him out.

"Jen!" I cry as she locks the door. Then I realize he's probably still within earshot. I run to the window and am relieved to see that he's entering his truck.

"Preparation plus opportunity equals success!" She spins in her doorway, snaps her fingers, and starts dancing the two-step. "We just landed a freaking whale!"

"I think I'm sick." I hold my stomach and keel over onto the floor. "I don't know. Do you think we can really do this?"

"There's only one way to find out," she giggles. "By the way, nervous Nelly, you need to get some professional help for that." She points at me sprawled on her new shag rug.

"Whatever. I have good reason to be anxious. Did you see the show he just put on?"

"I didn't want to interrupt." Jen raises her eyebrows. "I saw that LL lip action he was giving you."

"Oh my God!" I laugh, covering my eyes. "I can't believe this!"

"Believe it!"

"Well, we gotta watch him." I point to the door even though he's long gone.

"It was harmless flirting." She shrugs her shoulders. "I saw your face as soon as he did it. You looked a bit pale. But who cares? It doesn't matter." She turns and walks away. "Unless you like him."

"God no!" I shout. "He's an athlete. Besides, I told you that I Googled him."

"Then why haven't you stopped smiling?"

"What do you mean? We just signed our dream client!" I dust myself off, rise from the floor, and join her in the dining room. "That's why I'm still smiling. I assure you."

"Umm hmm." Jen rolls her eyes and grabs the stack of hundreds from the table. "You say you're not interested, but clearly he is. I mean the man's not blind. I fully expected him to be attracted to you. You're short with big boobs and long hair. What dude isn't? I really don't want to talk about this. Thanks."

"Fine, but what about the 'no fraternizing with clients' rule? I'm just saying."

"Never mind that. We've got six weeks. I'm going to need you to get your mind right." Jen splits the stack of bills and hands me half. "Now go get dressed."

"We're going?" My eyes widen.

"Yes!" she shouts. "And *this*, my dearest friend, is just the beginning."

For some strange reason, I have a feeling she's right.

At seven o'clock we head downtown to M&T Bank stadium, home of the Baltimore Nighthawks. It's located in a sketchy part of the city. Surrounded by warehouses and abandoned buildings, it's the perfect backdrop for a mugging. To make matters worse, the distant parking is scarce, expensive, and frequented by dancing junkies begging for cash. I know this because I've been to a few Nighthawks games (mostly by winning office draws for corporate seats).

They were fun, but none of them measure up to tonight's.

The skies are clear and the air is crisp, perfect for Thursday Night Football. It's a sold-out televised game and, thanks to Shane, we've got premium parking *and* our front row seats are on the 50-yard line.

The stadium is on fire. All the fans, dressed in every combination of Nighthawks colors—blue, black, and white—are on their feet. Drunken men dressed as birds complete with face paint, beaks, and blue spray-painted spiked hair. Dancing women in pink jerseys and cobalt-blue tinsel wigs. A row of teens with nude chests bearing the letters N-I-G-H-T-H-A-W-K-S, which when I look again, reads NIGHTHWAKS.

I excuse myself as we squeeze past cheering fans to our three empty seats. Leaning on the railing in front of them is a tall man. He's attractive and extremely well groomed (I think even his sweat pants are professionally pressed).

"Bryn." He grabs my hand. "I finally get to meet you. I'm Terry, Shane's assistant."

"Hello." I free myself from his grip. "This is Bailey." I pat my daughter on the head. "And there's Jen."

"Hi Bailey, how old are you?"

"Eight!"

"You are so beautiful. Has anyone ever told you that you look like your mom?"

"Yup," says Bailey, plopping into her seat. In fact, she hears it all the time. She really is a mini version of me with her naturally sun-kissed skin, long dark wavy hair, and bright round eyes.

Terry looks over my head at Jen. "Hello Jen, I'm Terry. Can I get y'all anything? Drinks? Candy? Shane wants me to make sure y'all are good before the game starts."

"I'm fine Terry, thank you." I wave and take my seat.

"Alright. I'm going to be over there." He scoots by us into the center aisle and points to the next section over. "If you need me, just wave and I'll come right over."

When I look in the direction he's pointing there's a girl with red hair staring back at me.

"Mom! Mom!" shouts Bailey, getting my attention. "There's Shane!" She points to the center of the field at the coin toss. "It's game time."

It's the battle of the beltways and it's not until the referee gives the two-minute warning that I realize we've been on our feet, cheering, all four quarters.

'WILL YOU PROTECT THIS HOUSE?' blares from the stadium's speakers as the Nighthawks defense takes the field.

"I WILL! I WILL!" roars the crowd in unison. Fireworks shoot into the sky. The marching band beat their drums in preparation for battle, as the defense line up to execute their infamous blitz.

"DE-FENSE!" I wail, pounding on my plastic seat. I bang and bang until the ball snaps, soars between the legs of the quarterback, and bounces freely onto the field behind him. "Oh shit!"

"Mom," whines Bailey.

"Sorry. Quarter in the swear jar."

Pure chaos erupts all around us, in the stands and on the field. Referees sprint from every direction towards a massive pile that's forming. Each time a player is tugged from the stack, another one jumps in. The Nighthawks' head coach, now red in the face, rips off his headset and charges onto the field.

Flags are flying everywhere. Three of our guys and two of theirs are throwing blows and wrestling for the football. Referees are shouting and trying to pull them apart. When they finally separate, the Pro Bowl linebacker and our newest client, Shane Smith, surfaces with the football secured in his arms. Fans go insane as he dances to *Got Money* by Lil Wayne playing on the loudspeakers.

"Girl, what an ending." My voice is hoarse from screaming.

"Bryn. This is freaking *awesome!*" We start high-fiving each other and the college students, reeking of Natty Bohs, jump around wildly in the seats behind us. When the music stops, Shane runs towards us with the ball raised high above his head and tosses it to Bailey.

I cover my mouth in shock. And just when I think it can't get any better, the cameraman finds my baby, bouncing and proudly hugging the ball. Enjoying her few seconds of fame, she keeps jumping and screaming as the Nighthawks offense take a knee and secure another win for the city of Baltimore.

Bailey is beside herself. Giggly, silly, and full of joy.

"Do you know Shane Smith?" An excited fan taps her on the shoulder.

Jen knocks his hand away. "Excuse me, do not touch her."

Nighthawks fans are known to be slightly insane so I grab my jacket and motion for Bailey to exit in the direction we came in. On our way up the stairway I hear my name being called.

"Come on!" It's Terry, waving us over with his lanky arms. "Follow me. Shane wants y'all to wait for him."

Bailey grabs my hand as we follow Terry across the stadium through a sea of people to double glass doors flanked by security guards. "They're with me," says Terry to the older one who shamelessly undresses me with his eyes. *Yuck*. I'm used to second glances and flirtatious looks, but this is blatant gawking. I cross through the doorway, pulling Bailey to the opposite side and avoiding Mr. Creeper McCreepy.

Inside what appears to be the Nighthawks' family waiting area, I overhear praises to sons, cousins, and brothers for their performance on the field, and watch them embrace their beloved Nighthawk as they exit from an elevator. Bailey's face lights up as the famous players pass her, but being in here makes me realize that they are just people with ordinary families like us.

Everyone *appears* normal until a six-foot, pale-skinned, pregnant girl with fire-engine-red pixie-cut hair and a toddler on her hip flings the lobby doors open. She huffs, switches the little girl to her other hip, and storms towards the elevators, where Shane finally emerges.

Shane swaggers out of the elevator dressed in a mousy-brown three-piece suit, complete with a knee-length jacket (like the preachers on Sunday's Best). Meanwhile, the girl—his wife? girlfriend? or just baby mama?—catches up with him. She strokes his arm and tries to steal a kiss. Shane brushes her off and lifts the little girl from her arms.

"Where they at?" He scans the crowd with a frown and finally locks eyes on Jen. "Go home and get dressed. We are celebrating tonight. Y'all need to see how I like to party."

2

<u>MISS INDEPENDENT</u>

Jen races to Betsy, the silver Honda Accord I've had since college, cackling like a silly schoolgirl. She's not ashamed of her behavior at all. "What is wrong with you? We *are* going tonight."

"Seriously? It's a school night."

"Suck it up and take one for the team." She signals for me to hurry and unlock the door.

"I—"

"I don't want to hear it. I'm cashing in that IOU for my services as Bailey's chauffeur last summer."

"Shame on you. You're her godmother." I unlock the doors and we all hop in.

"Call it what you want. Let's go." She loudly claps her hands.

"I secretly hate you, you know?"

I call my mom and convince her to watch Bailey as I race home. Breaking the speed limit the entire way, we arrive safely at our duplex in thirty minutes, which leaves us fifteen to get ready.

"What are you wearing?" Jen runs across the lawn to her front door. "I'm wearing a dress."

"Not sure yet. I can't think." *If it were left up to me, I'd be in jeans.* I nudge Bailey to wake up. She's curled up with her arms locked around that ball. "Let me get her settled and I'll call you." I tap Bailey a few times, calling her name, but she's out cold. I climb in the back seat, pull her out, and struggle to carry her all the way to my front steps, where she conveniently awakens.

"Do you have to go?" Bailey pouts and bats her long lashes.

"I don't. But I think I should. I'll tell you what, come and help me pick out a dress."

She perks up as I unlock the door.

I shower, moisturize, and apply my make-up at top speed. Next, we pick out a champagne-colored, BCBGMAXAZRIA dress with matching five-inch, nude, peep-toe Dior pumps I snagged half-off at a sample sale. They match perfectly. Standing in front of the mirror, I let my hair down and comb it with my fingers until it falls into place, reaching the small of my back. *Hmmm, not bad for twenty-eight.*

I check the time again and see I'm right on schedule. I apply another layer of mascara and my doorbell rings. I drop the tube on the bathroom counter and scurry over to my bed. "You can sleep in here tonight." I give Bailey a kiss on the forehead and grab my cell from the nightstand to call Jen.

"Please tell me you're ready?" I say as soon as she answers.

"I know how to tell time," she fusses.

"If you say so," I say, out of breath from hurrying down the stairs. I disconnect the call and open the front door. To my pleasant surprise, my mother arrives at the same time as Terry.

"Hey hey, hey," she says in her best Dwayne-from-*What's-Happening* voice. She bops through the doorway and hands me her favorite oversized knockoff Louis Vuitton handbag to put away for her. "You look gorgeous." She gives me a kiss on the cheek.

"Terry, this is my mother, Ms. Joan, and Mom—"

"I know, we already met. Where's Jenny Jen? I want her to see my latest find." She points to her over-the-knee leopard-print boots.

I stare with raised brows.

"They're my September issue. Just came in the mail today. I gotta get you on, *girl*."

Lately, my mother, a freckle-faced debutante from Long Island, has been acting as if she's from the hoods of Baltimore. I'm not sure why. For as long as I can remember, my younger sister and I were constantly reminded about how to act like proper ladies.

"You look incredible." Terry admires my dress before reaching for an embrace.

"Thanks." I give him a side-hug.

"Y'all ready? Because Shane is waiting in the truck."

"I believe so." I bang on the adjoining wall of our duplex. This is Jen's last warning before we walk out the front door.

When Terry and I get outside, Jen appears on my doorstep with her pashmina dragging on the ground. "Why must you always do that?" She shoots me an annoyed look and discreetly adjusts her Spanx. "You look good though." She points to my shoes. "Great choice." Then she looks through the screen door. "Hi, Ms. Joan." She waves, still shimmying in her dress.

"Alright, Ms. Thang," my mother answers. "How you doin'?" she says, impersonating Wendy Williams.

Embarrassed by my mother's behavior, I quickly shut the door. Jen struggles to hold in her laughter. She knows I want to shrivel, but the feeling dissipates as I approach Shane's shining black Range Rover parked in my driveway.

Shane gives Terry an irritated look as he hops into the driver's seat. "What took y'all so long?" He turns to the back seat to eye the two of us. "I bet Jen wasn't ready." The spotlight is on her. "Were you?"

"I was ready!" she shouts back.

He gives her a look of surprise and turns his attention to his two cell phones that are simultaneously sending alerts. He flicks through both and then grabs his iPod. "So what's up? Y'all find my venue yet?"

I give Jen a pissed look.

"Yes. We have a walk-through tomorrow afternoon."

"Bet." Shane starts thumbing through his iPod. "Did y'all listen to TGS's new track yet?" Without waiting for a reply, he pushes play and after a few notes, starts belting out the lyrics, "Girl, you know you want this."

Shane's so-called dancing and spontaneous outbursts continue during our ride to D.C. He finds it amusing to repeatedly disrupt the conversation Jen and I are having about his group's album release party. His silly behavior continues until we pull up to the valet in front of the nightclub an hour later.

Shane's the first to jump out and get the doors for us. He motions for Jen and me to walk in front of him. I take the lead and stop at the security booth. A hostess is waiting for us and takes us inside to a reserved area sectioned off by red velvet stanchions.

The space is small but decorated beautifully with velvet sofas, leather benches, and chandeliers. Splashes of amber up-lights against the fuchsia walls create an intimate glow. I take a mental note of the decor and sit on a purple loveseat. Jen scoots me to its edge to make room for Shane, and Terry sits on a gold tufted ottoman bench across from us.

Almost immediately, a young blonde hostess wearing a black bustier, booty shorts, and fishnet stockings sashays up to Shane and hands him a menu. He checks out her ass as she sets our table. Eventually, he realizes we're watching him.

"My bad," he chuckles. "What would y'all like to drink?" He leans in. "If you don't mind, I want y'all to try my favorite. It's pink and I want lots of this at my party—excuse me," he clears his throat and adjusts his collar, "my event." He places an order for a few bottles.

Terry orders a Sprite.

When our waitress returns, other girls parading in similar sexy black attire, each carrying a bottle with lit sparklers attached, follow her lead. They form a semi-circle and seductively dance with the bottles held high until the sparklers burn out. Then she opens a bottle of Nuvo and pours the first round of drinks.

Shane turns to Jen and me. "Cheers." He raises his glass. "To new partnerships."

"Cheers!" Terry joins in last minute with his soda.

"Now," he continues, "I signed with y'all cause y'all business minded. People always trying to get me to do stuff, but I can see that y'all are the real thing. With that said, the Squad will be here in a few weeks when they get out of the studio." He finishes his drink in a huge gulp. "Yeah, I can't wait for this event. It's going to be hot! Baltimore's not used to anything like this."

Jen chats with Shane while I people watch. The club is packed, and the DJ has the party jumping. Gradually, a variety of women make their way over and surround our section. I can only assume they're here waiting to speak with Shane since they're treating Terry like he's invisible. I'm slightly bored by it all until the DJ starts playing my song, *Miss Independent* by Ne-Yo. *Perfect timing.*

I hop up and tip-toe over to an open space in our little sectioned off area. "Miss In-de-pen-dent," I sing, dancing the two-step. Out of the corner of my eye, I notice Terry making his way over to me. He's awkwardly boogying to the beat and getting closer and closer to me. *And stop right there.* "Hey Terry." I wave to him innocently, trying to play it down.

"You know what? I was talking to Shane and we think you're a bad chick. And we bring you to D.C. and you are still the baddest chick in here. When I say bad, I don't just mean your body." He eyes me, cringing and biting his knuckles. "Girl, damn. What I'm trying to say is that you've just *got it*."

I smile awkwardly, not knowing how to respond, but at the same time thankful to the person who created shape-wear.

"You want to dance?" He opens his arms wide.

I hold my hands up in front of me. "Thanks, but I'm going to rest my feet for a little bit." I leave Terry and head back to the table to refill my champagne flute.

"You like it, don't you?" Shane's beaming, proud of his drink recommendation.

"I do. I really like it." I give him a friendly smile.

"I'll have some of that!" a woman shouts over the music. She shoves a glass in front of my face. "How are you?" She positions her flute for me to begin pouring.

I hand her the bottle instead.

"I hear you're working for Shane. How long have you known him?" she asks in a nasty tone.

I instantly become defensive. "Actually, we just met a few weeks ago." I return lots of attitude. "And yes, you're correct. We're planning the event for his group, The Gentleman's Squad."

"That's Jen?" She points and flicks her long, obviously fake, golden tresses towards Jen.

"Correct again." I smile and end our little chat. I can tell she wants more information, but instead she bites her tongue and scoots onto the sofa on the other side of Shane.

Good ol' Terry seizes the moment and finds his way back to me. "What did she say?" He laughs wholeheartedly. "That's his girl, you know?"

"That's *not* the same girl I saw earlier at the game, the red hair, piercings, and all."

"No." He leans in close and whispers, "That was Carice, his baby mama. That, over there, is his girl. Well at least one of them. Man, he can't go anywhere in D.C. without her knowing about it." Terry holds his stomach and tries to contain his laughter. "She's probably asking who you are because she knows that you're his type."

Shane's 'girl' glances over at me but I don't pay her any attention. If I felt so inclined, I would have told her I didn't want his ass and the only reason I was here, and *not* in my bed, was because he was paying me thousands of dollars.

I'm kinda over it all and I guess Shane can see it on my face. He checks his watch and signals to Terry that he's ready to go.

Terry is kind enough to leave ahead of us and retrieve the truck from valet, sparing Jen and me the cold wait outside. I'm so happy I could kiss him, but I wouldn't want to give him the wrong idea. I give him a brief pat on the shoulder instead. "Thanks Terry."

"You're welcome, B!" he replies, puffing out his chest at the attention.

I lean back onto the warm leather seat, cuddling my faux-fur wrap, when Jen grabs my shoulder and whispers, "Shane says Terry really likes you."

"You don't say." I cover my mouth to hold in the laughter.

"Wait, let me finish." She shields her mouth and tries to whisper in my ear. "I told Shane that you don't date the man standing next to the man. I told him that you only date alpha males." She giggles loudly into my ear. "He said, 'Like me?' I said, 'Yes! Like you!' I could tell he got excited." She falls around the back seat laughing hysterically.

"What's so funny?" barks Shane.

"Oh, nothing," replies Jen.

"Stop this." I hit her. "You better not have given *him* any hope." I laugh so hard my nose starts to run and I'm fresh out of tissue. I tap Shane on the shoulder. "Do you have any napkins?" I ask, slightly embarrassed.

He checks in his glove box and then the center console. "Nah." He looks out the window. "Terry, pull over." He points to a fast food drive-through.

Shane jumps out and knocks on the window. The lights are out. Regardless, he taps again. An older heavyset woman wearing a red headscarf appears behind the glass, but doesn't acknowledge him. He taps harder this time, getting her full attention, and points to a pile of napkins leaning against the glass.

She shakes her head no.

"Please," begs Shane, clasping his hands.

She stands motionless for a moment, looks left and right, and then cracks the window, handing a few napkins through. The next moment, Shane peels off three $100 bills. We hear the window fly back open.

"Did you see that? Did you see what just happened?" Jen, in disbelief, pinches my arm.

"Yeeeeessssssss." I try not to show any reaction.

"Here you go." Shane hands me the napkins before pulling his door shut.

"Thank you very much." I attempt to blow my nose as silently as possible.

"Girl!" Jen nudges me on the shoulder. "Those are some $300 napkins you're blowing your nose with!"

3

OFFICE SPACE

On my eighteenth birthday, I traveled to Trinidad for Carnival, and from Saturday morning until Ash Wednesday, participated in lots of underage drinking. I partied constantly, and after four days without sleep, even a single thought was painful. My head throbbed, my eyes burned, and my entire body ached. This morning, ten years later and after only two hours of sleep, I feel similar.

Wincing with every step, I trek down the hall of offices towards my desk, hidden in a maze of tall, gray cubicles in Merchant Bank's finance department.

"Morning, Imani." I yawn as I pass her office. Imani is a senior analyst and the fashionista of the department. She keeps her hair short and sleek and her attire is always runway ready. Her office is adjacent to our manager's, Alex, whose lights are still off. *Yes, I beat him into the office.*

"Hey girl." Her expression is perplexed. "You alright?"

"Girl, exhausted." I hope it serves as an excuse for my lateness and my sad wardrobe choice for today, wrinkled khakis (cringe: I should have ironed them) and a mint-green Merchant Bank logo polo given to me at a re-gifting party—it's simply pitiful. Even Bailey didn't want me walking her into school this morning. Oh well, it's casual Friday.

As I round the corner to my desk, I feel as if a large, black cloud is hovering over me. The proposal for Shane's event has taken over my life for the past two weeks. Beside my normal stacks of work papers there are fabric samples, catering menus, and venue floor plans. I stare at it all in despair, toss my laptop directly on top of all the mess, and pull my chair out. Someone's put a copy of today's paper on my chair. Shane, in full color, graces the cover. Feeling a surge of giddiness, I plop down, clear space for my feet and attempt to read the article.

"Aww man, that game was awesome last night. Shane was a monster." Brian, my young and impressionable junior analyst and football fanatic, pokes his head over our shared cubicle wall. He's so excited his face is flushed, blending in with his golden-orange hair. He widens his green eyes. "Did you go?"

"Yes, and guess what? He officially signed the contract yesterday."

"Sweet!"

"We hung out afterwards," I add on purpose.

"I'm so jealous." He slinks away, sulking like a five-year-old kid about to have a temper tantrum. When he returns to his senses, he comes back and I share the story of the most expensive napkins in the world.

"I would have flipped out. You're so lucky!" He walks to the main hallway and I hear him shout to someone, "Bryn went to the game last night and hung out with Shane Smith afterwards."

He marches back with Colin, our new payroll assistant. "That's pretty fantastic." Colin, dressed in a tailored suit, leans on the wall as if he's modeling for GQ. "King Smith! Man, he's one ugly dude. That scar!" he belts. "But he's a beast on the field. He kind of scares me." He shudders.

I try for a quick comeback to his insult, but am too busy staring in horror at the amount of product in his hair. He has the nerve to talk about somebody while he's walking around the office looking like Christian Bale in *American Psycho*.

"Come on now, that's not nice," I say in my best rendition of June Cleaver, when instead I want to snatch the silk hankie from his front pocket and shove it down his throat. "Shane may seem scary, but he can also be very sweet."

"Shoot. His money is sweet," Colin adds with an arrogant laugh.

I ignore this comment. I could come up with a few choice words, but I refuse to let him get to me. My head hurts too badly already.

"He likes you, doesn't he?" Brian laughs and gives Colin a shove to his shoulder.

"That came out of nowhere." I struggle to keep a straight face.

"I bet he does." He stares me down, taking a sip of coffee from his 'F***Off, I'm a Ginger' mug. "Everybody likes Bryn."

"We work together, *Brian*." I exaggerate his name. "I'm a professional. I don't mix business with pleasure. Besides, there's a 'no fraternization' clause in his contract."

"Aww man, come on, screw that. You should get with him," chuckles Brian. "I would *love* to meet Shane. Hell, I'll date him." He and Colin laugh together.

I make a face at them. Colin smirks and follows Brian out.

Exhausted from my headache, I pop four Advil and walk over to Alex's office to see that he has arrived. Leaning on his doorframe, I wait for him to acknowledge me.

"Morning." His eyes stay focused on his computer screen. "Come in. Close the door."

"Alex, you know Susanne hates it when we're in here with the door closed." I giggle. Imani taps the paper-thin wall to let us know we are too loud. Alex and I laugh even louder. Susanne, our CFO and office pit-bull, is bitter, self-righteous, and on an ongoing mission to destroy anything remotely fun. Most days she can be found pacing the floor dressed in her ankle-length khakis, turtleneck, and brown loafers (most likely purchased from JC Penney's), accessorized with a dumb looking nautical neck scarf (I think it's called a neckerchief). If she loosened it, she might be able to relax and remove that fake grin plastered across her face.

"Check this out." Waving me over to his computer, Alex turns his monitor towards me and points to the Orrstown, Pennsylvania police blotter. "Look at this. A woman called 911 because a *cow* knocked down her mailbox."

"You are so stupid. I come in here to talk about work and you want to show me a story about a cow." He is such a country boy. Standing about six feet, he's slim with blonde hair and vivid blue eyes, impressive for a forty-year-old. Most guys his age let themselves go, are half-bald, and have huge beer bellies. I wouldn't be surprised if there was a six-pack hiding under the button-up shirt tucked into his slacks. If he wasn't married, I'd be willing to find out.

"Bryn, stop being so loud and obnoxious," he jokes. "In fact, open my blinds. I want her to see you in here when she walks by."

"Alex, I need to take a long lunch. Do you need anything from me today?"

"Fine. Leave. I'll email you. Watch out for Susanne!"

"I—can—hear—you," warns Imani, enunciating each word.

I leave Alex's office, return to my desk, and open a complex spreadsheet to appear busy before the warden passes. I check my cell and see five missed calls from Jen. I punch some buttons on my keyboard to act like I'm working and call her back. "What's up? I missed your calls."

"I've got great news," she whispers. "Oris Odili, the designer I was telling you about, is going to design a custom suit for Shane." Her whisper turns to a squeal. "Finally . . . finally, I get him out of those big Ed Hardy jeans and long shirts. I can't have him play himself like that. He's got a hot body and I'm going to teach him how to show it off. I'm so excited! Hold on, there's Shelly again." She turns me over to piano music while I wait. Shelly is her manager who has concerns about Jen's side business. Jen has been tardy, ineffective, and borderline disruptive (due to her emotional outbursts) in her office since she launched Platinum Events. "Sorry about that, she just handed me one of Shane's receipts I accidentally printed on the main copier. Dang it! I meant to get it, but got distracted. This is the third one she's found after my warning last week."

"Yeah, that sucks. Especially since you just got caught yesterday. Now, so we both won't be in the unemployment line, let's get some actual work done. I'll see you this afternoon." I disconnect the call and stare at my monitor. I don't have the desire or the energy to focus on anything, let alone a budget for Merchant Bank. The only thing on my mind is sleep and this walk-through in a few hours.

I sneak out of the office a little after twelve o'clock and drive towards my dream venue. It's a new high-rise located on the west side of the harbor. I found it during an online search and became obsessed about booking it after taking the virtual tour. I called a bunch of times and the owner took forever to call me back. When he finally did, he told me the building was still under construction, but he was willing to pull some strings since he's a huge Baltimore Nighthawks fan. Today, I finally get to see it.

When I pull into the lot, I look in the rearview mirror at the concrete and glass building and see that it's raining. I know Jen will use it as an excuse for being late, but I'll call her anyway. "Hey," I say, watching Shane's black Range Rover speed past me into an empty space a few spots over. "He's here."

"Well, go and talk to him!" she shouts. "I'll be five minutes." She blows her horn and shouts nonsensical names at other drivers. She's famous for honking if she thinks a car wants to move into her lane.

I hang up, grab my pocket umbrella, and walk over to Shane's driver side window which is tinted the blackest black. As the window descends, a tired-looking Shane gives me a blank stare.

"Hi," I smile. "Jen is on her way. She shouldn't be more than five minutes." I lie. I know she will be much later but I don't want to upset him. I've already learned that he detests lateness.

"You want to get in?"

"Umm." I spin the umbrella and look towards the building, not knowing what to say. "I'm fine."

"I won't bite." Shane grins from ear to ear.

"Ahhh. That's nice." I look up, away, anywhere but at him.

"You would rather stand in the rain and get wet?" He looks down at my feet. The bottoms of my khakis are soaked.

"I'm okay," I assure him and turn my umbrella to shield my face from the rain.

"Have it your way." He shrugs his shoulders.

I look around, hoping Jen will appear and try to think of what to say next. "I think you're going to like this place." I point in random directions. "You know, from what you said you were looking for, I envision you here."

Shane looks around then focuses his attention at a mound of dirt, gravel, and a ghastly hedge wire fence. He looks apprehensive. I can tell he needs convincing.

"Just trust me. I know you'll love it. Wait until you see the inside."

"If you say so." He gives me an impartial look before turning his attention to his phone. "So, how long have y'all been doing this?" He glances at me. "You know, planning parties?"

"Unofficially, for some time now. A few milestone birthday parties, social gatherings, a sweet sixteen, and a wedding." *Would I ever forget Bridezilla?* Jen and I vowed never to take on another wedding because of her. "But Jen officially launched her company with a big charity fashion show a few months ago. I even suffered an injury." I point to my right foot. "One of the bases from our pipe and drape fell on my foot. It caused a nasty gash and I was wearing a boot for a few weeks."

"I didn't know event planning was that dangerous." Shane sets his phone down. "You know what I want?" He sits up from a slouched position.

I raise my eyebrows.

"I would be so happy if y'all could get Majestic or Houston to come."

Those reality vixens? Really? I hope my face doesn't mirror my thoughts. I haven't mastered the art of masking my emotions. "That is something I can definitely look into." I give him my rehearsed smile.

Our exchanges end in an awkward lull. Seeing Jen pull into a parking space gives me the opportunity to walk away without feeling like a complete idiot.

Inside the lobby, I ask for the owner, Nick. He comes right out. I lead the introductions and as we exchange handshakes, Nick, handsome and sporting a five o'clock shadow, rakes his hand through his sandy-blonde hair before handing us each an orange hard hat.

"You guys are going to love it." He leads us to the elevators and presses the thirtieth floor. "Awesome view, best in the city. I've been working on this project for the last four years. I've been up here every day just taking in the view."

We step out of the elevator and I stay close to Nick listening to him ramble on about the amazing building and construction details, past and present. He continues until we reach the end of the hallway and does his best to make a dramatic entrance, slowly opening the door and allowing only a small peek before flinging it wide open.

I'm the first to enter the space, which has twenty-foot floor-to-ceiling glass windows, a few steel and concrete columns, and a flight of exposed wooden stairs. "I love it."

"You haven't seen the best part yet." He reaches for my hand and walks me over to a large window ledge, which also functions as a door, onto the balcony that wraps around the entire building. That's when Shane appears from nowhere and grabs my other hand and assists me outside.

"Chivalry isn't dead yet." Shane takes my umbrella and opens it.

"Thank you." I nod.

"My pleasure."

I look for Jen but she stays inside. Nick walks out in the rain.

"Like I was saying, you can throw some heaters out here and you've got yourself an awesome party with a spectacular view. You can practically see all of Baltimore." Nick chuckles. "Look, the two buildings over there, that's Towson."

"This is *hot*!" Shane blurts.

Back inside, Jen and I take our time checking out the space and discuss design plans as we head back to the elevators, where Nick is standing holding the doors open for us. "Now—there's one more space I want you guys to see."

"What?" Shane's bark echoes down the empty hallway.

"The Penthouse." Nick gives me an 'I've-got-things-under-control' gesture. He presses a card key against a digital screen and the elevator takes us to the top.

"Nick," I whisper. "I thought this was the only space that's nearly complete?"

"It's okay. Seriously, it's fine," he says under his breath.

The elevator doors open and everyone's faces light up. Even Nick looks like he's seeing it for the first time and from what he's shared, he's seen it a thousand times. A sound of collective 'oohs' and 'aahs' fill the space. The forty-foot glass walls spanning hundreds of feet, steel columns, and an exposed ceiling are the focal points. From this view, we have front row seats to the expansive Baltimore skyline.

"Ladies and gentleman, I give you . . . The Monarch." Nick spreads his arms wide and bows. "It's seven thousand square feet and the space is lined with floor-to-ceiling windows. It's the length of the entire building. And did I mention the three-hundred-and-sixty-degree view?" He laughs at himself.

"I want it. How much?" Shane pats his pockets. "I'll write the check right now."

"It's twelve million, but I'm sorry, it's already sold. If we can get it completed in time, you can have the event here before we turn over the keys."

"Nick, I'm speechless. This place is phenomenal." I walk towards the windows and watch the rainfall. Nick joins me.

"This is where I come to escape, especially when it rains," he says.

"It's so romantic." I blush and regret that it's casual Friday.

"I want my party here!" barks Shane, startling me. "Make it happen." He gives Nick and me the evil eye.

I walk back to the parking lot completely stressed out. *Thanks a lot, Nick.* He just made my job a lot harder. Not only that, but when I check the time I realize I'm running very late. I rush to my car and call Jen. She doesn't give me a chance to speak.

"Don't stress. Nick is a businessman. He has no choice but to get it done. Remember, Shane's a Nighthawk so we've got leverage."

"I understand. Thanks for the reminder."

"But onto other more important matters . . . Shane wants to know if you have a man."

"I'm starting to feel like you are encouraging this. Why? No, I'm not interested. You could have told him that. Actually, I think I like Nick."

"I didn't peg Nick as your type. He's short. White . . ."

"Well, Shane certainly isn't my type. Besides, I read he's married or something."

"I don't know about that."

"Listen, I've read how he gets down. The women. Girl, please," I say in disgust. "No offense, he's a gentleman and all but nothing, and I mean *nothing* about Shane and his host of women is attractive to me."

Jen laughs until she cries.

I don't understand why she keeps bringing it up. Shane isn't my type. And from what I've seen so far, I'm even less his.

I manage to sneak back to my desk without running into Susanne. When I pass Brian, he rolls his eyes at me.

"You were with him, weren't you?"

I laugh and stick my tongue out at him. What I really want to tell him is that his instincts are right. Shane does like me. But I'll never admit it to anyone. They'll think it's the only reason we landed this contact.

Thinking about our coveted agreement reminds me I have to scan it for my file. I dig in my laptop bag and retrieve it. It's a mini hike over to the copier room, so I hide it from my nosy co-workers between work papers. I place the contract on the top tray for scanning and hit go. Simultaneously, a nasally voice behind me almost makes me jump.

"Bryn!"

The warden. I turn around to see Susanne staring down at me with a clipboard tightly pressed against her chest. "Yes?" *Just shoot me now.* I maintain eye contact while removing the contract from the bottom tray.

"I'm not a fan of the colors you chose for the budget template so I've emailed you a sample of the hues I would like to see. Can you get an updated copy to me by close of business?"

I match her grin.

"Sure. No problem." *Whew.* I wait for her to clear the hall.

4

THE MEETING

Shane will be here any minute and we're in a state of panic. Today is our first 'weekly' meeting with him since he signed the contract. Jen, Bailey, and I are trying to get Jen's house in order. I'm cleaning the kitchen, Bailey's vacuuming the living room floor, and Jen's upstairs in her office kicking her printer.

"Jack-Scrabbit!" I hear her scream, followed by a huge thud. "I can't take it! It stopped on the last one! The LAST one!"

"I don't need one," I call up to her. "Seriously. I'll look at your copy." Honestly, I don't *want* to look at anything. I'm not a fan of meetings. I loathe them. They bore me to death. At work, I have a terrible habit of falling asleep and so I try to avoid them whenever I can. Just last week, in the financial review meeting,

Imani said she tried to keep me awake. She said my chin fell to my chest and stayed there throughout Susanne's presentation. *Supposedly*, every now and again I lifted my head and let out a guttural moan. At one point, she thought I'd woken up. She said I sat straight up before leaning forward, grabbing my pen, and starting to write. But apparently, seconds later, I drew a long diagonal line before slumping onto the table. That's when she kicked me, hard. I remember that. I'm sure that's another reason Susanne hates me.

"Okay." Jen jogs down the stairs out of breath. "Are you almost done?" She runs her fingers through her hair, giving her bob hairstyle a lift. The emerald sheath dress looks radiant against her dark brown skin.

"Were you wearing that earlier?"

"I just changed."

"I thought so. I like that color."

"Thanks." She places an agenda on the table in front of two of the chairs.

"I feel underdressed." I'm wearing pink sweatpants, a white tank top, and fuzzy socks. My hair is in a high bun. "Should I go and change?"

"We're not going to have that discussion. Where are the bottled waters?" She runs into the kitchen.

"Right here." I hand them to her.

"Bailey, are you almost finished? Can you light a few candles?"

"Yes." Bailey turns off the vacuum and runs to grab a candle.

"I'll do it. I don't let her touch fire."

"Whatever, the lighter is in the kitchen drawer." She paces, touching things but not moving them. As I light the candles, the doorbell rings and Bailey runs to the door.

"Hey, Sweetie," belts Shane's deep voice. He picks her up and gives her a huge bear hug. "Good to see you again, Bailey baby."

"I made you something." She reaches into her book bag and pulls out a sheet of blue construction paper. She blushes and hands it to him.

"Read it to me."

"I love Shane Smith #50."

He smiles. "Bailey, I love it. I'm going to hang this at my house." He pats her on the head and walks towards Jen. He stops and points to me. "I love her. That girl is awesome."

"Thanks," I say and wave hello.

"Hi Shane," says Jen. "Just you today?"

"No, Terry is coming. He's outside inspecting my rims. His blind ass hit a curb on the way over here."

"Bailey. Upstairs," I say, signaling to Jen's office.

"Sorry, Bailey. Earmuffs," whispers Shane.

Bailey holds her ears as she runs up the steps.

Shane plops down in the chair and scans the agenda. "Bryn," he calls. "Terry says he sent you a friend request on MySpace. He said you ignored him."

"When was this?" laughs Jen.

He tried to holla at me through MySpace?

"Hey, Bryn." Terry walks in. "Hey, Jen." He joins Shane at the table.

"I was just asking Bryn why she didn't accept your friend request?" laughs Shane.

"Yeah, she broke my heart." Terry takes out his phone. "I'll show it to you."

"Stop." I wave my hand "You two are silly. There's no need."

"We're real friends now so you have to accept both of our requests." Shane picks up his phone. "Let me find you right now."

"Bryn. Can you join us over here?" Jen taps her agenda.

"Sure." I leave the kitchen and join them in the dining room. Jen wants to be formal, I guess.

"Thank you all for coming. If you will refer to your agendas we can get started. The first order of business today is design."

Shane leaps from his chair and walks into the kitchen. Jen goes silent. "Oh, you can keep talking." Jen rambles on about something while Shane stares at the photos on her refrigerator. He zeroes in on a photo of Jen and me at our high school ring dance. "Who's this?"

"Bryn and I," she says. "As I was saying . . . we're bringing on a designer, Christian. Would you like to meet him?" She stares at Shane, waiting for an answer.

"I don't care," he says in a monotone. "Where are y'all at in this one?" He points to a photo of us at Maracas Beach.

"Trinidad," she snaps, letting out a theatrical sigh. "Okay, never mind. Let's move on to guest lists."

"Who's she?" Shane's large finger presses the middle of someone's face.

"That's my sister."

"What's her name?"

"Taylor."

"Where is she?"

"She's home with her mother. Why?"

"Because y'all look alike. I thought she was your daughter."

"Are you saying I look old enough to have a sixteen-year-old?" She stands with her hands on her hips.

Shane laughs and then opens the refrigerator door wide and looks around. "No Orange Fanta? Gatorade?" He slams the door shut. Then he walks to the pantry and rummages through it. "Nothing sweet? Your food is boring."

"Shane. I'll add those items to my grocery list."

"Don't worry about it. Go on . . . go on."

"Guest lists." Jen takes a deep breath. "I've invited—"

Shane starts rapping and dances his way into her living room. I hold in my laughter and look over at Terry, who's not paying attention to anyone. He's busy playing Tetris on his phone.

Jen leaves the table and follows our silly client into the adjoining room. "How about models?" Jen's jaw tightens.

"There is something horribly efficient about you."

Jen returns a blank stare. Terry laughs. I guess he *is* paying attention.

Shane starts laughing hysterically. "You know where that's from?"

"*Quantum of Solace*," shouts Terry.

"That was perfect, wasn't it?" Shane looks at me to agree. At this point, Jen is the only one who isn't laughing. "Jen." He rubs her shoulders. "Lighten up, babe. This is going to be fun."

"Shane, I just want to keep you up to date with everything that we've done so far. We've gotten a lot accomplished in a week."

"I know. If it will make you happy, I'll sit down." He takes a seat and scoots his chair so that his abs are flush against the table. "Continue," he gasps. I laugh this time. Shane gives me a wink and pushes his chair back and balances on the two back legs. If looks could kill, he'd be dead. Jen's a boiling pot of water.

"Okay, I'm ready." He sets his chair on all fours and stares at Jen with his elbows resting on his knees. "You were saying?" He gives her his undivided attention.

Jen looks at her agenda. "I guess the most important thing you need to know is about—"

Without warning, Shane reaches down and yanks a stiletto off Jen's foot.

"SHANE!!!!" screams Jen.

He points to her toes. "Terry, look!" Shane laughs so hard that his eyes fill with tears.

"Do you take anything seriously?" she screeches, snatching her shoe from his hand.

"Nope. Not really."